"Would you prefer me to sleep in the spare room?"

Maggie was unable to look at Garrett as she voiced the question.

Garrett laughed bitterly. "Here I've been worried about whether or not we should make love, and you're not even interested in sharing bed space."

"That's not true!" she snapped back. "I just thought—"

"Sorry. I assumed we'd sleep together. After thirteen years, separate beds seemed foolish to me. I guess it doesn't to you."

Maggie snatched her pajamas from the hook and stormed out the door, her back ramrod straight.

Furious with Maggie, with himself and with the world at large, Garrett whipped back the blankets, took one look at the sheets and groaned. They had faded a little, but he remembered them well. More to the point, he remembered Maggie's creamy skin in sensuous contrast against the royal blue satin.

It was going to be a *very* long night.

Dear Reader,

It's summer. The days are long…hot…just right for romance. And we've got six great romances right here, just waiting for you to settle back and enjoy them. Linda Turner has long been one of your favorite authors. Now, in *I'm Having Your Baby?!* she begins a great new miniseries, THE LONE STAR SOCIAL CLUB. Seems you may rent an apartment in this building single, but you'll be part of a couple before too long. It certainly works that way for Annie and Joe, anyway!

Actually, this is a really great month for miniseries. Ruth Wind continues THE LAST ROUNDUP with *Her Ideal Man,* all about a ranching single dad who's not looking for love but somehow ends up with a pregnant bride. In the next installment of THE WEDDING RING, *Marrying Jake,* Beverly Bird matches a tough cop with a gentle rural woman—and four irresistible kids.

Then there's multi-award-winning Kathleen Creighton's newest, *Never Trust a Lady.* Who would have thought small-town mom Jane Carlysle would end up involved in high-level intrigue—and in love with one very sexy Interpol agent? Maura Seger's back with *Heaven in His Arms,* about how one of life's unluckiest moments—a car crash—somehow got turned into one of life's best, and all because of the gorgeous guy driving the other car. Finally, welcome debut author Raina Lynn. In *A Marriage To Fight For,* she creates a wonderful second-chance story that will leave you hungry for more of this fine new writer's work.

Enjoy them all, and come back next month for more terrific romance—right here in Silhouette Intimate Moments.

Leslie Wainger

Leslie J. Wainger
Senior Editor and Editorial Coordinator

Please address questions and book requests to:
Silhouette Reader Service
U.S.: 3010 Walden Ave., P.O. Box 1325, Buffalo, NY 14269
Canadian: P.O. Box 609, Fort Erie, Ont. L2A 5X3

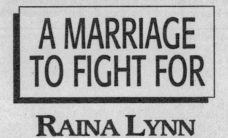

A MARRIAGE
TO FIGHT FOR

RAINA LYNN

Silhouette®

INTIMATE™MOMENTS®

Published by Silhouette Books

America's Publisher of Contemporary Romance

SILHOUETTE BOOKS

ISBN 0-373-07804-8

A MARRIAGE TO FIGHT FOR

RAINA LYNN

is married, the mother of three, mother-in-law of one and grandmother of two. She lives in a peaceful, secluded corner of paradise in the Sierra Nevada. To her unending joy, not even the U.S. Postal Service comes out there. Her favorite way of unwinding at the end of a long day is to disappear into the forest on her horse for a couple of hours, then curl up with a good romance novel.

I would like to thank my husband, John,
and my mother, Bee, for their support,
my daughter Cheryl for giving me a swift kick whenever
I need one, and my younger children, Matthew and
Angela, for their patience with boring meals and
postponed vacations so their mom could pursue a dream.
I would also like to thank Antoinette Bronson,
Mildred Lubke and Phylis Ann Warady for their
invaluable expertise and friendship.

Prologue

The captain's Texas drawl crackled over Flight 1251's PA system, and Garrett Hughes tensed, waiting for the next lie.

"Sorry for the continued delay, ladies and gentlemen, but the computer difficulties we're experiencing are being downright stubborn."

A collective groan from the nearly three hundred passengers filtered into the air.

"We've got lots of fuel, so we're just gonna keep circlin' San Francisco till we get the problem straightened out." He sounded bored, half-irritated.

Garrett hadn't bought the other two announcements, and he wasn't buying this one. Beneath the good-ol'-boy facade, that man was scared. Moreover, for the past hour, Garrett had watched the banked terror in the flight attendants' eyes deepen, and seventeen years of law enforcement wouldn't let him ignore it.

"For now, ya'll sit back, relax, and we'll be servin' complimentary cocktails in just a moment." Captain Perkins cracked a bad joke that sent scattered chuckles throughout the cabin. Then he broke the connection.

Garrett shared a skeptical glance with Tom White, a friend and fellow DEA agent. The sour expression on the smaller man's face had to be an exact match to the one on his own.

"A hijacking?" Tom murmured low.

"I doubt it." Garrett shook his head. "Hijackers thrive on passenger panic. We'd all know about it."

"True, but if it's really a mechanical failure, with all the backup systems these crates have, they should be able to land anyway, then fix the problem later."

A blond, very young flight attendant walked past them and into the forward galley, her overly bright smile so fractured it looked like a jigsaw puzzle a child had carelessly dropped. Garrett maneuvered his tall, square frame into the aisle.

"Where are you going?" Tom asked, frowning.

Garrett braced an arm on the seat back and leaned toward him. "Thought I'd flash my ID at a pilot or two."

Tom's large eyes widened to owlish proportions. "We're not FBI. You go in there, and they'll throw you out."

Garrett's lips thinned into an inflexible line, an expression that had frightened more than one suspect into settling down. "That's not my biggest worry at the moment."

"Garrett, I've never been to San Francisco before. I plan to enjoy myself. For the next two weeks, the words crime and suspects don't exist. One of these days, you need to add the word *vacation* to your vocabulary." With a resigned shrug, Tom went back to looking out the window at the boats in the ocean below.

Garrett stepped to the door leading into the flight deck and reached into his breast pocket for his ID. As he did, his fingers brushed against a black velvet jeweler's box. His life rested in that box and in the woman he hoped would wear the ring inside. But an unknown danger jeopardized his plans to win back his ex-wife, and assorted legal jurisdictions weren't about to keep him from finding out what it was.

The little flight attendant appeared at his side. Her fingers were locked together so tightly that the skin was white. The pieces of her smile barely held together at all. "Can I help you, sir?"

"Federal agent." Deliberately, he flipped his ID open and shut far too quickly for her to identify which law enforcement agency he was with.

Hope blazed across her face. "FBI?"

Something heavy was definitely going down, and Garrett sidestepped her question. "Is there someone on board who shouldn't be?"

It took a moment for her to comprehend the implication. "No."

"Good."

At his brisk knock, a member of the flight crew opened the door from the inside. Before the man had the chance to protest, Garrett took the little blonde by the elbow and pushed her through the doorway ahead of him. An angry chorus of four men greeted him, demanding that he leave, men with unbuttoned collars, sweat-drenched faces and damp white shirts. Perkins even had his sleeves rolled up. The flight crew definitely wasn't dressed for success. Garrett calmly shut the door and scanned the endless rows of indicator lights and dials on black instrument panels in the cramped compartment.

"Sir, it's against FAA regulations for—"

Garrett focused beyond Perkins's words. The man's outrage seemed more of a pressure release than genuine anger over the blatant intrusion. Rather than answer, Garrett flipped open his ID again and continued his visual sweep, looking for something wrong, a tough task when he didn't know what looked right.

Then he spotted it. A computer panel had been slid partially from its frame. Bolted to the inside was a thin, rectangular, metal box with a high-tech sensor display. The digital readout glowed a menacing green. Wires, like infinite tentacles, stretched from the box deep into the recesses of the jumbo jet's circuitry.

Odd that death should come in so small a package. He felt

no fear, just a dark sense of annoyance that settled over him like a familiar cloak.

For three years, he and Tom had worked deep cover. In the month since the operation had fallen apart, he'd struggled hard to detach from the cynical, cold-blooded persona that he'd adopted while living like a high-class animal with the cocaine import ring they'd infiltrated. Now, as he stared at the sophisticated bomb, he was sure he'd been less than successful. Where was the fear-pumped adrenaline?

So close. So damnably close. San Francisco was home, and Maggie and their son were the reasons he'd returned. Not a day had passed during that whole stinking operation that he hadn't dreamed of getting his family back.

Acid-hot anger boiled from deep within him. He'd survived the most complex case of his career, survived having his cover blown and the resulting attempt on his life. Now he was within minutes of seeing Maggie and Rick again, but some nameless, faceless terrorist threatened it all.

Garrett lifted his gaze to Perkins, who sat closest to the bomb. He successfully swallowed back the rising fury but was unable to do anything about the sarcasm. "I take it since jet jockeys aren't known for their prowess in bomb disposal, you're communicating with someone on the ground who is?"

The four men shared a look of frozen panic, and Garrett nearly swore. "Look. If you want to keep up your fiction that life's wonderful, you'd better do something about the employees dealing with the passengers." He jerked his dark head toward the flight attendant, now sobbing quietly.

The wiry man closest to Garrett was twitchy as hell and came half out of his seat. "Sir, the DEA has no jurisdiction—"

Garrett scowled him down.

Captain Perkins looked back at the box, then cautiously at Garrett. "You have experience with this sort of thing?"

"Some." *But not enough,* he amended silently. *Not nearly enough.* "I took a course in basic design and general disposal techniques, but I've never touched one. Not my specialty."

Perkins's breath hissed out from between his teeth. "Well, sir," he drawled, "that's more than we all got." He gestured for the first officer to vacate his chair in favor of Garrett. Then he stuck out his hand. "Welcome to the party. It's rigged so when we land, it'll be Lockerbie, Scotland, all over again."

"Wonderful," Garrett muttered and shook the man's clammy hand. He sat down and took the proffered headset.

As he identified himself to the experts below, part of his mind drifted to Maggie, her laughing green eyes and quick smile, the satin softness of her thick auburn hair as she lay in the hollow of his shoulder after they'd made love. And he thought of their son. Rick was sixteen now, and work had allowed Garrett precious little time with him during the past four years. Could they pick up where they'd left off? Or would his only child be a stranger?

Garrett's grim resolve to survive blocked out everything but the business at hand. To come this close yet fail was unthinkable.

Chapter 1

The skin on the back of Maggie Hughes's neck crawled. She leaned back in her chair and let the report slide from her fingers onto the mountain of papers on her desk. How long had this feeling of impending disaster plagued her? Thirty minutes? An hour?

One thing was certain. Her monthly reports were due today, and the Rutherford-Petrie Institute for Spinal and Head Injuries—like every other medical facility—ran on paperwork. Given her position as assistant director of physical therapy, the big boss jumped on her first if it didn't get done, and staring at the wallpaper accomplished nothing.

Besides, what reason did she have to be apprehensive? Life was surprisingly smooth, considering her status as a single parent of a teenager. Determined to quell the gut feeling that her world was about to fall apart, she left her office and headed down to the patients' rooms on the first floor. A smiling walk-through was as good an excuse as any to clear her head.

The physician investors who had built Rutherford-Petrie had planned everything with the patients' emotional well-being in mind, not just the health of their bodies. Equipment was state of the art. Each room featured a large picture window looking out onto the street or onto an inner courtyard or atrium. Most of RPI's patients' rehabilitative care required months of therapy. Depressing cubicles simply didn't exist here.

As she strolled past the nurses' station, Carl Sapperstein, her top therapist as well as her best friend, flagged her down. The man was built like an anorexic basketball player. He and a group of staffers were crowded around the staff's TV set. "Hey, Maggie. Come look at this. They defused the bomb! They're going to make it."

"Who? What bomb?" Maggie followed his gaze to the grainy, jerking image of a descending 747. Cheers and shouts nearly drowned out the reporter's jubilant voice.

"—Flight 1251 from Washington, D.C., is making its final approach. One can only imagine the euphoria felt by the heroic flight crew and the unnamed law enforcement officer who—"

Maggie's attention locked onto the aircraft, the sensation of crawling skin returning with a vengeance. Her pulse raced.

Only three times in her life had she felt like this. Each time, a police officer arrived afterward to tell her that Garrett had been injured in the line of duty. For thirteen years, she had lived through the hell of being a cop's wife.

Her eyes burned with unshed tears. "This is foolishness," she muttered under her breath.

"What is?" a nurse asked distractedly, her attention still on the TV.

Maggie clamped her mouth shut and forced herself to stare at the screen. The chances against her ex-husband being on that plane were astronomical. So why did a sudden knot in her stomach threaten to drop her to her knees?

On the screen, the camera showed the 747 coming in with smooth, textbook precision, its landing gear poised like talons beneath the wings. Then, fifty feet above the runway, a brilliant flash shot out from the base of the right wing. Pieces of wing, engine and landing gear ripped through the air and showered the ground. The jet crumpled like a dying bird.

Overbalanced, its left wing dug into the ground, throwing the plane into surreal cartwheels. A roiling ball of red-orange flame danced with opaque black smoke as both swirled from the tumbling wreckage. The fuselage corkscrewed on its nose, landed hard on its belly, then mercifully came to rest.

An involuntary scream tore from Maggie's throat and, with an agony too deep for words, her heart cried out Garrett's name.

Time and reality congealed into a muted mass around her, solid, unmoving, insulating her from the pain. As if from a distance, she heard muffled voices calling her name. Strong hands gripped her arms, and she looked dazedly into Sapperstein's worried eyes.

"Maggie, what's wrong?" he demanded. "Are you all right?" He gave her a restrained shake. From him, that meant it was only mildly bone jarring.

Reality eased into its usual forward momentum and, with a humiliated groan, Maggie remembered screaming. Abjectly, she wanted to crawl into a hole and pull the dirt up over her head. More embarrassing questions pelted her from all directions.

"Sorry." Her voice cracked, and she cleared her throat. She was their supervisor, for crying out loud, and they didn't need to see her falling apart. She glanced sheepishly at the TV. Emergency vehicles swarmed around the flaming wreckage, and billowing white foam covered it like grotesque whipped cream. "That accident really got to me for some reason. I'm fine."

Relieved murmuring followed, but she didn't miss the appraising glances a few of the staffers shared. They thought she was nuts. Frankly, she was tempted to agree.

"Why don't you go home early?" Sapperstein urged. "With the overtime you put in, I know you need it."

Maggie's face burned. She attempted a scowl, but from everyone's unimpressed expressions, she knew the effort failed miserably. So she rolled her eyes, instead. "Get back to work, people. Other than royally humiliating myself, I'm fine."

After few more protests, her scowl became real. "Go."

The reactions varied as much as the personalities, ranging from amusement to skepticism to annoyance, but everyone did, in fact, return to what they should have been doing before the TV had distracted them. For a moment, silence surrounded her. Then the reporter's strained voice broke through, the horror of what he'd witnessed evidenced in his broken sentences and wordless pauses. Worse, though, was that despite all, Maggie's deep-seated *knowing* didn't fade. *Garrett was on that plane!*

She had to put her mind at rest or go insane. Returning to her office, she propped her elbows on her oak desk and buried her face in her hands.

"Get a grip, Hughes." The worry spread into a raw, bleeding wound. Disgusted, she picked up the phone and called the neurology wing at San Francisco Community General Hospital. "Dr. Blake Hughes, please. This is Maggie Hughes at Rutherford-Petrie." The floor nurse put her on hold. "He's going to think your little red choo-choo has really gone around the bend this time," she muttered to herself. After an interminable wait, the line clicked open.

"Hi, Mag. What's up?" Blake sounded cheerful but distracted.

She leaned back in her chair. "Darned if I know."

"Oh?"

She half sighed, half groaned. "Are you ready for a stupid question?"

He gave a startled laugh. "Fire away."

"Did you ever find out where your brother is?"

The pause on the other end of the line was annoyed, but not at her. "Are you kidding?" he grunted. "My last round of badgering a pencil pusher in Washington got me the usual tripe. 'I'll get a message to Agent Hughes when it's feasible, and he'll call you on a safe line when it won't compromise the operation.'"

"Did Garrett ever call?"

"No," he said in a small voice. "And it's been six weeks."

Maggie willed down an involuntary shudder. "What do you think he's doing?"

"The usual. Something that neither of us wants to think about too hard."

"Oh." A pain-filled moan escaped her throat without her permission.

"Worried about him?"

"Yeah," she admitted bleakly.

Blake sighed. "That doesn't go away just because a divorce says it's supposed to."

"I know. I should have fallen in love with an accountant. Or maybe a pharmaceutical salesman. Anything but a cop who doesn't understand the concept of 'duck.'"

Blake chuckled. "Look, Mag, I can't talk now. A 747 just smeared itself all over a runway at SFO. Trauma's gearing up for war. I'm headed there myself. When the dust settles—provided I'm not dead on my feet—we'll go out for coffee."

Maggie's lips thinned in a feeble attempt at a smile. "Sounds good. Sorry I bothered you."

"Don't mention it. The kids are at a slumber party, and this'll give me a good excuse not to go home to an empty house."

"Faith's still in Europe?" His wife was a world renowned photographer and was often gone for weeks at a time.

"I wasn't cut out to be married to a globe-trotter," he muttered. "It gets lonely."

She laughed. "Be strong, little soldier."

"Thanks a lot." His pager shrieked in the background. "I've got to go. We'll talk later."

They broke the connection, and Maggie attacked the paperwork mountain on her desk. Four hours later, the mountain had been conquered—if not entirely eliminated—and she'd convinced herself she was okay. It was six o'clock. She could have gone home at five, but Rick—being sixteen and the proud owner of a driver's license and a job—wouldn't be home until midnight curfew. Blake wasn't the only one who hated empty houses.

Her phone rang, and she picked it up. "This is Hughes." At first she heard nothing but the hollow emptiness of an open line. "Hello?"

A hoarse clearing of a male throat. "Mag? It's me."

"Blake?" Every shred of hard-won calm vanished.

He inhaled raggedly. "You always know. I've never understood how, but you always know."

The mental vision of the jet cartwheeling down the runway played behind her eyes. Tears burst over her lower lids and down her cheeks. She wanted to ask, but she couldn't force out the words. Terror-spawned anger sharpened her voice. "Garrett's dead. Isn't he!" It wasn't a question.

"Not quite." Blake's ragged indrawn breath was louder than his voice. "We're taking him to surgery as soon as a suite's free, but it doesn't look good."

Her heart and mind recoiled in self-preservation. "I don't want to know."

"I need you, Maggie," he pleaded, clearing his throat and fighting the choking tears. "Mom and Dad are coming in from Vallejo. Mom can't handle this and take care of Dad by herself."

Maggie felt herself recoil further. This was too much like scenes that had played out three other times. Garrett injured, the family called together, and her heart being torn open. Then, when it was all over, and she and Garrett made love, her fingertips brushed an old scar or the bandages from his latest wound, and the horror came back in a violent rush.

Wasn't avoiding this why she'd divorced him? For years she'd tried to tell herself that across the country thousands of police officers lived to be comfortably old and happily retired. But that hadn't helped; she hadn't married any of them. He swore he never took unnecessary risks, but she also knew him well enough to know he never compromised, never backed off if he thought he could control a situation.

For thirteen years she'd smiled bravely every time he left the house, then jumped every time the phone rang. His transfer to undercover narcotics had made the constant worry intolerable, and their quarrels increasingly bitter. The death blow to their marriage came at his acceptance into the DEA. Something fractured deep inside, and she filed for divorce. No matter how much living without him hurt, the bottom line was that it had been easier to push him away than to live with the constant terror of not knowing when—if ever—he'd be taken from her.

"Blake, I freed myself from this once. I can't—*won't*—walk back into his life again."

An engulfing silence stretched out on the line before Blake managed a broken, "Please?"

She wanted to slam down the receiver and pretend the call hadn't come, but her fingers tightened as if they had a will of their own. A question welled up in her throat, demanding to be voiced, refusing to be swallowed back.

"How bad is he?" She hated herself for asking, hated Garrett more for making her ask.

"Third lumbar is fractured and fragments are pressing against his spinal cord. The cord isn't severed, but both legs are paralyzed. He's also got assorted broken ribs, a fractured right arm and internal injuries." Blake's voice shook. At the moment, he wasn't one of the hottest young neurosurgeons in the country. He was simply a man whose older brother, his childhood hero, crept closer to death—again.

Maggie wanted to scream out her anguish. Loving Garrett had nearly destroyed her. How could Blake ask this? "No."

"Please, Maggie."

"No! Playing bullet tag with drug dealers and crazy people was more important to him than Rick and me. I'm out of it."

"This accident has nothing to do with being a cop."

"He's still hurt, and if he dies, I don't think I could stand to watch. And if he lives, I'll be right back where I started."

"Think of Mom."

Guilt added its weight to the emotional overload. Laverne and Patrick Hughes were the only real parents she'd ever had. Her father had deserted her mother when Maggie was six. Her mother—an alcoholic who couldn't hold a job—preferred the company of fellow barflies over making a decent home for her frightened, confused little girl. Child Protective Services stepped in when she was eight. From then on, she bounced from foster home to foster home, always the outsider, never sure if "home" one month meant the same address the next.

"Throwing Mom at me is fighting dirty, Blake."

"She's going to need you."

Maggie felt her resolve slip, sending new ripples of panic roiling through her.

His voice dropped to a whisper again. "Just be here. I can concentrate if I know the family is taken care of."

Knowing no matter how she protested she'd never be able to stay away, Maggie groaned.

Her ex-brother-in-law correctly interpreted the sound and breathed in relief. "Thanks."

They shared a moment of mutually needed silence. Maggie ran the whole conversation through her mind, then mentally listed the specialists Garrett would need. One of them was a neurosurgeon. "Wait a minute. What did you mean by 'concentrate'? You can't operate on him yourself. He's your brother!"

"No, I called in every favor I had and got Rollins, Tellerman and Kelly. They're going over the pictures now."

Maggie sucked in her breath. Rollins was one of the best neurosurgeons in the world. If it was humanly possible to pull Garrett through this, Rollins would find a way.

Blake's voice dropped so low, she could barely hear him. "Maggie, there's very little chance we'll get him off the table alive. He was pinned in the wreckage too long. His vital signs are so unstable, just putting him under could kill him, but surgery is his only hope." The tremor in his voice worsened. "I'm going in with him, Mag. I won't let my brother die alone."

For another heartbeat, her world spun in circles, then finished falling apart, just as she'd known all afternoon it would.

* * *

Maggie strode into the trauma center at San Francisco Community General with her chin tilted up and her emotions clamped down. For a stunned moment, she could do nothing but survey the chaos. The small hospital's security personnel rode herd on the dozens of reporters—complete with camera crews and unwieldy equipment—keeping them a respectful distance from patients and frantic family members. Medical personnel barked out orders. Patients screamed. The din of voices blended together into a hideous roar of human misery.

Somewhere in this horror was Garrett. Her pulse quickened with a fresh wave of fear.

People stood ten deep at the front desk, all shouting demands for information at the two harried nurses. Maggie paused to thank God she still wore her white uniform and name badge. Then she elbowed her way through the crowd. Angry glowers greeted her efforts, but the sight of her tunic, pants and sneakers gained her the path she needed.

Bracing her fingertips on the desk, she leaned across it. "I'm from Rutherford-Petrie. Where's Dr. Blake Hughes?"

The nurse glanced at the badge and didn't even blink about why a surgeon coping with one of the worst air disasters in U.S. history would call for someone from a rehab center. "Trauma nine." She pointed toward a garish, black-and-white-tiled corridor. "That way."

Maggie nodded crisply, then waded through the river of people, gurneys and wheelchairs, scanning room numbers painted on the doorjambs. The next number was...*nine!* She whipped through the doorway and plowed into her ex-brother-in-law.

Blake Hughes was dark like his brother, but a little taller and more lean, with the classic male beauty right out of a woman's fantasy. But today, his rich olive complexion was a pasty gray, his sapphire-blue eyes—another trademark of the Hughes men—haunted and half-wild.

"You made it." He pulled her into a desperate hug. "Garrett refused further medical treatment until you got here."

Maggie's jaw dropped. "He's *conscious?*"

Blake nodded, trembling. "Given his injuries, that's probably the only reason he's still alive." Blake jerked his gaze over his shoulder. "Hurry. I want him in the next available operating room."

Taking a steadying breath, she folded her hands and walked into trauma nine. Four patients on gurneys and their medical teams were crammed into a tiny room designed for only one crisis at a time. Garrett lay on the gurney second from the left, staring at the ceiling, his face set in silent, clench-jawed agony.

His square, chiseled features looked like Hollywood's version of a 1940s Mafia don, darkly handsome, seductively compelling, lethal. Little wonder he'd made such an effective undercover officer. He looked like the quintessential bad guy.

His only covering was a sheet draped over his hips. Pressure bandages covered various wounds on his muscular, tanned legs and chest. His right arm was splinted, multiple IVs in his left. A grim-faced technician checked readouts on monitors. But the most frightening sight was the steel braces strapped to Garrett's body, completely immobilizing his spine and legs.

Maggie had loved Garrett since she'd moved next door to his family at sixteen, loved the quiet confidence that radiated from him as naturally as breathing, loved the way he turned their world into paradise whenever he held her. Now he lay broken, his indomitable strength drained nearly to its end.

"You need it *now,* Mr. Hughes," growled one of the hovering doctors, a syringe poised over a Y-connector in an IV tube. At Garrett's sharp glower, the harried physician looked pleadingly at Blake. "The call just came. They'll be ready for us upstairs in five minutes."

"I said no." Pain thickened Garrett's voice, but his strength of will cut through the room like satin-wrapped steel. "Not until my wife gets here."

Wife? Maggie's heart twisted in her chest. *Not ex-wife?* She swallowed hard and stepped to his side. "I'm here." Despite her best effort, her voice quavered.

He turned his face toward her, the familiar power of his

piercing blue gaze drawing her in, surrounding her with his possessive warmth. He forced a smile.

"Hi, babe."

Beyond conscious will, she took his hand in both of hers. His skin was cold, and she tightened her grip, willing strength back into the dynamic man who had taught her the ecstasies of love, the man who—even after four years—she still burned for alone in the bed they had once shared. The simple act of holding hands, touching once again after the years' long absence, sent her blood tingling up her arms. She'd been afraid it would be like this. That was why she'd refused to see him those rare times he'd stolen enough time from work to come see Rick.

She took a shuddering breath and projected a hopefully cheery-looking smile. "Hi, yourself. Other than giving your insurance a workout, what are you doing in California?"

Despite his grave condition, she truly expected him to attempt that crooked smile he used whenever he knew she was sidestepping an unpleasant subject, but he didn't. After a timeless moment, his gaze became more possessive, blocking out the rest of Maggie's world. Had Garrett's eyes really become more blue, more sexy? Or did they just seem that way because for so many years she'd only seen them in her dreams?

"I came back for you."

Her heart slammed against her ribs.

"I love you, Maggie. Too much to let a damned divorce keep us apart." His broken ribs gave his words a frighteningly breathy quality. Exerting tremendous effort, he drew her fingers against his lips and kissed them.

The tingling in her blood burst into open flame, and she nearly wept.

When they'd met, Garrett had been twenty-two and a college senior, godlike to a high school sophomore. Instant fire had ignited between them, but he confined their passion to fevered kisses, denying them the fulfillment they both craved. His father would have killed him if they'd slept together. Moreover, his personal sense of honor wouldn't allow it. He'd said she'd been through too much in her life. If their love didn't work out, he didn't want the memories tainted with regrets.

So honorable, this Boy Scout, this knight in shining armor who held her heart. But for thirteen years of marriage, loving each other hadn't been enough, would never be enough.

She cleared her throat of the choking memories. ''We'll talk later when you feel better.''

Resolve flashed in his eyes, momentarily overshadowing the pain. ''Where's Rick?''

The abrupt subject change didn't surprise her. It was typical of Garrett. When he'd come to a decision and knew she wouldn't like it, he simply moved on.

Inwardly, she sighed. ''He's out with friends. I called the grocery store where he works, but his boss gave him the night off.'' She squeezed his hand. ''He'll be here when you wake up.''

Garrett opened his mouth to speak, but his face abruptly tightened in anger and he whipped his head back around to the IV pole where his brother stood calmly injecting the contents of a large syringe into the Y connector.

''Damn it, Blake.'' The snarl was no more than an unsteady whisper. ''I told you I needed to talk to her first.''

''We have work to do, big brother.'' Blake, like Garrett, was most at home when a decision had been made and he could proceed accordingly. The fact that he had no authority to do the anesthesiologist's job never entered the equation. ''Somehow, I don't think you'll sue me. Say 'good night, Gracie.'''

Maggie saw Garrett's eyes go unfocused, and he groaned with the effort to stay conscious. ''Where's my coat?''

''For Pete's sake, Garrett,'' Blake moaned. ''Why can't you just lie there and be impressed with us like a regular patient?''

Garrett gritted his teeth, and Maggie felt a slight shift in pressure on her fingers as he tried, but failed, to secure his grip. ''Breast pocket. There's a box.''

Watching him struggle was more than Maggie could take,

and she clamped her teeth down on her trembling lower lip and wrapped her fingers more tightly around his. Blake took one look at her face and rummaged through the bloodied rags on the floor until he found the velvet jeweler's box.

Opening it, he swore under his breath and turned it toward Maggie. "I take it this is for you?"

A two-carat, marquise-cut, diamond solitaire ring winked in the glare of the ER's overhead lights.

"Oh, Garrett, no." Acid tears slipped down her cheeks. "This isn't the time."

"Probably not… Got your attention *now*." His voice had begun to slur, and listening to him fight to make himself understood tore out her heart. "Love you, babe. Marry me, again…. We'll get it right…this time."

The need to throw herself into his arms surged through her with renewed intensity. She stiffened, knowing if she gave in at all, she'd cave in completely. "We'll talk later—when you're out of surgery."

Garrett's grip weakened further. Whatever Blake shot him full of didn't waste time.

"Not…till you say yes. Conscious…can refuse treatment."

"Go ahead," Blake butted in. "I'll declare you incompetent. As a family member, I'm allowed."

Garrett ignored him, focusing his rapidly fading consciousness on Maggie's face. "I'd planned to propose…under more romantic circumstances…. Wanted to put the ring on your finger…myself. I'll settle for…knowing you're wearing it while they…put me back together."

Maggie couldn't handle looking at him anymore, but was helpless to look away. *How can I say no, then send you off to a surgery you may never wake from?* Her mouth took on a will of its own. "Yes, I'll marry you." She glowered at him. "But it won't be until you're out of here, and we've talked— extensively. Hospital rooms make lousy backdrops for wedding pictures."

He puffed out his breath, probably the closest he could come to laughter. With trembling fingers, she dislodged the ring from its case and slipped it onto her left hand. Then she took his hand again, and he tried to give it one last squeeze.

"One more thing." He could barely keep his eyes open, and his words were slurred almost beyond recognition. "My partner. Find him for me. See…if he made it…too."

At first she was too stunned to react, too stunned to think, to feel. Then came the blistering rage. *Your partner? You're here on a case? What had you planned? Squeeze a wedding into your spare time?*

She swallowed past the anger. "Okay."

His expression eased into the placid gray of the dying. His eyes closed, and the trauma team rolled the gurney out the door and around the corner.

"What have I done? Even if he lives, he'll never change," she whispered, trying to ease the heartache. "He can't. He doesn't want to." A sick despair crawled through her heart. *You couldn't live with it before, and you never will.*

Taking one last longing look at the engagement ring, she pulled it from her finger, dropped it into a tunic pocket and went out to wait for her former in-laws.

The blue plastic, chrome-framed chair she found in the main corridor of the surgical floor was built for durability, not comfort. The corridor's walls were gray, relieved only by periodic scuffs and gouges. All in all, the decor suited her mood. The bright, cheery colors of RPI—a subtle psychological touch to lift spirits—would only have increased her agitation. Maggie wrapped her arms around herself, her thoughts a numb collection of disconnected pieces of hell.

At the click of street shoes against the floor tiles, she looked up. Worry lined Laverne Hughes's thin features as she searched for Maggie and kept one eye on her husband. Patrick, the Hughes patriarch, distinguished with his salt-and-pepper hair, seemed preoccupied with his hands today, turning them over and over, staring at them as if divining the secrets of some great mystery. He'd always been such a vibrant man. Seeing him this way hurt. First there had been the stroke. Then something nastier set in. It wasn't Alzheimer's, but no one knew exactly what it was. Whatever the name of his affliction, his periods of lucidity grew steadily shorter.

"Maggie, dear." Laverne enveloped her in a warm hug loaded with genuine affection. Miraculously, she and Patrick hadn't taken sides in the divorce.

Maggie turned to Patrick and projected her voice a bit to get his attention. "Hi, Dad."

His head jerked up, and he apparently noticed his surroundings for the first time. "Maggie!" He turned to Laverne. "See, my love? Didn't I tell you everything would be fine?"

Laverne patted his hand and returned his adoring gaze.

"Where are my sons?" Patrick demanded to the air in general.

Maggie took his arm and waited until his gaze swung back in her direction. "Garrett is in surgery. Blake is with him."

Laverne's jaw dropped, and Maggie cast her a quick glance. "Blake pulled in some real heavyweights," she explained quietly. "Rollins, Tellerman and Kelly."

"My boy's the best surgeon in the country," Patrick said. "His brother's in good hands. He'll come out just fine."

An ugly lump formed in Maggie's throat, and she was acutely aware of the engagement ring in her pocket. "Sure, Dad."

He looked thoughtfully at his hands again, and she and Laverne spent a quick moment comparing notes.

"We won't know anything for twelve to fifteen hours," Maggie explained. *Unless, of course, he dies on the table first.* "So we might as well go find some coffee."

"Garrett's going to be okay," Laverne said, her face set in desperate determination. She urged Patrick to his feet.

Patrick was instantly alert, and he beamed down at Maggie. "Speaking of Garrett, how long have you two been married now?"

For a moment, she thought she might throw up right there in the corridor. Patrick's memory came and went, and no one knew what he was likely to remember. One thing he'd never remembered, though, was the divorce. "Next week it'll be seventeen years."

He sighed rapturously. "I don't mind telling you, I thought too many years separated you. Six is a lot for young people." He patted her hand holding his arm. "Sure glad I was wrong."

"Me, too, Dad." Her stomach churned, and the lump that had been in her throat earlier came back, bringing three or four of its larger cousins with it. She could hardly breathe.

Garrett had proposed the first time the day he entered the police academy. They were married six months after he was accepted by the San Francisco Police Department and had a steady paycheck. Her personal Boy Scout wanted everything perfect.

"Where is that boy, anyway?" Patrick frowned. "Haven't seen him in a long time."

Maggie couldn't answer.

"Patrick dear," Laverne said, coming to the rescue. "He and Blake are busy. We'll see them later."

Patrick made an accepting noise in his throat. "Probably out playing basketball. I've never seen two grown men play such serious half-court in my life. You'd think it was the NBA playoffs or something." He gazed fondly at Maggie. "Do you think when we get home, they'd be interested in a little threesome with their old man?"

Maggie forced herself to inhale. She'd heard Blake's tone when he'd talked about the bone fragments pressing against Garrett's spinal cord. Fourteen years' experience in rehabilitative medicine left no illusions, and her mind traveled down all the ugly roads Garrett could take. If Garrett lived at all, there'd never be any more hard-fought matches between the two brothers, the loser having to wash and wax his sibling's car.

Get a grip, Hughes, she told herself sternly. *No one knows anything—yet. And the cord* wasn't *severed. Anything can happen.*

"Did you know Garrett went to college on a football scholarship?" Patrick rambled on as they walked toward the cafeteria. "I really thought he might go pro, but he had his mind fixed on being a cop. Has had ever since he was knee-high to a hubcap."

Maggie glanced at Laverne, hoping for another rescue, but the older woman seemed lost in her own dark reverie. "Dad, do you think we could talk about something else?"

"Sure," he said cheerfully. "By the way, where do you suppose Blake and Garrett hightailed it off to?"

Chapter 2

"**M**om! Where *are* you? I've been worried sick. Do you know what time it is? Two o'clock, Mom. *In the morning!*"

"I know the time," Maggie answered low, fixing her gaze on the pay phone's battered faceplate.

The sixteen-year-old had himself wound up in a real coil of righteous indignation. "The last time *I* wasn't home when you expected and *I* didn't leave a note, you grounded me for a week. It cost me a date with Sandy Walker!"

"Slow down, Ricky. There's something I need to tell you." Maggie steeled herself for what she had to say. Rick and Garrett had been so close before Garrett's move to Washington. Garrett had spent hours teaching their son how to shoot baskets, pass a football and build the perfect doghouse. Maggie could barely stand the thought of Rick's devastation. *Please, God, watch over him. He'll probably drive like a maniac to get here.*

"We have a rule, Mom. We both leave notes so the other one knows where we are." His voice dropped to a mocking sarcasm. "I checked every magnet on the fridge. No note. Not even a little one. Have we discovered invisible paper?"

Maggie winced at having her own words thrown back at her. She'd been so worried the night he strolled in after curfew, she had really popped off. No wonder he'd balked. "Point taken. I shouldn't have said those things. I'm sorry."

The apology seemed to take all the starch out of him, and he asked softly, "Are you okay, Mom? I've been really worried."

"I'm at Community General, and—"

"Were you in a wreck?" His voice went up an octave.

"Slow down. No car accident. I'm fine."

An audible sigh of relief came through the phone.

"Rick, did you hear about the plane crash this afternoon?"

"Yeah. Almost two hundred people died. That psycho only told them about the bomb in the cockpit, not the one set to blow the wing off."

Two bombs? So that explained it. She'd been so absorbed with Garrett, she hadn't thought about the details of the crash.

"Every cop in the world must be after that guy."

Maggie took a deep breath, held it, then let part of it out very, very slowly.

"So you're there for that? Weird. I thought rehab was the cleanup crew. Sort of like the guy who picks up the trash in the bleachers after a big game." He chuckled at his own joke.

"Honey, sit down." Maggie paused to give him a moment to prepare himself. "Your dad was on that plane." Tears crowded her throat. She inhaled and held it. *I absolutely won't break down. Rick needs my support, not hysterics.* She needed to tell him that Garrett was still alive, but her vocal cords seized up.

"Is he dead?" The frozen lack of emotion shocked her.

"No," she wheezed. "He's in—"

"Too bad." A short pause. "When are you coming home?"

Maggie flinched as if hit by a powerful electric jolt. The receiver fell from her hand and swung inanely by its cord. Adolescent rebellion was one thing, but this was an entirely different, and vastly uglier animal. What had happened? Rick had worshiped Garrett.

As if having fallen into a nightmare, she picked up the receiver and put it back against her ear.

"Mom? Are you there?"

"Richard, he's your father," she cried. "He's badly hurt."

"My father," Rick mimicked sarcastically. "Well, why don't you remind him of that. You've gotten your child support checks—thanks to some setup at the bank—and his accountant never forgot my birthday or Christmas. But *he* usually did. He didn't have to be here, but a phone call on the right day would have been nice." The secret pain Rick had borne alone leaked out like droplets from a crack in a dam.

"How often has he come to see me? Five times in four years. The first time he came mostly because Grandpa had that stroke." The droplets of pain quickened into a stream. "Did *my father* ever send for me so I could spend the summer with him? No! Stupid me, I settled for a few days here and there." The stream rushed into a river, and Rick's voice cracked under the force.

"He told me he was going under for a while, on a case. That was okay. But he hardly ever called, and when I left a message, sometimes it was a week before he'd call back. Even then, it wasn't really him. It was his voice, but it was like talking to a stranger." The sixteen-year-old openly wept now, and the anger she heard was directed as much at himself as his father.

"Ricky, very often police officers have to become different people to work complex undercover operations. It's like acting, but they have to live it twenty-four hours a day for weeks at a time. That other person is impossible to shed just for a phone call home. I imagine it's worse for a DEA agent because they can stay under indefinitely, no time restrictions."

Angry sobbing was all she heard.

"Oh, Ricky," she groaned. *How could I not have noticed how hurt you were?*

"And my name's not Ricky. It's Rick!"

"Right." Raising a teenager was like tiptoeing through a minefield, and in her own turmoil, she'd stumbled on a forgotten land mine. Without his saying another word, she could feel her son retreating. She had a better chance of sprouting wings than accomplishing anything meaningful with him tonight. "Okay, honey. Your dad will be in surgery for hours yet."

"So? I'm not coming down there if that's what you're getting at."

Maggie swallowed the urge to snap at him. "I don't know when I'll be home. Get some sleep. We'll talk when we're both rested."

He mumbled some sort of noncommittal reply, then hung up.

Maggie stared blankly at the old, beat-up pay phone. This morning she had awakened blissfully unaware that her ex-husband was plotting a reconciliation—possibly getting himself killed in the process—and that her son hated him so much that he refused to come to the hospital. What other comfortable illusion would be shattered before her head hit the pillow next?

Fourteen hours and thirty-two minutes after the surgical team wheeled Garrett into surgery, Blake trudged into the waiting room. Maggie leaped to her feet. The morning sun shone through the window, giving a stark clarity to the mottled gray of his face and the haggard lines carved by exhaustion. But it was Blake's eyes she needed to see. When he looked up, what would she find? Grief? Joy? Maggie's pulse pounded at the base of her throat and in her ears, blocking out all other sound. Blake pulled the slump from his shoulders and took in his surroundings as if dragging himself from far away. Desperate for a tenuous lifeline to hope, she reached into her pocket and slipped the heavy diamond and gold ring onto her finger.

"Oh, please, God," Laverne prayed under her breath.

Blake wrapped his arms around their shoulders. "By all

rights he should be dead. His heart stopped twice while we were closing. The second time was real touch and go.''

''But he's alive?'' Maggie backed off enough to see his face.

Blake nodded. ''His condition is extremely grave. He's in recovery, and the ICU team is with him now, orienting themselves to his case. A nurse will be at his side constantly for the next twelve hours at least.''

Maggie swallowed. *Put simply, you're measuring his life in minutes.* ''Can we see him?''

Laverne was laughing and crying and blessing her son's face with a shower of kisses that he accepted almost numbly.

Blake nodded wearily. His bloodshot gaze locked onto Maggie's face. ''Mag, he's alive for one reason. He wants to be. I just hope to God he's not ready to give up.''

It was nearly noon before ICU had Garrett settled. Maggie took her turn to see him after his parents were through. When she first looked at the man in the chrome-framed bed, it took her several moments to believe it was really Garrett. He was swathed in bandaging and braces to keep him absolutely immobile. IVs and monitor wires stuck out of him like weird vines. Because he was too weak to breathe on his own, a respirator breathed for him. And he was so still, so frightfully still. If not for the beeps of the monitors and the rasps and clicks of the respirator, she would have thought he'd died.

Hesitantly, she grasped his square, powerful hand. The skin was warmer than before. His core temperature was coming up, a small straw to cling to, but the only one she had. Jumbled emotions, hot and bittersweet, coursed through her veins.

''Garrett, I'm here.'' Her voice broke up so badly that the words were unintelligible, and she cleared her throat. It was on the tip of her tongue to tell him how much she loved him, but she couldn't. ''I love you'' was too close to ''I surrender.''

Squeezing his hand, she tried again. ''Garrett, why is your life never simple?'' *Better! Be strong. Be yourself.* ''The worst is over, I think.'' *Sure it is.* She looked up at the monitors.

The readouts weren't good. Between his injuries and the two heart attacks caused by fourteen hours of anesthesia, he wasn't merely unconscious; he was in a deep coma. Prudently, she looked away. "When you're out of here, we've got a lot of talking to do."

Despite what the monitors said, Maggie half expected him to open his eyes, to fix her with that penetrating blue gaze of his, then grumble, "No, babe, we're going to talk about it now." But he didn't.

Maggie fought a surge of love and regret, hope and fear. She gazed down at him, and deep in her chest, her heart slowly bled. "I don't want to love you."

Garrett heard Maggie's pain with a clarity he didn't understand. It was as if a new sense had awakened, one that allowed him to feel her turmoil as clearly as if it were his own. Moreover, it wasn't only Maggie's emotions he sensed. Across the room, a nurse sat reading a medical journal, her disgust at whatever she read as clear to him as if she'd complained out loud. Yet he had no physical sensations. It was as if his mind and spirit were fused together, but without the rest of him. He sensed the presence of his body, but felt no personal connection with it. A ribbon of disquiet sliced through him.

Is this some sort of weird, near-death experience that crackpots talk about? Or is this what everyone goes through when the body shuts down?

He thought about that for a while, but without concrete data, he couldn't form any conclusions. Then a new thought struck him. Pain. For the first time since the crash, there was a merciful lack of it. *That* he could handle.

He sensed Maggie's withdrawal, but he couldn't open his eyes or squeeze her hand to let her know he wanted her to stay.

"I'm going home for some sleep, I'll be back later."

Don't go, Maggie. Not yet. I need you.

She patted his arm, then moved toward the door. Garrett couldn't let her leave. Focusing his mind on trying to move—

a concept that for some reason seemed strangely abstract—he shifted.

The high-tech sterility of ICU screamed into vivid focus, and a buzzer wailed. Maggie whirled around, her delicate face pale with horror. The nurse launched herself off her chair and rammed her palm into a call button on the wall.

"Code Blue in three! Code Blue in three!"

A red light pulsed in the hall outside his door. A small army of people rushed in, crowding Maggie against the far wall.

"Give me a rundown," ordered a doctor.

"Forty-two-year-old white male," the nurse barked, then rattled off the long list of Garrett's injuries and the details of his surgery, ending with, "This is his third cardiac arrest since midnight."

The doctor swore. "Give me the paddles. Let's start him off low—fifty. This guy must have a tremendous will to live to have made it this far. I don't want to do any more damage."

Garrett glanced at Maggie. Her fingers were clamped tightly over bloodless lips. Her pain washed through him as if it were his own. *Oh, babe,* he groaned. *Is this what you went through when that clown shot me eight years ago?* That had been the worst of his injuries while on duty.

Garrett was only distantly aware of the ICU staff trying to get his heart started again. In the face of what he was learning about Maggie, their efforts didn't seem particularly important. He'd always dismissed her reaction as overactive female hormones. *I was a real idiot, wasn't I, babe? With your childhood, how could I not have realized how badly you still needed security, stability? I thought my love fixed all that. I thought you were just using it as an excuse to get me to quit the force. I didn't understand, babe. I swear I didn't.*

A gently enticing pull distracted him from his self-recriminations, beckoning him to let go. Focusing on his body, he struggled to force himself back inside where he belonged, but the flesh and blood frame he'd occupied his entire life didn't quite belong to him anymore.

"Don't go," Maggie pleaded in an anguished whisper.

I'm trying not to, babe, he muttered dryly. *I'm a little out of my element here. Literally.*

"V tac, Doctor."

Garrett watched them all check the readouts, vicariously feeling their collective commitment to doing their jobs, their suppressed fear.

"Lidocaine."

The pull on his soul intensified as they injected the powerful heart stimulant. Death held no fear for him. He'd made peace with God years ago, exactly six months to the day after he'd shot and killed a suspect. He didn't mind dying, but he minded very much leaving Maggie and Rick. Somehow he had to fight back.

"No good. V fib."

"Epinepherine."

He mentally turned away from Maggie and focused again on the abstract sense of shifting. Something, somehow *connected,* and he couldn't see anymore. He was back in his body, not that he understood exactly how he'd gotten there. But back was good.

"Now we're getting someplace," the doctor grumbled. "The cardiac waves are coarser."

Another burst of electricity surged through Garrett, and his body convulsed in response.

"Don't hurt him," he heard Maggie sob softly.

"Again." They repeated the procedure.

This time when his body convulsed, he felt Maggie cringe.

"Sinus rhythm."

"It's all right, Mrs. Hughes," the original nurse assured her a moment later. "What you saw looked pretty frightening, but he didn't feel anything. He wasn't at all aware of what happened just now."

Like hell! Garrett shot back, annoyed.

Maggie shrugged. "Maybe you're right. But I like to believe that co...coma patients are more aware of their surroundings than we know."

Garrett gave a wry mental grin. *So I've learned.*

"Mrs. Hughes, go home and rest. We'll call you if there's any change."

Garrett tensed as he felt Maggie's hesitation. He didn't want her to leave. For the first time in his life, he suddenly felt as if he truly had a chance to understand the only woman he'd ever loved, and he didn't want to lose that.

"Not…just yet."

Garrett would have shouted for joy if he'd been able.

"All right," the nurse agreed dubiously, "but wearing yourself out won't help him." Standard hospital tripe and, as Maggie ignored her, pure elation rippled through him.

As the team filed out of the room, Maggie moved closer, and his inability to see aggravated him beyond all reason. *I want to see your face again, babe. I need to tell you I love you.* Inwardly, he groaned in frustration. Seeing meant leaving his body, and he'd courted death too much since he'd walked onto the airliner's flight deck. *When I wake up, am I even going to remember any of this?*

He felt her turbulent emotions rising and falling, the anger and guilt and confusion. When she finally spoke, her words came so softly, he doubted the nurse could hear them from her chair across the cramped room.

"Garrett, you always did know how to shred my life." She swallowed hard. "You can't keep doing this to me. I can't take it." Her voice dropped even lower. "I love you too much."

Without warning, she moved away, and he felt her presence retreat down the hall.

Maggie, come back here. My being this way doesn't have anything to do with my job! Stop running!

Within seconds she was out of reach. Without thinking, he rose to follow her, and the cardiac monitor's alarm screamed in retaliation.

Oh, hell.

Maggie turned the key in the lock with the same white-knuckled intensity with which she'd gripped the steering wheel all the way home. Today, the normally welcoming creak of the old door sounded less like a friendly greeting and more like a lonely echo of her mangled emotions.

"That you, Mom?" The voice coming from the dining room sounded much younger than its sixteen years.

She sighed heavily. "Yeah." The aroma of fresh brewed coffee floated in the air and, like an automaton, she walked into the dining room. Rick, a young version of his father, nearly Garrett's height of six foot one and just beginning to fill out, sat at the table idly tapping a fingernail against the handle of a coffee mug.

Desperate to lighten the mood, she quipped, "Why can't you get your caffeine from tooth-rotting sodas like a normal kid?" The effort at humor fell flat.

Rick shrugged but didn't look up. The dark shadows under his eyes emphasized the downcast set to his features. He hadn't slept last night either.

"I made a whole pot of coffee if you want some," he murmured as if unable to think of anything else to say.

Maggie retrieved a steaming cup for herself and sat down. More than the expanse of the cherry-wood table separated them. "You want to talk about it?" she asked.

Rick quit tapping his mug and pulled both hands into his lap in a defensive posture. She took a sip and waited him out.

"I know you're mad at me, Mom, but I just can't go see him."

"Why not?"

"When you divorced him, I guess he sorta divorced me."

Not flinching took all her willpower. If Rick realized how close she was to collapse, he'd clam up, and she'd never get to the bottom of this. "His move to Washington didn't change his feelings for you. I know you're hurting, but we've always been open and honest with each other. Hiding something this important isn't like you. And it couldn't have been an accident. What gives?"

Rick shot her a bitter look. Then, with a willpower to match her own, he quelled it and returned to staring into his coffee.

"Because I loved you both." His voice wobbled, and he cleared his throat. "Admitting you were right was like choosing."

Maggie's own throat clogged with tears she didn't dare shed.

He raised his eyes. "I never told you that I tried to call him six months ago."

She took a steadying sip. "You've called him a number of times since the divorce. What's special about that one?"

"The phone company didn't have a listing." Rick's whole body trembled, and he hunched down in the chair. "All I had was the safe line number where I could leave a message."

Maggie ached for him. "He told us both he'd been assigned to a case that had gotten extremely complicated. After paying rent for a year on an apartment he never used, he let it go."

"That was two years ago!" The dry disbelief sounded so much like Garrett that Maggie shuddered. "Mom, he had to be living somewhere. If he cared about me, I'd have more than a message number."

"Then ask him about it."

Rick recoiled as if she'd suggested something vile. "Nice try, Mom, but no thanks."

Under normal circumstances she wouldn't have tolerated such an attitude. Then again, under normal circumstances Rick wouldn't behave this way.

"Sweetheart, don't condemn him without giving him—"

"A chance?" Rick shot to his feet. "You were right, Mom. All he cares about is busting drug dealers."

Maggie winced. "I never said that. Never."

"You didn't have to. I knew how you felt!"

Maggie took a couple of rapid breaths and fought for her words. "He loves you. But there's a part of him that demands he try to make the world a little safer, a little more decent. Good cops aren't just logging in hours at a job. It's who they are."

Rick gave her a scornful look. "Like I said. Dad's only interested in his work."

"Sweetheart, you're not listening." Garrett might not have been with them physically, but the emotional desertion Rick claimed simply hadn't happened. Deep inside, Rick had to know it, too, but the volatile emotions of the teenage years weren't letting him see it.

"What about you, Mom? Does he love you, too?"

The answer sat on her finger, all two carats of it. Thankfully Rick hadn't noticed. "More than you know." Maggie sighed. Her shoulders sagged a little under the weight.

Rick crossed his arms defensively across his chest. "He wrote us off. That's not love."

Rick's accusation clawed its way through her conscience. Hadn't she been guilty of writing off Garrett when she heard the code blue as she was leaving? Hadn't she refused to be there when he really needed her? She took a shuddering breath. Time to change the subject and give them both breathing room. "Were there any phone calls after I talked to you?"

He gave her a sharp, penetrating look. "Like who?"

"The hospital." She took her half-empty coffee mug to the kitchen and poured the contents into the sink.

Rick growled something unpleasant under his breath. "I'm going to the arcade for a while." The chair legs scraped against the hardwood floor as he scooted his chair back.

She didn't attempt to stop him, and listened morosely to the agitated tread of his footsteps on the living room carpet. When the front door slammed, she jumped, then wrapped her arms around herself, longing to wake up from the nightmare.

Garrett discovered that, although he didn't sleep per se, he could drift in and out of awareness. Passionately, he wanted to somehow communicate, but whenever he tried to move, his heart stopped. It was a real nuisance. Grudgingly, he allowed that his body needed time to heal. Patience was a skill he had learned early on in police work, but that didn't mean he liked it. The largest hurdle—surviving the plane crash—had been overcome. Before long, he'd walk out of here, then he could concentrate on getting his family back.

Since the divorce, Blake had kept him posted. Maggie rarely dated, and that pleased him immensely. He wouldn't have to worry about destroying any romantic entanglements she might have.

A warning voice told him his cold-bloodedness was a left-over from Gary Reeves, the identity he'd assumed three years ago. Reeves wouldn't have let a simple thing like morality interfere with whatever he'd wanted.

"Good morning, Garrett."

Maggie! He had been lost in thought, and she'd sneaked up on him. He soaked up the emotions she radiated—hurt, confusion and resentment, all hidden beneath forced cheerfulness. *Someday soon, babe. I don't know how, but somehow I'll make it right between us.*

The memory from when he'd accidentally left his body the day before had a crystalline clarity. Her soft features had grown more beautiful over the years, and her hair still hung to her shoulders in a soft, fluffy, auburn cloud. He wanted to reach out and stroke her satin skin, run his fingers through her hair, but he contented himself with reaching for her the only way he could, with his mind. What he touched stopped him cold. *Guilt?*

"The nurse said you've been more…stable since I left."

Oh, so that's it. Babe, staying here wouldn't have helped. My heart stopped because I don't have a handle on this yet.

Maggie cleared her throat. "The tendons in your arm are damaged, and I need to massage them. That will help until you're strong enough for more surgery." There was a long pause as she worked, struggling to find something neutral to say. "Do you remember that cabin we almost bought? Good thing we didn't. A fire wiped out that whole area last summer."

Garrett mentally shook his head. *Babe, I know you're upset, but don't hide in trivia. Tell me what's eating you.*

She skipped from one subject to the next. By the time she

began sharing anecdotes about Blake's girls, he realized something odd. In her wandering monologue, she never once mentioned their son. *Where's Rick?*

"I'm putting in a new flower bed in the backyard." Beneath the calm voice, she was a wreck, hiding behind trivia to keep from falling apart.

It unnerved him. *What's wrong with Rick, babe?*

"I'm redoing a whole section of sprinkler pipe. It's kind of fun. Working in the yard, I can see something accomplished when I'm through. And unlike housework, it stays done."

Talk to me! Frustration and worry gathered like storm clouds, and the cardiac monitor's bleeps came faster, keeping time with his agitation.

"Well—" she cleared her throat again "—I suppose I'd better get to work."

Don't go, he pleaded. *There must be a way I can communicate with you. Give me a chance to figure it out.* He felt her ease away from the bed.

"Mom's coming back as soon as she gets someone to watch Dad."

Watch Dad? Garrett suffered a bout of mental whiplash. *Why does Dad need watching?*

"Blake will be by later. He needed some sleep. Between you and another crash victim, he hasn't had much sleep lately."

Fear congealed into anger. *I don't want to talk about my brother's insane work schedule. He's been doing that for years. Maggie, what's wrong with Dad, and where's our son!*

"I'll come back as soon as I've got work covered."

Agitation boiled unchecked. Quite unintentionally, he moved—not his body, just him. An obnoxious buzzer sounded.

Maggie gasped. Garrett froze. The buzzer went silent.

Within seconds, a team of nurses and their assorted cronies surrounded him, checking readouts and poking at him.

"Just a little cardiac flutter, Mrs. Hughes," one of them

assured her compassionately. ''Actually, we've upgraded his condition from grave to critical.''

He felt Maggie gratefully take in the dubious good news.

Didn't mean to scare you, babe. The need to wrap his arms around her became overwhelming. His family needed him, and he couldn't even open his eyes. *How in the hell does one revive a comatose body?*

Chapter 3

Blake set the large pepperoni pizza on the table between himself and Maggie, and they took a seat. "Mag, the problem is that you're fighting all the old issues that tore up the marriage the first time."

"Tell me about it." Maggie took a large bite of too-hot pizza and chewed slowly as if in thought.

Blake leaned back in the padded booth, his lips pressed together in a flat line. "My point is that it's not just his being a cop. If he'd been an accountant or a pharmaceutical salesman, you'd still have climbed the walls every time he walked out the door."

Her hackles went up. "I'm not a clinging vine."

"No, but you're so convinced that those who love you will desert you in the long run that you reject us first."

"That's ridiculous."

"Is it?" He skewered her with a look that said she'd hear him out even if he had to tie her up with surgical gauze. "Then why, after the divorce, did it practically take an act of Congress to get you to rejoin the family?"

"What do you mean?"

"You were so convinced that blood was thicker than the heart that you assumed we'd written you off."

Uncomfortable with the memories of the Hughes clan arriving on her doorstep with a picnic basket and announcing it was past time for a *family* dinner, she looked away.

During the ten years of her childhood that she'd been a ward of the state, she'd been in so many foster homes she'd quit counting. Each new address meant nothing more than the label of the next place she would live for a while. Sort of like the brand on a loaf of bread, only important if you were looking for a specific one. Until the last one when she was sixteen— right next door to Patrick and Laverne Hughes and their two sons.

Her new foster parents paid everyone an allowance for certain chores. Her first week there, she'd been scrubbing dead bugs off a car windshield when two boys pulled up next door in a beat-up truck that probably had been red at one time. Now, it was mostly rust, primer and a lot of good intentions.

The older of the pair was more man than boy and handsome in an inflexible sort of way. He maneuvered a football helmet and assorted sports gear from one arm to the other and crossed the lawn to where she stood. His sapphire-blue gaze raked over her with lightning speed, and softened in surprised approval. A solid strength radiated from him. His stance labeled him as a rock, someone his friends could always count on.

"I'm Garrett." His seductive, smooth voice shot straight to her heart. He tossed a glance over his shoulder at the other boy, a teenager about her age and impossibly good-looking. "That's Blake."

Thunderstruck by Garrett, she barely noticed.

He cocked his head expectantly, and she wondered if he had a clue that he'd shut down her nervous system. It took an embarrassingly long time to make it work again. "I'm Maggie Jean Kincaid."

"The Smiths's new foster kid?" Blake asked.

Maggie barely heard him she was so locked into Garrett's

mesmerizing presence. Why was she out here washing the car, wearing grubby clothes? Why couldn't she have met him when she had her hair combed and makeup on? Or better yet, wearing a swimsuit? Instead, she looked like a refugee from a thrift shop.

Maggie stared helplessly, unable to think. As if he couldn't help himself, Garrett reached out and brushed a strand of long auburn hair from her cheek. His touch warmed her like a fire on a foggy winter night.

"Are you going to be living here a while?" Garrett gave her a tenderly hopeful smile that she still treasured after twenty years.

"Earth calling Hughes. Come in, space cadet." Blake's amused voice and his knuckles rapping loudly on a table interrupted her reverie.

Maggie blushed and chuckled at herself.

"Where did you go?" Weary merriment danced in his eyes.

"Just remembering the day we all met." Feeling strangely shy, she picked a mushroom off her pizza. "I sort of melted into a little puddle at his feet that day. It's a wonder you two didn't laugh your heads off."

"Big brother made a bigger puddle than you did. It took two weeks of reciting 'jailbait' like a divine mantra before he was human again." Blake took a generous bite and worked it to one side of his mouth to talk. "Oh, by the way, don't ever heckle a college senior about love at first sight, especially one who's there on a football scholarship. It can get painful."

Tension melted away. She couldn't find the right words, but she smiled at him in gratitude. Garrett had always been her love, but Blake had always been the brother she could turn to.

"Think about what I said, Mag," he whispered. "Rejecting people first has hurt you as long as I've known you. I know you're aware you do that, but seeing a problem and confronting it aren't the same."

"Eat your pizza, Doctor."

* * *

Maggie walked into Garrett's room and checked the monitors before she could bring herself to look at his motionless form lying in the steel-framed bed. Better. Not great. But better. Only after she studied his chart, too, and assured herself that he wasn't in any immediate danger of dying, did she settle into the chair beside his bed.

You're a coward, Hughes, she chastised herself silently. *What would you have done if he'd been worse when you walked in? Run? Desert him before he could desert you?* She didn't realize she was crying until a fat tear dropped onto the back of her hand. Fishing in her pocket for a tissue, she sniffed loudly.

The sound jolted Garrett into awareness. *Maggie?* He searched with his mind, found it sluggish to respond. He knew Maggie was in the room, but he couldn't quite locate her, nor could he sense her emotions. The unnatural ability had unsettled him, but losing it was even worse, especially since he still couldn't feel his body. *Does this mean I'm getting better? Or worse?*

She took his hand. And he felt it! Sort of. It was more like a numb pressure. But it was something. Sheepishly, he imagined her rubbing it between her own like she used to while they'd nuzzled on the couch watching a movie and he'd fed her popcorn.

"Garrett, it's me."

Her voice was heaven. He'd spent too many hours alone in the solitude of his mind. Worry over Rick and his father had taken some imaginative and vicious turns. His mother had come alone that morning, and she was tired, more so than he could believe.

"Blake and I had lunch today. In case you're interested, that man can still pack away more junk food than any human being I know. A doctor should know better."

He took a mental breath. *No trivia, babe. Where are Dad and Rick? Did Dad have another stroke?*

She explained the massage technique she used on his arm

to keep the tendons from becoming atrophied until Dr. Kelly could get him back into surgery. The physical sensation wasn't strong enough to call pain, more of a vague discomfort, but he had the sneaking suspicion that if he were fully conscious it would send him through the roof.

My arm's not important now, babe. Tell me what's going on with the family.

"Do you remember my eighteenth birthday?"

Annoyance over her choice of subject flashed through him, but he took a deep mental breath and accepted it. Maggie had no intentions of telling him anything she deemed unpleasant, and he was just going to have to live with it. For now.

"Mom gave me the most incredible party."

Despite himself, he smiled inside. *How could I not remember? I'd been counting the days until you'd be legal. I nearly proposed that night, but I hadn't been accepted to the academy yet, and I wanted to wait until I knew I had a job.*

"I'd loved you for so long, and I really expected you to propose. When you didn't, I stupidly cried myself to sleep." She laughed. "I sure had some growing up to do."

He chuckled. *You were worth waiting for.* Love swept through him, and he envisioned himself wrapping her into an inescapable embrace. *I never told you I'd already bought the engagement ring. I couldn't afford much, and the size of that microscopic diamond chip embarrassed me for years. Why didn't you ever want a larger stone?* He paused. *Well, babe, you've got a respectable rock now. Maybe this one will still stay on your finger.*

"I love you, Garrett. More now than I did then." Her voice cracked, and she cleared her throat self-consciously. "You need to get well. One-sided conversations leave much to be desired."

I noticed.

"Rick, he's your father." Maggie had bolstered herself the entire trip home for this confrontation. Now they faced each other, invisible battle lines drawn on the living room carpet.

The sixteen-year-old's arms hung boardlike at his sides, his hands clenched into white-knuckled fists, and his jaw tilted in implacable defiance. Maggie tasted failure but plugged on.

"What do you want me to do, Mom? Walk in there, wave and say 'Hi'? 'Let me introduce myself'? 'I'm the son you forgot'?"

Maggie died a little inside. How could she have lived every day with him and not seen this? "If he lives, you two can argue all you want. But if he doesn't, twenty years from now you'll feel differently than you do today. I don't want you to live with that kind of regret."

"Not damn likely."

"Watch your mouth!"

His lips pursed together, and he turned toward the stairs. "I've got studying to do." He reached for the banister.

Maggie latched onto his arm and levered him back around. Young muscles bunched rock-hard beneath her fingers. "Running solves nothing." Inside, she winced, condemned by her own words. "Tomorrow morning, you and I are going to the hospital—together." The wheels turned behind his eyes, and his mutinous expression slowly transformed into one of cold reason.

"I have school, and my boss needs me right after."

"Your family is more important than school or your job."

"Really?" Beneath the sarcasm, she heard the hurt of a little boy's hidden wounds. "I'm just following in my old man's footsteps. He'd be proud."

Rendered speechless, Maggie's hold on his arm slackened, and she stood helplessly as he strode upstairs. How could she condemn her son for running away from the pain when that was exactly what she'd done? Condemn, no. Understand, yes. And getting him to deal with this before it hardened into a permanent scar was critical. With a heavy sigh, she trudged up after him.

A total stranger would have known which of the two upstairs bedrooms was Rick's—the one with the closed door. She raised her hand to knock, but a muffled sob from inside

stopped her. It was followed by the sound of something break-
able shattering against a wall. She listened intently as he raged
against his pain in a garbled, tear-filled whisper. Parental instincts screamed that she needed to charge into that room and
comfort her child, but hard-won wisdom held the impulse in
check.

In some ways, boys were more vulnerable than girls. Despite twenty years of Alan Alda's influence, society still dictated that real men didn't cry, and a teenage boy would rather
die than seek solace in his mother's arms.

Her heart broke, and she leaned against the door, caressing
the wood. Another splintering crash punctuated the sobs, but
a tenuous hope rose within her. As long as Rick's emotions
were this raw, he hadn't written his father off completely.

"Dear Lord," she whispered so softly that no one but God
could hear, "Garrett's got to live. Our son needs him."

What little time Maggie spent at work the next day was
hell. Two new patients arrived at Rutherford-Petrie, one of
whom was combative and had to be placed in restraints. The
other had a load of self-pity that would have choked an ox.
The day's only saving grace was her success at lining up people to cover the most important of her responsibilities.

For the next two days, she carried photo albums to Garrett's
room in ICU, described the family snapshots and added her
own commentary. Seeing those ghosts from the past tore her
heart out, but she kept her voice light and nostalgic for his
sake. He needed the stimulus of the human voice, an anchor
for his mind to hang on to. When she ran out of albums, she
read magazines.

No amount of coaxing could get Rick into the hospital. Out
of desperation, she nearly had Laverne try, but it seemed more
than a little underhanded to set the kid's grandmother after
him. Rationally, she knew Rick had to work through this himself, and as long as Garrett remained in a coma, he had time.

Five days after the crash the doctors upgraded Garrett's condition from critical to guarded and weaned him off the respirator.

"Rick's going through a tough time right now," she murmured, "and you're the only one who can help him." She couldn't believe what just slipped out. Drained, she closed her eyes and rested her head on the mattress. *How much longer, Lord?*

Garrett's fingers trembled. Maggie's eyes flew open, and she stared at their joined hands, watching in joyous fascination as his fingers curled weakly around her own. She leaped to her feet, her gaze desperately seeking his face.

"Garrett?" she wheezed, unable to get air past the sudden constriction in her throat. "Garrett, can you hear me?"

She bent close, drawing his hand with her. As if by supreme effort, his eyes fluttered open. His gaze was unfocused, but he was definitely conscious.

With a glad cry, she scattered teary kisses across his cheeks and mouth. He didn't kiss her back, but that didn't matter. Tears flowed freely, and she laughed a bit hysterically.

"You always told me you were tough to kill. I should have believed you."

Blake's solid footsteps sounded behind her. "Maggie?"

Casting a euphoric grin over her shoulder she pronounced, "He's awake."

Blake's eyes rounded in terrible hope as he made long strides to the bed. But as Maggie turned back, Garrett's eyelids drifted closed.

"No! Don't you dare fade out on me." She knew she wasn't being rational, but she didn't care.

Blake leaned over his brother, his voice rasping and unnaturally loud. "Come on, bro. You've come this far. Let's see those eyes again."

Garrett's stillness was all the more frightening because of the hope preceding it. Maggie clenched her jaws and swallowed back a fresh wave of hysteria.

"It's okay," Blake assured her softly, laying a hand on her

shoulder. "Only people in movies come out of a coma bright-eyed and demanding cheeseburgers."

She knew consciousness usually returned in stages, but she badly needed to hear the words anyway. Still clinging to Garrett's hand, she hugged the only brother she'd ever had.

Pain.

It hit Garrett during the night, starting hazy and shadowlike. Doggedly it grew into a blinding inferno, dragging him from a surreal world that he couldn't quite believe in to a no-man's-land of hell's own torment. Fractured ribs screamed with every breath. His right arm pulsed fire from elbow to fingertips, and the agony in his lower back defied description.

Think, man.

Pain.

Endless throbbing fire.

The pull of death's call flooded back, tempting him to reach for it, embrace it totally. Anything to escape the flames. But what little coherent thought wasn't pain-blurred fought back.

My son's in trouble. Maggie needs me.

His eyelids felt as if they belonged to someone else. Nothing worked. Maggie clutched his hand with both of hers. He focused on the long-denied sensation of skin against skin, a lifeline to keep the mind-numbing fire from burning him to ash.

Mentally clawing his way toward Maggie and consciousness, he closed his fingers around hers. Her glad shriek settled into his ears like a soothing balm. Summoning his meager strength, he dragged his eyes open. Light! And Maggie leaning over him, kissing his face.

He wanted to smile, tell her out loud he loved her, but a thick fog closed around him, smothering the white-hot fire under a blanket of peaceful oblivion.

The next time Maggie entered ICU her step was distinctly lighter. Rick had taken the news with a silent trembling and a falsely nonchalant nod, another cause for hope.

She tiptoed with inexplicable shyness toward Garrett's bed. "Are you awake?"

His eyes opened immediately. They were clear, focused but dark with pain. He seemed to devour her, and she framed his face in her hands and planted a kiss squarely on his mouth. His lips moved in response. Although she couldn't call it a proper kiss, it affirmed life, and that made it all the sweeter.

"Can you talk?" she whispered, unable to break the contact between her palm and his beard-stubbled cheek.

She watched, fascinated, as he swallowed laboriously. "Yeah." His voice was hoarse from disuse.

"Is this where I ask how you feel?"

"You don't…want to know." His brows lowered in puzzled contentment. "You really stayed."

Self-reproach washed through her. After the divorce, she'd given him ample reason to believe she wouldn't be here for him.

"I've become sort of a fixture at this place lately."

He swallowed again, a little more easily this time. Tension lines bracketed his eyes. "Where are Rick and Dad?"

The question hit her like a blow to the stomach. How to answer? She refused to tell him the truth, not with him this weak. "Well," she hedged, "Rick's at school, and Dad doesn't get around like he did before his stroke."

Garrett's expression became anguished, confused, accusatory. "Why the games, babe? What's…going on?"

Maggie nearly swore. Even in his fragile condition, he'd seen through her lame attempt at avoiding the subject. For the first time in her life, she wished she'd cultivated a talent for lying. "What makes you think anything's wrong?"

Anger flashed across his square features.

His body may be a mess, she thought, chagrined, *but his brain works just fine.*

"Don't." His voice, still hoarse, took on a faintly demanding note. "You said he…needed me…. Didn't sound minor."

Her breath hissed in between her teeth.

"Why does…Dad need…watching?"

Choking on her panic, Maggie whispered, "You heard what we all said?"

Garrett nodded, his gaze an agitated plea for answers. "I don't...understand what I went through.... And I don't know...if I remember everything.... But what I do remember..." His expression softened heartbreakingly. "Talk to me."

Stunned, Maggie could only stare at him. She'd always believed that coma patients were aware, but was there more to it than she suspected? Then a miserable—and admittedly selfish—thought descended on her. *Does he remember when I told him I still loved him?*

Her abrupt uneasiness was foolish, she knew, but Garrett was awake, and that meant *she* was the vulnerable one now. And she'd had a week of being by his side to erode her resolve not to get drawn back into his life.

He tightened his grip on her hand, rubbing her fingers between his own as if to reacquaint himself with touch.

Think, Hughes. You've got to distract him. "Do you remember the...ah...accident?"

A slow frown creased his brow. "What'd I do? Get plowed into by a drunk driver?"

Amnesia is normal, she told herself. *You know that.* Then she realized she had stumbled onto the perfect subject change. "No, you really put your special touch on this one."

His attentive expression told her he'd picked up on her wry tone. *He should, it's genuine enough.* She then told him the details as she knew them.

"Suspects?"

"Spoken like a true cop," she muttered sadly.

He suddenly started thrashing in bed, his breath ragged gasps. "That case I was on... My cover got blown...but I didn't think the cartel...learned who I was.... Oh, God...you and Rick! Call—"

Maggie shut him up the most effective way she could think of, by clamping her hand over his mouth. "It's okay. The bomber was a disgruntled employee, a basic psycho. It's been all over the news. The investigator asked the plane crew to keep quiet about you, considering your undercover work, and Blake has kept everything quiet from the hospital's end. You should almost be glad you missed the first excitement.''

The tension melted from his body, and he closed his eyes.

''Apparently, he wanted everyone dealing with the bomb to think they were safe once they disarmed the first one. He didn't tell anyone about the second one. He just let it go off on its own. When the FBI closed in on him, he committed suicide.''

Garrett nodded in acceptance. ''Anything else?''

''Your partner survived, too.''

His eyes widened. ''What was Tom doing...with me?''

''He said you two were on vacation and simply flew out on the same plane. You can ask him more when you're a little stronger. Right now he's in a burn ward across town, and they're getting ready to transfer him to a hospital back east near his sister.''

A subtle tensing of his body told her he wasn't handling the unknown details well. Frankly, neither was she. *Had there been more than a reconciliation on your agenda when you came home?*

He grunted, accepting but far from satisfied. His gaze made a slow sweep of the ICU cubicle. He took in his broken arm and the assorted medical equipment as if they were what he expected, familiar even. Gradually, his attention focused on their joined hands, and the diamond ring she wore.

A slight smile warmed his face. ''I remember this. We're getting married again.''

The deep contentment in his voice set off alarms. ''What I agreed to,'' she said, ''was that we'd talk about it.''

His eyes glittered. She'd known him long enough to recognize when he believed a subject was settled and no longer warranted discussion.

''We'll talk, Garrett,'' she said, stepping hard on her fluttering heart. ''And now isn't the time.''

He blinked slowly, as if humoring her. Despite his weak-

ened condition, Garrett Hughes's force of will was still im-
pressive. "What day is it?"

Maggie almost told him the day of the week, but remembered something more relevant. "Well," she said with a sigh,
"if we were still married, today would be our seventeenth
anniversary."

"I lost a week?" he said, shaken. "I'd planned to propose
today. But I guess…" He squeezed her hand. "Happy anniversary anyway, babe."

She could practically see thoughts churning behind his penetrating gaze, and a dark sensation of entrapment crept over
her. *For Pete's sake, the man can't even move, and I'm running from him!*

An uneasiness returned to his features, and his gaze settled
determinedly on her face. "Can we talk about Rick now?"

Maggie tried not to flinch but did anyway.

"I need answers, Maggie."

"Rick's fine. He'll be here later this afternoon."

He searched her eyes for truth, and she let him. *That kid'll
be here if I have to club him over the head.*

Garrett dragged himself from sleep as Blake walked in, a
stethoscope slung around his neck.

"Morning, big brother. You awake?"

"Unfortunately." The painkillers made living tolerable, but
the fuzzy-headed side effects left much to be desired. Much
of yesterday was a blur, and he suspected entire chunks were
missing. Maggie had said she would bring Rick by. Had she?
Garrett searched his memory.

No, Rick had come down with the flu. His parents had been
here, though. The memory of his mom's joy-filled, tear-
streaked face was vivid. Dad had seemed unusually quiet, but
nothing to worry over. Maybe some of his coma memories
weren't all that reliable after all.

A tranquil sense of victory crept through him. He'd survived
a plane crash—which he now remembered in detail—and

Maggie had accepted his proposal. "I've got my family back, Blake. Would you be my best man again?"

Blake was too long in answering. "You got it, but we need to talk about your injuries first."

Despite the relaxed inflection, the younger man's body language radiated tension like a warning beacon. Moreover, he wore his best doctor face. Blake's blue-collar background and laid-back attitude drove stuffier colleagues nuts, but right now Garrett saw no trace of anything less than the polished, medical professional. He knew his injuries were extensive. The news couldn't be good, but he'd gotten through the worst and would easily handle whatever his brother was about to drop on him.

"Out with it, little brother. The broken arm and ribs already introduced themselves. So did my wrenched back. What else?"

Blake let his breath out slow. "How much have you tried to move around?"

Evasion? That's not like you. Acid ribbons of dread burned their way through his veins. "Almost none. You medical wizards have me in restraints. Why? New ICU policy to keep patients from falling out of bed?"

For an olive-skinned man, Blake turned shockingly pale. "Not restraints exactly. You're trussed up to keep your spine immobile."

Garrett watched, patiently, intently, as Blake drew back the covers. The brace reminded him of a straitjacket without sleeves. "No wonder I couldn't move."

"Tell me when you feel something." He pulled something pointed and shiny from his pocket and prodded at the bottoms of Garrett's feet.

No sensation at all. A corner of his mind recoiled as Blake poked both calves and thighs. Reflexes were checked, then checked again, but Garrett's legs remained as limp as those of a corpse. Needing reassurance, he tried to move them, but got nothing for his trouble. Blinding panic threatened to engulf him, but he flattened it. "What's wrong with my legs?"

Blake covered him back up and sagged heavily into the chair. "You got slammed around pretty bad during the crash. The damage to internal organs was messy, but fixable."

"Okay," he said warily. "What wasn't fixable?"

Blake's face became masklike, a caricature of professional composure. Blood throbbed in Garrett's ears, and terror-spawned adrenaline surged. Unwillingly, he looked down at the blanket-covered ridges that were his legs and feet, and he tried to flex his toes. Nothing.

Nothing!

He tried again, struggling for the slightest twitch.

Nothing!

A horror too deep for words screamed through his mind. "What won't fix?"

Blake's voice cracked. "Your spinal cord."

The horror blackened, obliterating Garrett's defenses, leaving no light to see, no air to breathe.

"The damage is low—third lumbar," Blake added quickly. "That's good. Bone fragments—"

"Quit dancing around!" he snapped, his voice harsh, fractured. "Bottom line."

"Bottom line?" Blake echoed, equally shattered. "Right now, you're paralyzed from the hips down. No one knows how much you'll regain with therapy. In cases like yours, it's a real crap shoot."

A wholly inadequate groan of anguish ripped from Garrett's soul. He tipped his head back and closed his eyes in a futile attempt to escape from the waking nightmare. He took a deep and brutally controlled breath. "Meaning you're not expecting much."

"I won't lie to you. It's…difficult. At this point, we can't find any nerve response at all, but that could be due to swelling." Blake gripped Garrett's shoulder. "Give it time."

Garrett swore softly. He wanted to rage at the top of his lungs, but the all-consuming shock left him without the breath.

"That's not all of it, but that's the worst."

"What else?"

"Your right arm."

He spared a defiant glare at his forearm strapped into a steel brace rather than a traditional cast. A fuzzy memory surfaced of Maggie massaging that arm. She had to have worked around the bars. She'd mentioned surgery. And surgery meant repairs. "What about it?"

Blake took a couple of shallow breaths before he continued. "Kelly's got you scheduled for surgery tomorrow. The tendons should have been operated on that first day, but keeping you alive took priority over restoring function to your hand."

"Restore?" *How much of me have I lost?* He forced his mind to remain calm, analytical, anything to keep the panic at bay.

Maggie rounded the corner into his cubicle. "Good morning," she chirped. Her gaze darted from him to Blake and back again, and her happy smile froze.

She knows. She's known all along.

His control shattered, leaving a black pit of uncertainty and self-doubt. He'd always been the strong one. Now, in the blink of an eye, his entire world had blown apart.

In a gesture beyond conscious will, he reached toward her with the one limb left to him that worked. Panicked indecision clouded her eyes. A memory returned of something he'd learned in the coma, the emotional price she'd paid for loving him. Now this.

"Maggie?" he whispered.

Tears dribbled onto her cheeks. Her indecision deepened, then vanished. An instant later she crossed the room, and fell into his one-armed embrace. She was warm and real, and he devoured the long-craved need to hold her.

The next few minutes were a jumble of hard embraces and futile reassurances that he'd walk again. He wanted to believe, but instincts screamed that she and Blake were lying through their collective teeth, as frantic to convince themselves as they were him. The pit sucked him in deeper as more and more implications of Blake's diagnosis rained down on him.

He needed an anchor to cling to until he had his emotions

in check. But asking that of Maggie was too much. He broke
their embrace and gently wiped away her tears, then his own.
Unable to resist one last touch, he stroked her rich auburn hair
and trailed a finger down her damp, porcelain cheeks.

"I'll be okay," he said, his voice not as steady as he would
have preferred, "but right now I need time alone."

The color leached from her face. "I don't like that idea."

Neither did he, but right now he couldn't cope with anyone
seeing him so completely unhinged, especially not the woman
he loved and the brother who'd idolized him when they were
kids.

Blake paced the floor, a doctor helpless to heal. Garrett
quirked his lips into a crooked smile. "Time will tell, little
brother."

"Damn right. We've got four years worth of basketball
games to catch up on." Blake's expression became fierce.
"Rehab gets you by the end of the week."

The door had barely closed behind them when Garrett
yanked away the blankets and lifted his head to stare at his
legs. Beyond assorted cuts and bruises, they stretched out before him looking unnervingly normal.

He tried to move. But it was as if they belonged to someone
else. There was nothing, no feeling, no indication of life. He
tried again. Failure followed failure, leaving only a simple
black truth.

Paraplegia.

Wheelchairs.

An end to the life he'd known and the man he'd been.

Alone, with no brave front to keep up, he let go and let the
grief do its work.

Blake eased himself and Maggie into a couple of chairs in
the corridor. Maggie barely felt the stream of tears that flowed
down her face and dripped onto her lap. Blake wrapped a long
arm around her and pulled her against his shoulder.

"He needed me so badly just now." She sobbed, her voice
muffled against his shirt. "And all I could think about was

running away. He knew it, too. I felt him pull back, trying to protect me. What kind of person does that make me!"

"A very human one, Mag." He kissed the top of her head.

They held each other in silence, soaking up support. Eventually, she gave him a wordless kiss on the cheek.

Wearily, he propped both elbows on his knees and buried his head in his hands. "How is Rick's 'flu'?"

"Just ducky," she replied bitterly. "This morning, he's not threatening to run away, provided of course I don't make him come to the hospital."

"Do you want me to talk to him?"

Maggie sighed heavily and rubbed at her face as if she could wipe away reality as well as the tears. "Thanks, but you've got enough on your plate. I'll figure something out." She shuddered.

An alarm screamed. "Code blue in three!"

Maggie and Blake lurched to their feet. He pushed her back down. "Stay put." He charged into Garrett's room, a team of nurses at his heels. A moment later, he sauntered out, his expression wry. "He's fine. He just tore off all the lead wires to the monitors."

"He what?" she demanded, coming to her feet.

Blake made a calming motion with his hands. "I'd be happier if he'd left them alone another couple of days, but it's okay."

His attitude appalled her, but the voice of reason made itself heard. Garrett's actions weren't anything she hadn't seen dozens of times. "He's lashing out."

"Exactly. Very normal. Very healthy." Blake shuddered. "God, what an oxymoron."

Chapter 4

Even a local anesthetic had been rough given the shape he was in, Garrett acknowledged, but the surgery on his arm had proceeded uneventfully. No one would know anything definitive until he'd had a lengthy shot at rehab. At least he was out of ICU and in a regular room in the neurology ward. The sanitary cubicle that was his new home sported a World War II–style gray- and black-tiled floor and drab off-white walls with matching privacy curtains. Its only redeeming qualities were the quiet and Maggie's presence.

"Does Rick really have the flu?" he asked.

The awkward distress that flickered across her face confirmed his suspicions and reopened that whole line of worry. He sighed, leaned back into the pillow and stared at the ceiling.

"He hasn't come once, not even while I was in a coma."

Her tiny gulp hurt him. He didn't like pinning her to the wall, but he had to learn what he was up against.

"You even remember who was here?" Her emerald eyes were huge. "How aware of your surroundings were you?"

If I answer that one, you'll never stop running from me. "Level with me, babe. What kind of trouble is Rick in?"

She broke eye contact, her gaze darting around the room as if looking for a safe haven, but there was none.

"Spit it out," he demanded.

"Garrett, he's not in a good place right now, and—"

His deepest fears had swirled through his mind, taunting and whispering. "Is it the law?"

Stunned, Maggie sat down hard in the bedside chair. "Never!"

A knock on the open door drew their attention.

"I'd shake your hand, son," Patrick said jovially as he, Laverne and Blake strolled in, "but I think I'll pass until your busted flipper mends."

Maggie's sigh of relief at getting off the hook didn't go unnoticed.

"Thanks, Dad." He cast a telling look at her that said the subject wasn't closed, only interrupted. "I heard you're not doing too well yourself right now. What's up?"

From the corner of his eye, Garrett saw his mother tense.

Patrick's gray brows shot up in surprise. "Not a thing. Fact is, I've been repairing your practice net."

Puzzled, Garrett blinked. *Practice net?*

"The cord was rotted." The older man frowned. "I can't find the receipt or I'd take it back. We paid too much for that thing to put up with shoddy workmanship. You won't get a scholarship if you can't practice throwing the ol' pigskin."

Garrett felt his jaw sag as another section of his world spun out of control. The man standing before him looked like his father, sounded like him, but was, in truth, a shadow. His mother looked old, worn. Haggard lines had aged her beautiful face ten years since he'd been home last.

"So much has happened," she whispered. Tears glistened in her soft brown eyes.

Speechless, he shot a look at Blake and Maggie, neither of whom seemed surprised by his father's senility or his mother's exhaustion. Was he the only one who hadn't known? Guilt, grief and anger added themselves to the emotional soup that had taken up residence in his gut.

Laverne turned to Patrick and pasted on a brave smile. "Honey, let's put the net away till next year."

Patrick mulled that over as he appraised the cast on his son's arm. "You're probably right." He brightened visibly, a caring parent's attempt to soothe a child's bitter disappointment. "Junior varsity is important, but not critical. You can still show them your stuff next year."

The heartache on his mother's face left Garrett no hope that he could be misinterpreting his father's condition.

His original plan had been to get Maggie and Rick to move back east with him, but he scrapped that. His parents needed him, and he was going to be here.

A nagging voice whispered the word *paraplegia,* and he recoiled. What if he became just one more burden for his family to bear? Everything within him rebelled at the idea. *I'm not spending the rest of my life in a wheelchair. My family can't afford it. No, I'm walking out of here.*

Fear whispered its doubts. *But what if you don't?*

Maggie sneaked out, a sense of purpose on her face. But he didn't have the faintest idea what she was up to. It was just as well, he decided. The effort of maintaining a cheerful facade drained him. Frankly he no longer had the energy to pry Rick's problems out of her. All he wanted was sleep.

Another hour dragged by before he and Blake were alone. Garrett felt a scowl tighten his face. A faint, rational voice said he was on the verge of doing something stupid, but the emotional overload was too strong to contain. "Why wasn't I told about Dad?"

Exhausted himself, Blake bristled. "You were in a coma."

"Dad's senility started a week ago?" he snarled.

The younger man rose to the bait. "For the past three years you weren't exactly easy to get hold of, big brother. Part of the time, we didn't know if you were alive. Now you're griping about a lack of medical updates?"

"That excuses how you underplayed everything when I

asked about him? Whenever I talked to him on the phone I knew something was wrong, but you brushed it—''

"So shoot me at dawn! You were in deep cover and weren't yourself—even on the phone. Talking to you was like talking to Mafia Central." The anger drained away, and Blake's voice softened. "I was afraid if I worried you, you'd lose your edge and get killed. I planned to tell you as soon as you started sounding like yourself again."

The logic took the wind out of Garrett's sails. Both men lapsed into a silence that hung thick in the room. "Sorry, Blake. Seeing him like that was a hard blow."

"I can understand that. I've had time to adjust. You got hit all at once." He shook his head and stared off at nothing. "He thinks I'm still dating Sue Murray."

A slow tension filled the room, a tension caused by too many problems with too few solutions. *Despite what you think, little brother, I* will *walk out of here. You've carried this alone long enough.*

A light knock on the door tore his attention from one set of devastating problems to another. Maggie stood in the doorway, a grimly determined smile glued to her face. She had an equally determined, one-handed grip on their son's upper arm.

Blake tugged nervously on his ear. "I, ah, think we'll talk about Dad later."

He started to leave, but his pager went off. He glanced from the doorway to the phone then back. After a moment's hesitation, he grabbed the phone and made a call. His face slowly transformed into an uncompromising mask. Fury rolled off of him in waves, and Garrett's attention was torn between visually devouring the son he hadn't seen in far too long and trying to figure out what was wrong with his brother.

Blake snarled some orders into the phone and slammed the receiver down.

"What happened?" Maggie asked.

"A five-year-old boy went through a windshield. Wasn't wearing a seat belt. If his mother hands me a Cousin George story, I won't be held accountable." With that he was gone.

Garrett's attention latched onto Rick with a heart-hunger for his only child. Rick's face was carefully blank, but his green eyes—so much like Maggie's—were mutinous. *My son wants nothing to do with me,* he realized with sick horror. He couldn't think of a relevant thing to say. "Hi." *That didn't come out as insipid as it sounded, did it?*

Maggie stepped into the room, discreetly propelling their reluctant offspring before her. "Hi, yourself," she chirped.

She cast a glance at Rick, who turned his face away, the last vestiges of a lost battle of wills. "Since he's over the flu, I went home to get him."

Her grip tightened subtly. If Garrett hadn't been watching for nuances, he would have missed it.

Rick jammed his hands into his jeans pockets, hunching his shoulders in belligerent defeat. "Yeah. I feel great."

The tone of voice was one reserved for a hated teacher, and Garrett's heart sank. He wanted to sweep his wife and son into a tight embrace. Only neither attempted to approach him and, for all intents and purposes, he only had one arm.

During the past three years, work had swallowed his life, and somehow in the unbearable loneliness he'd convinced himself that winning his family back would be easy. How wrong he'd been. How pathetically naive. "I've…missed you, Rick. I'm glad you're here."

A wary hunger lit the boy's eyes briefly before he snuffed it out. "No sweat, Dad."

Nothing in those three words or in Rick's body language allowed for a next step in building a conversation. Garrett's nervousness transmuted into full-blown fear of failure.

The boy turned to Maggie, obviously dismissing him. "What's a Cousin George story?"

Maggie glanced between the two of them, clearly preferring the conversation to go in a more constructive manner, but she answered anyway. "Everybody who doesn't believe in seat belts seems to have a Cousin George who got stuck on the railroad tracks one night. The only thing that saved him from getting hit by the train was that he wasn't wearing a seat belt and he didn't have to waste the time undoing it before he got out.'' She shrugged, casting a discreet look at Garrett, a subtle pleading for patience and understanding. ''RPI is full of Cousin George's relatives. On our gallows humor days, we call it job security.''

The words fell lifeless, swallowed by the tension that sang in the room.

Garrett tried again. ''Rick, you've grown nearly a foot.'' *Inane, but better than nothing.* ''Are you into basketball?''

The muscles in Rick's jaw flexed. ''Soccer. City youth league. We won the championship last year. Remember?'' The last was a challenge.

Why? Garrett knew he was treading on dangerous ground but didn't have the faintest idea what was going on, and he glanced at Maggie for insight. Her slender body was as taut as an overstretched rubber band. The slightest increase in pressure, and she'd snap. No clue there.

''I remember,'' he said quietly. ''I couldn't take any leave because of the case. I wanted to be here.''

Rick stuffed his fists deeper into his pockets. ''Nobody forced you to move.''

''Rick!'' Maggie let go of his arm as if she feared she might break it otherwise.

Garrett locked his gaze onto their son's face. ''I love you, son, and I need to know why you're angry. And why your mother had to force you to come here.''

Rick's face took on a bitter cast. ''You're going back to D.C. as soon as you leave the hospital, anyway. So what does it matter?''

Garrett took a slow breath and mentally sat on the urge to swear. *Just like his mother. If the subject gets too uncomfortable—change it.* ''I'm not going back east—ever.''

Their jaws sagged in unison. Another flicker of unguarded hunger lit the boy's eyes, but suspicion quickly erased it.

''Why?'' he asked belligerently. ''It sure isn't because of me.''

''You're a big part of it,'' he said softly.

Rick's face flamed with disbelief. "Yeah, right."

Keeping his peace cost Garrett everything he had. He knew he wasn't physically up to this right now. Resorting to scorched-earth heroics would only damage future chances to sort out this mess. He needed to talk to Maggie—alone. He needed details, but she didn't look up to providing them.

Instead, he reached for her, offering what comfort he could. She stared at his open hand for a moment before slipping her palm across his. Warmth radiated up his arm, rekindling a love he'd never been able to cool. Only God knew whether they had a future together or not. At least she was with him now.

Rick's gaze latched onto the ring she wore. His eyes widened in revulsion, and his face darkened with rage. "Mom, where'd you get that?" His voice shook.

Through Garrett's grip on Maggie's hand, he felt her flinch, although nothing showed on the outside.

"Nothing's settled yet," she said. "That's why I didn't tell—"

"You're gonna *marry* him again?" The bellowed demand echoed in the small room. His gaze ricocheted to his father. "No!"

Sick despair ripped through Garrett. Every time he thought he'd finally hit bottom, the black pit opened up a deeper cellar. He exploded. "What's wrong with you!"

Maggie raised her hands in a calming gesture and started to speak, but Rick yelled over her.

"You haven't come home in a year. In the past two months I called you eight times on the safe line, and you didn't call me back *once!* Now you come back and act like you belong or something." Rick opened and closed his hands as if unsure what to do with them. *"Well, we don't need you!"*

Garrett recoiled, stunned by the venom. "When they assigned that case to me three years ago, no one knew it would open up like it did. The last month was ugly—real ugly. I didn't dare call you again until I was out of it. Even then, my head was such a mess I needed another six weeks before I was fit to be around."

"You haven't sent for me in a whole year, *Dad,*" Rick snapped, ignoring him. "You had days off."

"You're not listening." Garrett struggled to quash the rising anger. "I didn't send for you because I wasn't me."

"Oh, give me a break," the teen snarled.

Maggie jumped into the battle. "Sarcasm won't accomplish anything." Rick rolled his eyes at her.

"Son, I'd been undercover too long. They were on the verge of pulling me in. I could no longer separate myself from Gary Reeves, the identity I'd assumed. I don't *ever* want you around men like him."

"Yeah, right, Dad," he said with a sneer. "You missed my whole life, but it was for my own good."

Garrett sucked in a deep breath. Broken ribs screamed, but the pain paled compared to the searing helplessness. When had his son become such a self-absorbed little punk? "That's not at all what I—"

"Enough!" Maggie snapped. The authority in her voice stopped them both. Garrett let out his breath slowly, and Rick slumped into the green vinyl and chrome chair. "We're not getting anywhere."

Rick lunged to his feet. "I'm taking the bus home." He glowered one last time at his father as he turned away. This time Maggie made no attempt to restrain him. Her head hung slightly, and her shoulders sagged.

"Rick, get back here!" Garrett ordered, but he might as well have talked to the wall. Maggie sagged into the vacated seat. Her head rolled back, and her brow furrowed.

"He didn't hear a word I said."

"Welcome to sixteen," she said, sighing.

Garrett returned to staring at the ceiling. Just before the crash, he'd wondered about the changes in his son. Never in his worst nightmare had anything like this occurred to him. He suddenly felt so alone. "Would you sit beside me, babe?"

She stiffened like an animal who feared being pounced on. "Please?"

Hesitantly, she perched on the edge of his bed. He slid his

hand along her side, desperate for the warmth of her body beneath her blouse. She shivered, refusing to look into his face, refusing to see his need. Deliberately, seductively, he ran his fingertips up her spine and drew her to him. She didn't resist.

Their lips touched, and all coherent thought fled under the onslaught of passion, exhaustion and stress. He drank as a man dying of thirst, and Maggie answered the force of his kiss with demands of her own. They tasted and nibbled, driving each other higher. A moan rolled from her throat and fueled the fire. He wanted to pull her beneath him and bury himself in her right there on the hospital bed. But he couldn't move, and her efforts to put her arms around him while avoiding taped ribs, a broken arm and a body brace only called unwanted attention to his helplessness.

Then yet another dawning horror settled on him. His brain was in the midst of hormonal storm, but the relevant part of his anatomy wasn't hearing the message at all. *God, no.*

She must have sensed his mental withdrawal. She backed off enough to look down at him, her eyes questioning, her hair forming a warm curtain around their faces.

Behind them came an outburst of wordless outrage. Maggie sat up, and Garrett allowed his tenuous one-armed hold on her to slip away. Rick stood in the doorway, looking murderous.

"I came back to apologize, Mom. I thought maybe I'd hurt your feelings, but I see you don't think about me any more than he does." He turned to go.

"Honey, wait." The anguish in her voice as she leaped from the bed tore Garrett up as much as Rick's rejection. In a flash, the two most important people in his life were gone, and he could do nothing.

Rick's battered, green Chevy sat in the driveway as Maggie pulled up beside it, and she breathed in relief and dread. He was home, but what could she say? How could she help him when her own emotions hung in shreds? And what exactly constituted help?

"Kids really ought to come with an owner's manual."

Reluctantly, she walked into the house and called out. No answer. When she reached his bedroom, her jaw dropped. It was *clean*, not only clean, but *dusted*. It actually looked like a human being lived here instead of a Neanderthal. Posters of rock stars covered the walls, and a life-size, glow-in-the-dark plastic skeleton stood beside his desk. A sticky note tacked to its forehead read No Fear.

A metallic clank sounded downstairs followed by muffled grumbling. Curious, she followed the assorted noises.

She found him in the master bathroom, lying on his back, working industriously inside the cabinet under the sink. A hand and arm appeared, looking strangely disembodied. Fingertips felt around blindly until they brushed a set of vise grips. A quick grab, then all promptly disappeared back underneath the sink.

"What are you doing?"

"Oh, hi, Mom," he said, his voice dull, lifeless. "You said the drain was clogged, so I'm fixing it. I tried that stuff in the can, but it didn't work, so I'm taking the pipes apart. I've about got—" The sound of gushing water accompanied an inarticulate screech.

Maggie gasped as she remembered the primary ingredient in drain cleaner. "Rick, get in the shower quick, and give me your clothes! That backed up water had lye in it. It'll eat holes in your skin."

Rick leaped into the shower, clothes and all, and turned the water on high.

"Did you get any in your eyes?"

"No." He stripped out of his sodden jeans and T-shirt, then handed the dripping garments over the frosted-glass shower door.

She ran them into the laundry, then came back to rinse drain cleaner from the inside of her wooden cabinets before it did any serious damage to the finish.

"Botched up big-time, didn't I?" he murmured, defeated.

"Don't worry about it." Actually, Maggie silently blessed

this little catastrophe. It gave them both something immediate to deal with, something other than the real catastrophe at the hospital. "Just consider this a crash course in better living through chemistry."

"You're not mad?" He sounded so much like a little boy expecting the lecture of his life that she had to grin.

"I needed to clean out these cabinets anyway. It just wasn't on my agenda for today, that's all."

He didn't answer.

"You okay in there?" she quipped. "Hair falling out or anything?"

"Ha, ha," he retorted dryly.

"Then I'll leave you in peace." She laid a clean, dry towel on the counter before heading to the kitchen.

By the time he joined her, a tremendous amount of tension between them had eased, and she smiled at him. Despite his current bizarre behavior toward his father, Rick was a good kid.

As she handed him a cup of coffee, she took a good look at the son she and Garrett had created. His auburn hair and green eyes were the only resemblance to herself she could see. It was as if those two features had been placed on a younger version of Garrett's face and body. Some days, looking at him made her remember things she wished she could forget.

"What's with the Mr. Fix-it?" she asked.

He took a sip and shrugged. She knew that shrug and hated it. It was identical to his father's I've-got-everything-under-control-so-let-*me*-worry-about-it shrug.

"Not that I don't appreciate the thought," she injected into the silence when it was clear he didn't want to talk.

"You're welcome." Again, so Garrett-like she wanted to ask if he'd practiced.

"Your father's lack of explanations caused some of our worst fights. Today isn't a good day to see if I'll put up with it any better from you."

Rick's gaze riveted onto her own. Unguarded rage blazed

in the sea-green depths before he masked it. "I'm not like him."

"If you say so," she said mildly, then went on the offensive. "Why were you fixing my sink?"

"It needed doing." His body language gave nothing away.

"And your bedroom?"

"That, too."

"Great projects, but what gives?"

She could see the turmoil behind his eyes as he weighed different responses, dismissing each in turn. Finally, he looked her straight in the eyes, his expression the bleak vulnerable one of a teenager who'd decided to own up to the truth. "When I was ten, Dad said that a child sees to his own wants. A man looks beyond himself and takes care of what's important." Rick glanced in the general direction of the bathroom. "Or tries to."

"Honey, what were you trying to do? Pay penance?"

"Sort of." He didn't quite look at her. "I don't know." The last came in a very small voice.

Time for definitive action. She put her hand on his shoulder. "I'm sorry his being away hurt you. I'm sorry he missed your soccer games. I know how important they are to you, but you've got your priorities a little out of balance."

The answering bark of laughter was bitter. "Give me a break, Mom. Soccer's not my life."

That startled her, but no worse than anything else.

His young body telegraphed indecision then stiffened in challenge. "How about this, Mom? Do you know what it's like to be the only virgin in high school?"

Maggie's jaw sagged, praying that her face didn't betray that she'd just been poleaxed.

"Dad said sex was too special to treat like a game, that with all the diseases out there I'd be taking my life in my hands. But he didn't tell me about the razzing I'd get."

"Why didn't you talk to *me*?"

He looked appalled. "No offense, Mom, but you're a woman."

"Your uncle isn't."

Rick's face twisted in misery. "Blake said to use a condom and pray it didn't break."

"Oh, very helpful," she snapped.

"We were joking around, and I don't think he knew I was serious. I didn't bring it up again." Clearly uncomfortable, he took another step away from her. "I needed my dad."

Your macho was on the line, and you needed him closer than a DEA safe line. More puzzle pieces fell into place, each with soul-jarring clarity. It would have been easier for him if Garrett had died. Rick could have grieved and learned to live with the loss. But rejection—even if only in his own mind— had ripped a hole in his heart that he'd carefully hidden until little remained but a festering wound and all its assorted toxins.

"No matter what you say is the right thing to do, Mom," he said miserably. "I just can't go back to the hospital."

She nodded in understanding. There was more to all this, but at least now she had the right pieces to the puzzle. "We'll work through it, honey."

He snorted in disbelief.

With clench-jaw determination, Garrett concentrated on the pathetically small wavy lines on the computer screen. Electrodes attached to key points along his leg muscles measured the electrical activity of the nerves. Most of the lines were flat, a feat nearly impossible with normal nerve signal in a conscious person, but at least something was getting through his damaged spinal cord.

For three months, the therapy sessions had been the same, intense exercise, massage, measuring nerve signal and stimulating contractions artificially so the muscles and nerves didn't atrophy. Even if he regained no more function than he had now, his overall health would be better.

The therapist standing at the foot of the table bent Garrett's leg at the knee. "Push toward me, Mr. Hughes."

Garrett's muscled body tensed from effort. White hot fire

slammed up his back. He forced his mind away from the staggering pain. Three of the lines rose slightly then flattened. He'd used every force of will he could gather, but it hadn't been enough to manipulate the weight of his own leg, much less put any pressure against the therapist's hands.

"Again," the man ordered.

They repeated the familiar routine for seemingly endless minutes, then switched to the other leg.

Determination and hard work hadn't accomplished a thing except drive home brutal reality. Life in a wheelchair was no longer a fear. It was a fact. He'd never wake up one morning and leave the hospital under his own power.

"I've had enough for one day, George."

The therapist looked up in surprise. "But we're only about half finished, Mr. Hughes."

"You may be, but I want to go back to my room."

"Look, Mr. Hughes, I know we're not seeing the progress we'd all like, but—"

Garrett exploded at the condescending tone. The man had done everything but pat him on the head and give him a cookie. "Cut the *we* crap! You're not the one whose life was flushed down a sewer." He ripped electrodes off his thighs, levered himself into a sitting position and grabbed for the ones below his knees.

The therapist stood off to the side, stunned. Garrett felt like a fool. His pain and frustration weren't this guy's fault. As he opened his mouth to apologize, he caught a motion out of the corner of his eye and glanced toward the door.

Rick stood there, his young face pinched with pity and disgust. Humiliation burned. "Well, son, you picked one hell of a time to show up. Thank you. I'm a little busy right now, so if you don't mind, I'd like some privacy."

Rick recoiled as if Garrett had punched him. He turned and fled.

Garrett shook his head to clear away the insanity. "Rick! Wait a minute."

"I'll get him." George sprinted from the room, leaving Garrett to drown in remorse. How could he have done that?

A moment later, the man returned alone. "I don't know where he disappeared to, Mr. Hughes, but I couldn't find him."

Garrett sighed. "Thanks for the help. I also owe you an apology."

"No, you don't. Patients blowing up comes with the job. You've been so even-keeled that I was beginning to wonder if you were superhuman or something." He smiled. "Can I replace the electrodes so we can get back at it? We only have today and tomorrow left before you're transferred, and I'd like to make the most of both."

"Please." Garrett couldn't begin to imagine how he'd undo the mess he'd created with Rick, but he'd have to find a way.

The next day, Maggie braced herself to enter Garrett's room. Accepting limitations had never been his strong point, and he was starting to crack. Tomorrow, he'd be released into the care of a spinal rehab center. She wondered if he secretly saw it as this hospital giving up on him.

Then there was the problem with Rick. Despite the boy's adamant refusal to set foot in the hospital three months before, he'd come sporadically anyway. He kept the visits polite, but resisted every attempt she and his father made to get past the wall he'd erected around himself. Garrett believed the best course was to wait him out.

The emotional load it added to what Garrett already carried made her nervous. During the past week, his emotional state had taken a frightening downhill slide, and now they needed to deal with the fiasco that had erupted yesterday. How much more pressure could he take before he snapped completely?

She shut the door, her heart inextricably entwined with the man sitting in the bed, his eyes closed, his sensuous full lips pulled taut in a frown or grimace of pain; she couldn't tell which. Popular myth aside; paraplegics often experienced a great deal of pain. Garrett endured it all with single-minded determination. Often the only evidence of the price he paid was the clenching of his jaw or breath a little too controlled.

Some days he spent in a wheelchair reading the newspaper or staring at the walls. It grieved her that the rooms here didn't all have windows like at RPI. Some days—like today—he sat in bed, the TV on but unwatched, his thoughts closed.

Maggie pasted a perky smile on her face and stepped toward him. During the past three months, the broken vertebra had healed and, through herculean effort, he'd retrained his lower back muscles so he could sit unassisted. He'd always been such a dynamic man. Having such a simple thing as that be a major accomplishment half killed her. "'Morning."

His head snapped around. He hadn't noticed her—odd for him. He always seemed so aware of his surroundings that she'd often accused him of having eyes in the back of his head.

Longing flickered across his square features but vanished as quickly as it had appeared. She wanted to throw herself in his arms, to feel the satin of his skin against her own, a shield against the ugliness their world had become. The ferocity of her love terrified her. It always had.

He said nothing, choosing instead to feign interest in the TV's morning news.

"Garrett, we have to talk," she said gently.

"About what?"

The disinterest daunted her, but she pressed on. "Yesterday, among other things."

Another kind of pain tightened his features.

Easing down onto the edge of the bed, she took his hand. It remained passive to her touch, but she refused to let him isolate himself. She squeezed his hand and waited him out.

He sighed heavily. "I've made a lot of mistakes as a parent." His gaze remained fixed on the TV, his voice brittle with self-condemnation. "Yesterday was the worst. And I don't know how to undo it."

"All things considered, losing control now and then is to be expected," she said firmly.

"Expected?" He speared her with a black look. "Does Rick understand that? Maggie, after three months of being dragged here against his will, he came to see me—on his own. He even tracked me down in rehab. I'm finally reaching him. So what did I do? I threw him out!" He pulled his hand from hers and curled his fingers into a fist. "What excuse can there be for that?"

"I've heard Rick's version," she murmured. "Tell me what really happened."

A blanketing silence fell.

"Garrett?"

He drew in a long breath. "Week after week I've lived for the next therapy session—lived for it and dreaded it."

"I know," she replied silently. *Few patients have your internal drive to give to their recovery. You're impressing people, my love.* "There's a reason we call it torture."

"I've lost ground." He faltered.

"That happens sometimes. Three steps forward. Two steps back. Just keep in mind that nerve signal is getting through to your legs. There's hope."

"Not much," he murmured. "Of either." After a long agitated pause, he went on in a rush. "Yesterday! It all suddenly seemed so pointless. I felt like a side of beef, not a man. I got frustrated, angry, and took it out on the therapist. About the time I got myself together enough to apologize, I looked up. Rick was standing in the doorway. He'd seen it all." Garrett's voice cracked with self-loathing. "His anger I can handle. But seeing pity and disgust on my son's face—"

"No," she said quickly. "What you saw was confusion. At that moment your paralysis became real to him."

A snort of humorless laughter erupted from his chest. "Nice try, babe, but I know what I saw."

"Another thing, Garrett," she continued doggedly. "You've always been larger than life to him." *To me, too.* "Yesterday, he saw you as a human being, not a hero who'd let him down."

Garrett's breath hissed in through his teeth. "And I threw him out."

"Cut yourself some slack. It's not the end of the world."

"Look, Maggie, somehow I have to find a way to handle this." He indicated his legs with a sweep of a hand. "I won't risk making a worse hash of things than I already have."

A wave of impending doom swept through her. "Meaning what?"

He gave her a long level look. "I need to spend my energy on learning to walk again, and I can't seem to do that without hurting my family." The declaration cracked with the finality of a judge's gavel.

"Meaning?" Air sat in Maggie's lungs like rocks.

His expression softened. "Babe, why'd you agree to marry me? Were you granting a dying man's last request? One you thought you've never have to honor?"

She blanched. "Partly."

Rather than answer, he brushed the back of his damaged right hand down her cheek, a not so subtle reminder of the changes and all they represented. His hand couldn't move beyond closing in a weak, clawlike motion.

"Babe, for thirteen years love wasn't enough. You said so yourself. And now our lives are in an uproar."

Maggie's heart twisted in her chest.

"Proposing when I did was a mistake. I thought I'd wake up from surgery and get on with my life. Either that, or I wouldn't wake up at all. Saddling you with a cripple for the rest of your life never entered my mind."

Her stomach twisted into knots. *No! No!*

"I'm being transferred to the rehab hospital in Vallejo tomorrow. I think that's a good time to go our separate ways."

Separate ways? Angry hurt flooded her. She'd tried so hard to protect herself from getting too wrapped up in his life again, and now the tables had turned. "If you don't want this reconciliation that's one thing, but don't make decisions for me. 'Saddling' as you put it—"

"Don't be noble, babe. Neither of us can afford it right now."

"Noble? What do you call what you're being?"

He didn't answer.

A strange unnatural calm settled over her. At that moment it seemed as if nothing could ever hurt her again, but a corner of her mind recognized the condition as only temporary. Hysteria, she assumed, oddly detached. Emotional whiplash of epic proportions was just around the corner. "It'll be a little hard to avoid each other."

He arched a brow in inquiry.

"Blake and I pulled every string known to man, and we *finally* got you a bed at Rutherford-Petrie. That's where you're going in the morning, not Vallejo."

His eyes flashed blue fire. "And no one thought to tell me?"

"I just got the word. You don't want to go?"

"What I want," he growled, "is to be *consulted*. I'm not a child or mentally deficient."

"I'm sorry. I guess you're not the only one who makes decisions without asking. We'd talked about it before, and I thought you still wanted RPI if we could get you in."

He stared at her, frowning. "You don't sound like yourself. Are you all right?"

"Sure." She shrugged, determined to salvage some pride if nothing else. "Why wouldn't I be?"

His eyes narrowed in skepticism, and Maggie broke eye contact, drew the engagement ring from her finger and laid it on his palm. Her fingertips brushed his skin. The accidental touch shot fire up her arm.

He pushed the ring back at her, but she stepped out of reach. "I called it off, babe. You keep the ring."

She shook her head, no longer trusting her voice, and backed away. "I don't want it." *I only want you.* Then she turned and walked to the door before she broke down in front of him. "By the way, you're stuck with RPI. I don't have the nerve to waltz into my boss's office after all the groveling and say 'Never mind about the bed, he changed his mind.' Learn to live with it.'' She left before he could answer.

The emotional whiplash she dreaded held until she reached the relative privacy of the parking lot. Then a violent trembling settled in, and she stabbed ineffectually at the door lock with the key several times before she got the car unlocked. Once inside, she braced her elbows on the steering wheel, lowered her face into her hands and let the tears do their worst.

Separate ways. Separate ways. Garrett's words echoed relentlessly, tormentingly. She'd lost him yet again.

Four years ago, she'd pushed him away out of fear. It had been better to lose him at a time of her choosing rather than never knowing when or if he'd be taken by a drug dealer's bullet. Now he was gone, and she had no one to blame but herself.

What was wrong with me? He'll never return to police work. Never. He'd be safe. Why couldn't I have embraced the chance to rebuild our lives? I had the chance. But I held him at arm's length until now he doesn't want me.

His words sliced bloody paths in her heart as they swirled in ever tightening circles. *Separate ways... Separate ways...*

Blake's observation long ago in the pizza parlor came back. He had been right. She'd spent her whole life rejecting people before they could reject her. Now, starting tomorrow, she'd be in the same building with Garrett nine hours a day, five days a week, wanting him and not being wanted in return.

If she hadn't gotten the divorce, she and Rick would have moved back east with him, Rick wouldn't be so messed up, and the plane crash wouldn't have meant anything more to her than an impersonal tragedy because Garrett wouldn't have been on it.

And it's your fault, Hughes. All your fault.

"Aren't you going to see Dad tonight?"

"Nope." Maggie didn't dare look up from the paper. If Rick saw her eyes, he'd know something was wrong, and she couldn't talk about it, not yet. "Since you have the night off, are you game to risk your reputation and see a movie with your mother?''

She made a very obvious show of scanning the listings. Rick, rather than firing off a wisecrack as she expected, gave her a probing look so much like one of Garrett's that a strangling lump formed in her throat. How often had Garrett watched her that same way, silently trying to unravel her thoughts? *How often did you shut him out when he came home with a torn uniform and you couldn't bear to hear the details?*

Rick ignored her movie question completely. ''Why aren't you going to the hospital?''

Unconsciously, she shook her head. ''I saw him this morning. Now, are you coming with me, or do I brave the snack bar alone?''

To her horror, he zeroed in on her left hand and grabbed it. Newsprint fluttered to the floor. ''Where's that ring?''

Maggie reclaimed her hand and bent to pick up the scattered paper. ''I told you nothing was settled.'' Her voice caught, and she froze. He couldn't have helped but hear her pain. She wanted to swear, but there wasn't a word vile enough.

Rick's eyes narrowed, and she felt the sixteen-year-old's version of Garrett's hard-eyed stare.

''He dumped you?'' His bewildered outrage threw her. ''He can't do that!''

She swallowed past the heartache of Garrett's rejection and took a shaky breath. How to explain? ''Your father was dying when he proposed and I accepted. His recovery has been a dictionary definition of a *miracle,* but the life-and-death battles are over now. Emotions are—'' she almost said ''normal'' but caught herself ''—not as out of control. We both had reservations, and this was a good time to take a few steps back.'' She forced a chipper smile. ''There's a thriller playing in an hour. You want to come or not?''

''He dumped you.''

If I told you how much like your father you are you'd take it as a mortal insult. She sighed. ''Yes, sweetheart, he did.''

His young face darkened with fury. ''He can't do that.''

"Why not?" she asked, dazed. She'd have thought Rick would be overjoyed. "I *divorced* him once. One good dumping deserves another." Even to her own ears, the weak attempt at humor sounded strained, near tears. *Swell.*

Rick dragged his car keys from his jeans pocket and headed for the door.

"Where are you going?"

"To see Dad." The squeaky wooden door slammed behind him before she could reply.

For a moment, she nearly went after him, then decided against it. Maybe a good row was what he and Garrett needed.

A touch of black humor overtook her, and she chuckled tremulously. "Two cases of testosterone poisoning in the same room. That ought to liven up the neurology ward."

Chapter 5

"**Y**ou really hurt Mom."

Garrett whipped his head around so fast he thought his neck might snap. His heart constricted at the sight. Rick stood just inside the doorway, an enraged half-grown pup determined to defend his turf. But he'd come on his own. Again. After yesterday. "I'm glad you're here, son. I owe you an apology."

Rick's flexed his fists and stepped forward. "This is about Mom, not you and me."

You and me? The words slammed through his brain like a bullet. *Once, "you and me" meant a team.* "I didn't raise an ill-mannered, self-centered hothead. Now, if you want to act like who you *are,* fine, but check the attitude at the door."

Obviously startled, Rick gave him an evaluating look as unnerving as it was long.

Now, where did you learn that?

His shoulders lost their combative set. "You're right, Dad. I'm sorry."

Stunned relief flooded every fiber of Garrett's being. A concession. Not the whole war, but a start. "Pull up a chair."

Rick did so, raised his eyes and said without rancor, "You really did hurt Mom."

"Holding her unfairly hurt her worse."

"Unfairly?" His brow furrowed in confusion, and not a little suspicion. "I thought since you're getting better you figured you didn't need her anymore."

I need your mother like I need air to breathe. "What gave you that idea?"

Rick hunched down miserably in the chair. "If that's not it, then why?"

Garrett groaned silently. *She deserves better than someone who's less than a man.* "She told me once she didn't want to love me. That I always shredded her life."

"When did she say that?"

While I was in a coma. "It doesn't matter. The point is that I've turned her life upside down and given nothing in return. It's time to let her go."

Rick flung himself to his feet and paced the room. "It's wrong. Wrong! It's *all* wrong."

Garrett could only mentally shake his head at the fractured emotions. *Poor kid, you don't know what you want.* "Would inflicting myself on her be right? I have nothing to offer now."

"What do you mean?"

Garrett puffed out a soft bitter laugh. "Other than old TV reruns, how many cops in wheelchairs have you seen?"

"I'm confused."

Heartfelt laughter rolled from Garrett's chest. "Welcome to the club." It was tempting to try to get Rick to open up about the problems between them, but he doubted the unexpected truce was strong enough to handle the weight.

He watched as Rick gave a furtive glance toward the door then make one more agitated pass around the room, the only sound being the soft squeak of sneakers on the freshly waxed floor.

"There's a ball game on as soon as the news is over," Garrett probed gently. "Interested?"

Hesitantly, the boy looked up at the TV bolted to the wall, and Garrett held his breath.

"Sure. Why not."

Garrett sighed in deep, parental relief. Nothing had been settled. He didn't even know whether or not Rick had forgiven him for yesterday—or anything else. But watching a game together was a solid step forward.

By the end of Garrett's first week at the Rutherford-Petrie Institute, Maggie wanted to resign. The first few days, his rebuffs had been gentle. But now he bristled whenever she walked through the door, his jaw set in unyielding disapproval, subtlety a thing of the past. She couldn't pass his room without going in, and if her duties didn't take her downstairs to the in-patient wing for several hours, she made up excuses to make a special trip. So much for pride.

Once again, she found herself standing outside his room, needing to be with him. Once again she didn't have an excuse to enter. She ran a fingertip across the embossed plastic nameplate on his door, the name "Garrett Hughes" stark and unmistakable, like a nightmare she couldn't wake from.

Unlike a paper nameplate in a regular hospital, the ones here were semipermanent. Patients in facilities such as RPI stayed from a few months to well over a year, far too long for the dubious longevity of paper.

"Checking on baby, Mother?"

Maggie jumped. Behind her, Carl Sapperstein, her top therapist, leaned indolently on an empty wheelchair, the smirk on his long, narrow face a combination of mischievousness and compassion. Since RPI policy forbade any employee to directly oversee a family member's care, that left her with her next best choice for Garrett—Sapperstein.

Her attention settled on the wheelchair in front of him. Shiny new chrome glistened in the hallway light, the dark blue upholstered back and seat unmarred by the inevitable scratches and scuffs of use. Pristine. Untouched. Garrett's. Built for his specific needs, not just a generic pulled from a closet for a quick trip to therapy and back. This one he'd take *home*.

Sapperstein didn't seem put off by her lack of a retort to his gibe. "You want to be in on this?"

No! Yes! She shuddered.

"Yea or nay, *mi capitán*." Sapperstein waggled his bushy brows in a gesture that from anyone else would have been grossly insensitive. But from a friend it restored her backbone.

Without a word, she turned and shoved open the door. Garrett had elevated the head of his bed to a comfortable reading position, a magazine spread open on his lap. His eyes met hers and pure sexual fire ignited, heart-pounding in its intensity, heartbreaking in its futility. His dark features closed, and the moment vanished, leaving emptiness in its wake.

It was then that she noticed his choice of reading material— a professional magazine for law enforcement officers. Inside, she recoiled.

"Just because I can't go back to it, Maggie," he snapped, "doesn't mean interest in the subject died."

Maggie, she observed painfully, *not babe.* "You're not accountable to me, Garrett. Read anything you want."

He opened his mouth to reply, but Sapperstein came in and whatever he'd been about to say was lost. Within the depths of his eyes she watched him scrutinize the wheelchair, his expression an unholy war between loathing and determination.

"Okay, Mr. Hughes," Sapperstein said, wisely dropping all traces of his acid humor. "You've been practicing transferring from a bed to a wheelchair. This puppy's top of the line. Among other features, most of which we'll explore over the afternoon, the arms are low and out of the way. Transference should be a snap. Also, see these?" He tapped one of the projections bolted at regular intervals on the right hand rim. "With these grips, you'll be able to propel yourself regardless of hand function."

Moments passed as Garrett stared venomously at the chair, his eyes the color of sapphire ice, a stranger's eyes. "Maggie, I'm sure you have other patients."

The unnerving cold bothered her more than the not so subtle dismissal. "I'd rather stay," she replied in as near a detached professional tone as she could muster.

His expression darkened. "If we were still married, fine. But since we're not, I don't need the audience."

Courtesy demanded that she respect his wishes, but she couldn't seem to make her feet walk out the door.

"If the boss lady wants to stay," Sapperstein drawled, "she stays. Now, let's get at this." He gave Maggie a you-owe-me-one look.

Garrett glowered at them both, then refocused on the chair. The deep, fortifying breath he took was discreet, and she wished she hadn't seen it. It tore her heart out.

With a meticulous care that marked the awkwardness of a newly acquired skill, he swung his sweatpants-clad legs over the side of the bed. His right hand and wrist could support no weight at all, but by supporting himself on his left hand and his right elbow, he shifted his body, beginning the as yet arduous process of getting out of bed.

She watched, her heart in her throat, wanting to reach out to help him, to hold him—to have him hold her. She froze under the realization of how much she needed his reassurance. *She* was the professional. This was *her* turf, and it appalled her how badly she needed Garrett's strength, needed the other half of her soul. She crossed her arms and stayed out of the way, holding her breath as Sapperstein and Garrett worked together as a team. For a moment Garrett poised precariously between bed and wheelchair, then settled into place as neatly as if he'd been doing this for years, not a week.

"So life in four-wheel drive begins." The words rolled from Garrett's mouth like an exotic poison.

Wheelchairs freed so many people, but to her eyes it imprisoned him—her knight in shining armor—sentencing him to life without possibility of parole. His tall broad-shouldered frame should be standing proudly, not sitting supported by an upholstered metal frame on wheels. Tears burned behind her eyes.

He took hold of the hand rims experimentally, his jaw hardening. "Might as well take it for a test drive."

Maggie let Sapperstein take over at that point, retreating instead to her office and the safety of paperwork and other patients, patients who, if they locked her out, it didn't sear her alive.

Garrett sat in the RPI cafeteria, sipping coffee and staring out the window that faced the inner courtyard, his black depression taking a brutal inventory of his life. He was slowly mastering what they called basic living skills. Learning to feed himself left-handedly figured prominently on the list. Vegetables weren't that hard, but cutting meat required strapping a knife to his right hand. Sweat suits and Velcro seemed to be the "physically challenged" person's best friends. God, how he hated politically correct terms.

His first trip to the cafeteria had shocked him. The tables had no chairs; everyone—including him—brought their own. Family members who wanted to eat here had to scrounge from the stackables along the far wall.

He took another sip of his coffee and watched through the plate-glass windows as a young woman helped her toddler place a big red ball onto his father's thighs. Only with the greatest effort could the man roll the ball off his own lap. Throwing it was a pipe dream. The child squealed and picked it up. Devastation racked the young man's face. His wife held him tight, speaking what appeared to be encouraging words.

Unable to watch, Garrett turned away. How little did he have to give his own family? For twenty years—minus the last four—he had always been there for them to lean on. Now he was nothing, a crippled shell starting over at age forty-two.

"I *will* start over," he vowed under his breath. "But I *won't* inflict this on my family."

Maggie. What did she really think of him? Was she as repelled by his deficiencies as he was? Did she know about his impotence? Probably. She'd known everything else. It made him feel like a bug under glass.

He ran the memories of their last kisses through his mind. They had been liquid fire, but his body hadn't noticed. Supposedly, the brain was the most important sexual organ. Maybe, life would have been kinder if the brain had shut off too. Perhaps, then, what he'd lost wouldn't matter so much.

Not that it changed anything. Maggie had divorced him and built a life for herself. He'd intruded enough. Maybe if the crash hadn't happened he'd have won her back by now. Then again, maybe not. His decision to give her back the life she wanted was the right one. He just wished she didn't make it so unbearable for them both with her constant hovering.

More than once he toyed with the idea of seeing about a transfer to the regional facility in Vallejo. That would put distance between them, but his parents lived in that town. His mother would make certain she visited every day, and he refused to put her through the extra strain.

Blake had told him how he'd tried to hire help for her, but she wouldn't hear of it. Instead, she stubbornly drove herself into the ground by doing all the work alone. Mom had never listened much to Blake. She still thought of the accomplished neurosurgeon as her baby, always would. But Garrett, as the elder son, carried more weight. Once he was out of here, he'd throw some of it around.

Burying the emotional turmoil, he returned to the business of getting his *own* life back, and retrieved a small, gray rubber ball from a utility bag that hung from his wheelchair. Not a very high-tech piece of equipment, but supposedly it would help restore mobility in a hand that was little better than a claw. Microsurgery immediately after the crash might have given him full range, but as Maggie had said, they'd had to save his life. His hand had been a luxury they couldn't waste time on.

Using his left hand to keep the ball centered in his right palm, Garrett gritted his teeth and tried to curl his fingers around it. The abysmal lack of success was no worse than usual, and he tried again. Once again, he failed.

"You know what they say," he growled. "It ain't over till

the fat lady sings.'' The world receded as, with solitary intensity, he fought one more day of his private war.

For the fifth time since the accident, the monthly reports came due and Maggie found herself buried under the paperwork mountain on her desk. In the days since the last quarrel, she had stayed away from Garrett's room, telling herself the heartache would eventually go away. She wasn't the first woman to get dumped and, if other women got over it, so could she. Too bad she didn't believe it.

Maybe it would be easier to bear if Patrick and Laverne didn't make their twice-a-week pilgrimage to RPI, and maybe if Blake didn't hang around visiting whenever he made rounds. Blake also came by in the evenings with his wife, Faith—who was in town for a while—and their two girls. So did Rick. Everyone was welcome but her.

At the quick knock on her office door, she lifted her eyes.

Blake sauntered in and grinned at her. ''How's Grumpy Bear today?''

She leaned back in her chair and crossed her arms defiantly. ''Who do you mean? Him or me?''

''Both.'' His grin faded into something gentler, more compassionate. ''You okay?''

''No,'' she snapped. ''I didn't want that man back in my life. He barged in anyway, rearranged my whole world, got me to love him again—not that I'd ever stopped—then he tells me to take a hike.'' Tears of rage burned behind her eyes. ''And as far as his grumping is concerned, according to Sapperstein, he's grumping along quite nicely. If we give him twenty minutes in the pool, he wants forty. Sapperstein is threatening to let him max out and fall on his face.''

''Relentless. That's my boy.'' Blake chuckled proudly. ''Let's let him. He'll learn.''

Maggie blinked stupidly in surprise. He hadn't pursued her emotional state. Weird. ''You're the M.D.,'' she said warily.

''His living skills are coming along well. Another couple of months and I can take him home. Faith and I have the house all ready. He wants his own apartment, but I've finally convinced him he's not up to independent living yet. Not to mention that he's a long way from reentering the workforce.'' Blake's expression became fondly nostalgic. "We used to spend a lot of time in my gym. It's going to be great having him around.''

The family togetherness Blake conjured made Maggie ache with loneliness. She wanted Garrett home with her where he belonged, not with his brother. Being shut out hurt beyond belief. "Did you come by to wax poetic, or to interrupt my workday?''

His eyes widened in innocence. "Mag, I just came by to ask you to lunch.''

"You're almost as bad a liar as I am," she shot back. "You're up to something.''

He tried to look hurt. "I'm just hungry.''

"Yeah, right.'' Maggie grabbed her purse. "You're buying.''

Chlorine fumes assailed Maggie's nose as she entered the room that housed the indoor pool. It had been a week since she'd last seen Garrett and a full day since her lunch with Blake. An hour of hearing the details of the good times ahead for the two brothers had pushed her over the edge, and she was back to caving in to temptation and checking up on Garrett. Then, again, that had probably been what Blake had planned all along.

When she saw Garrett in the sling lift suspended above his wheelchair, a sob nearly escaped her throat. A staff member maneuvered the swing arm over the decking while Sapperstein waited in the water below. Every time she saw him she thought she could handle it, but every time it tore her apart.

The RPI-issue swim trunks fit well, baring Garrett's broad chest to her gaze. He'd lost weight, typical in cases like his, but she would have preferred to forgo seeing the evidence. His dark olive skin spared him the pasty look a lighter-skinned man might have had, but the months of not being out in the sun still showed. His white-lipped expression spoke more eloquently of his feelings of degradation than words ever could.

She walked toward him, disgusted with herself for loving him, hating him for the hold he had on her heart. *Well, Hughes,* she grumbled silently, *you always knew there was a fine line between love and hate.* She took a deep breath. *So why can't you just cross it already and be done with it?* "Good morning."

He swung his gaze around to her but said nothing. Was it a trick of her imagination or had she seen welcome and longing in his eyes before he swept them away beneath a harsh glower? The possibility pulled at her heart.

"Good morning," she repeated sarcastically. "I'm Maggie Hughes, Assistant Director of Physical Therapy. How are we doing today?"

After a quick glare, he looked away, his jaw clenched so hard she wondered if he might crack a tooth.

"Good...*morning.*" She enunciated the words as if she were a teacher in an elocution class. "Are we not talking today?"

"Hilarious, Maggie," he grumbled. His piercing gaze took in the lift, pool and two staff members. "Cattle are loaded onto ships with more dignity than this."

If ever she'd doubted the wisdom of RPI's policy of no direct responsibility for a loved one's care, she didn't now. Too bad she couldn't seem to follow her own better judgment. "Humiliation is all part of Club RPI's service."

His glower darkened. The lift operator lowered him into the water, and Garrett sucked in his breath.

"A little cold?" she quipped, desperate to break some of the tension that sang between them. "The water's really pretty nice. Inactivity makes the human body more sensitive to temperature."

Garrett's attention swung unnervingly back to her. "I noticed. Care to join me?"

Beneath the anger, she saw near desperation. He needed her, yet despised himself for the weakness. Her heart thudded painfully at the unexpected revelation. The intensity of the sudden temptation to slip into the water with him shocked her. Following through would be an act of errant lunacy.

"Let me check in first. Then I'll get my suit."

Garrett paled. "You've got work to do."

"So you've reminded me. Repeatedly." Unwilling to let him see the turmoil in her eyes, she walked to the wall-mounted phone, made the call, then trotted into the staff locker room.

Her fingers, stiff from nerves, made unbuttoning her uniform an adventure in aggravation. Pulling on the one-piece swimsuit didn't prove any easier. When finished, she smoothed the straps and scrutinized her figure. Trim and in better shape than most women ten years younger, she was comfortable with her body. The occasional cheesecake indulgence scarcely caused a problem, but having Garrett see so much of her skin after all this time made her strangely shy. Would he still like what he saw?

"Oh, get off it, Hughes," she snarled under her breath. "This isn't a date, and you're not trying to get him back." Her voice trembled on the last, and she rolled her eyes in disgust.

With almost violent motions, she secured her hair in a knot at the back of her head. "He's a patient. Treat him like one." She slammed her locker shut. "The big cheeses here are going to hate this. Helping on my own time is fine, but taking over on company time and under their liability insurance?" She shuddered at the probable repercussions, then padded out to the pool.

By now, Garrett was free of the sling, and he kept his head above water by holding on to one of many chrome exercise bars bolted to the side of the pool at water level. His expression at her approach could only be called horrified. "Maggie, I've got enough baby-sitters."

"Tough. You're not in charge." *Boy, saying that felt good!* She grabbed the edge of the decking and slipped into the water.

"Maggie, for God's sake, you can't be serious!"

Determined, she moved toward him, the water swirling softly around her breasts.

He glowered savagely. "I said no."

She cocked her head and asked sweetly. "By some chance do you know how much I'd make per month on unemployment?"

He blinked in puzzlement at the non sequitur, and her own confidence rose a notch or two. She reached out to him then, her fingers grazing his shoulder. His pupils dilated with a heat so intense she half expected the water to boil.

"Go back to work." He shrugged her hand away.

Sapperstein held back, smirking, while Maggie moved behind Garrett and locked her arms around his ribs. Her breasts pressed against his back, sparking a surge of sexual need that raced to her core. She didn't speak, didn't dare try.

"Maggie, stop it." The order was broken and guttural, harsh.

Fighting flames the water couldn't hope to cool, she clenched her teeth, leaned back and drew him toward her. Then she walked backward to give his body the chance to float free of its own weight.

"What are you doing?" he demanded.

She drew a quick breath. "Nothing you haven't done every day for weeks."

"Take me back to my room."

"Sorry, *Mr. Hughes*," she chirped, struggling to sound cheerfully unaffected by the play of his muscles beneath her hands as he shifted in her hold. "You'll go back when we're finished."

Then she did something really stupid. She rested her cheek against the side of his head. She couldn't breathe. They'd made love in a swimming pool more than once. Did he remember? Was he remembering those times now? The freedom? The playfulness?

With a virulent oath, Garrett twisted out of her grasp. In one fluid motion he slid his right arm through an exercise bar to hold himself in place and swept his left around her shoulders. Before she had the time to react, he kissed her. The press of his lips against her own was hot, real, consuming. Every nerve ending in her body screamed to life and demanded his touch. She lost her balance under the storm and scrambled for footing, her arms wrapping instinctively around his chest.

We're both going to drown, her brain complained, but her fevered body didn't listen.

He continued the sensual assault, very much the Garrett she had loved for twenty years—secure, confident and in control.

Her brain kicked in, finally. *Don't kiss him back, you idiot. It'll only make the next rejection that much harder.* Yet her lips parted, demanding more. She tried to grab a bar but missed. *Turn your head away! That's all it takes to stop this…heaven.* The protest weakened under the storm, then died completely. She sighed in long-denied pleasure as their breath mingled, as they drank deeply of each other. It had been so long, so very long.

"Boss?" Sapperstein called out, sounding somewhat uncomfortable. She and Garrett jolted apart, maintaining just enough hold on each other and the exercise bar to keep Garrett's head above water. "You want us to leave you two alone?"

Despite her auburn hair and fair skin, Maggie rarely blushed, but she felt her face crimson. Garrett muttered something unpleasant under his breath, and Maggie groped futilely for a witty comeback while she attempted to reestablish a more appropriate hold on Garrett's upper body.

Garrett found his voice before she found hers. "We'll be fine here—alone."

Both staff members looked to Maggie for confirmation. She nodded. As they left, she muttered, "The higher-ups are going to hang my skin from the nearest flagpole." Her voice echoed eerily in the room.

"Why?"

"Do you know how many rules I'm breaking?"

"Not really."

"Good."

They let the silence spin out. Garrett moaned, then turned back to her. "Why couldn't you leave well enough alone?"

She bristled, but kept her voice level. "That didn't feel like a go-away kiss."

He looked at an unfocused point across the pool. "It was a mistake. I'm sorry."

He loved her. She knew he did, but now, she wasn't the only one fighting against it. That made it somehow worse.

The anguish in his eyes matched that in her heart. "Maggie, look. You shouldn't be here. I shouldn't have sent Sapperstein and his shadow away."

She swallowed past the lump in her throat. "I take it you want me to call them back?" A firm nod was the only answer she got. "Too bad," she said. "I'm already in hot water—no pun intended."

"Meaning?" His brows lowered in annoyed suspicion.

"I just elected myself chief baby-sitter."

He did swear then, a pungent phrase filled with earthy explicitness. Without warning, he pushed off, turned and swam away, his arms moving in slow, even strokes. She shrieked and scrambled to catch up. "What are you doing?"

He rolled onto his back, continuing without pause. "It's called swimming. I've been doing it since I was five. Although my legs used to take a more active role than just trailing along behind," he added bitterly.

Maggie sputtered incoherently. "All you've done lately are exercises. You could have warned me you were going to try something new."

He didn't answer, not that she expected him to. Swimming with just arms and body was an art, one that took more energy than he had to spare. She swam beside him, watching for signs of fatigue. It wasn't long in coming. Before he'd made it to the far end of the pool, his face took on that telltale lined look, but he pushed himself onward.

"That's enough, Garrett. Too much exercise and you lose the benefit and keep all the bad."

He ignored her, and she grabbed for him but missed. He swam on, her protests falling on deliberately deaf ears.

"Testosterone," she muttered, "is the bane of humanity."

When his stroke faltered, she tackled him, and they both went under. When they broke the surface, Garrett spewed water and painted the air blue.

"You never used to swear." She panted as she flipped him neatly onto his back.

"You never tried to drown me before!" His body trembled from overexertion.

They moved to the edge of the pool, catching their breath, silently fighting the awareness that blazed between them.

"You don't find me repellent," he observed quietly.

Startled, Maggie gave him a sharp look. "Why would I?"

Breathy laughter puffed from his throat. "At the moment, what you see is the sum and total of my physical prowess. That's enough to repel any woman."

Her heart screamed to comfort him, to hold him, but she kept her place half an arm's length away, close enough for the ripples created when he moved to sizzle across her body. "You don't know how far you'll come back."

His eyes hardened. "I'm not cut out for life in four-wheel drive. I won't be an object of pity."

"And *I* won't lie to you, Garrett. Wheelchairs aren't for sissies. But you're strong. Inside where it counts. Men like you are the ones who succeed."

"I'll make sure I tell people that."

She gave him a level look. "Demand respect. You'll get it."

A long pause followed where she felt shut out of his thoughts. Then he sighed with an aching vulnerability. "I'm scared, babe."

She nearly cried out under the shared pain of this dynamic man reduced to such a confession. "I am, too," she managed past the constriction in her throat. "I am, too."

Chapter 6

Maggie assumed that her willingness to walk away from her career was probably responsible for her continued employment. The director grumbled and whined about the liability potential of an employee overseeing a former spouse's care, certain that the slightest ripple of an old quarrel between the ex-Hugheses would erupt into a malpractice suit. Maggie held her ground. Finding a replacement with her qualifications without notice wasn't that easy. In the end, he nearly gagged, but gave her the go-ahead.

Over the course of the next six weeks, she and Garrett fell into a tense routine. They never discussed the desperate kiss in the pool, nor was it repeated. Most days he mentally locked out the world, excluding even her from his obviously troubled thoughts. She didn't even try to figure out where he stood with Rick. As near as she could tell, it was still a powder keg waiting for a lighted match.

Maggie held her breath as the indicator lines arched on the computer screen, lines that marked nerve activity in his muscles, each small increase hard fought. His skin was sweat streaked. Veins stood out at his temples from the strain. Her gaze traveled to his left leg, bare below green shorts and girded with electrodes. The flaccid muscles twitched. Her heart pounded.

"You're almost there."

She expected one more all-out effort on his part, but he relaxed and leaned back. The lines on the screen plunged. He took a deep breath, marshaling all his reserve strength from deep within. The lines rose, faster at first, then more slowly. Then it happened. Garrett moved his leg an inch.

"You did it!" she shrieked, leaping to her feet. The rush of victory coursed through her, slamming to a confused halt as she saw Garrett's ravaged face.

No happiness, no joy, only an agonized relief, punctuated by eyes too moist. He lowered his lids and turned away. She wanted to hold him, but he needed this moment of mental privacy, and giving him that took more willpower than she thought she had.

Eventually, he turned back to her, his turmoil shielded. "Not much for six months worth of work, but a start."

She brushed her hand across his cheek and gave him a none too stable smile. The poignancy of the moment made speech impossible. He captured her hand and kissed her palm. The sensation of his warm, firm lips against her flesh arrowed straight to her heart.

Soon, he'd be ready to leave RPI. She briefly entertained asking him to come home, not the wisest move if she hoped to retain her sanity. But the vision of him back in the bed they'd shared during their marriage tempted her. It had been far too long since she'd nestled in his embrace, warmed by his body.

Days crawled by, the progress minimal. They clung to each other, yet held part of themselves back, fear and insecurity creating an emotional buffer zone that neither dared cross.

The day he slid each foot in turn a few inches across the floor, Maggie didn't think first, she simply threw herself into his arms. He caressed her spine with his good arm, and his breath puffed against the tender flesh of her neck. Pleasurable chills raced from her scalp to her toes, and she tilted her head back, exposing her throat.

Groaning low, Garrett began a leisurely exploration along the pulse point with his lips. Maggie pulled away just enough to kiss him full on the mouth. He held her tighter, his firm lips demanded compliance, and she unreservedly opened to him. Maggie was completely awash in the sea of passion, drinking in the spicy scent of his skin and answering his kisses with a pure, wanton fire of her own. Running his fingers through her hair, he began a sensuous massage of the back of her head and neck. Her breasts ached, and she groaned a wordless plea as he one-handedly unbuttoned her blouse and unhooked her bra.

His strong, square hand slid along the edge of her breast, and she turned, pressing her flesh into his palm. Again, her head lolled back, and she bit her lip to keep from moaning aloud with the pleasure. He played her body with maddening skill. Distantly, Maggie knew this wasn't the time or place, but the sexual frustration she'd battled for four-and-a-half years had them both fully in its grip.

She gave a chagrined laugh under her breath. "You always did enjoy making me suffer."

"If something's worth doing," he said, chuckling, tasting her throat, "it's worth doing right."

She wanted to snap off another retort, but his foray was taking him on a thorough exploration of the skin along her ribs. The ache at the junction of her thighs burned to the point of pain, and she clenched her jaws.

When he shifted her trembling body and trailed kisses along her collarbone and lower, voices in the next room brought sanity to the storm. She started to pull away, but he made a curt, negative order low in his throat, holding her in an iron, one-armed grip. Maggie panicked and braced her palms against his shoulders and pushed away.

"We can't do this," she whispered, her voice trembling. "Someone could walk in any time."

"So? Lock the door," he murmured low and enticing. Even with one arm, his strength was notable, and he easily pulled her against him for another searing kiss that stole her breath away.

"I could lose my job."

"Babe, I want to take you. Right here. On the floor."

The thought of a cold floor against her back wouldn't ordinarily sound erotic, but memories of some of their past adventures of the body added another spark to her dangerously overheated frame.

"Yeah, well, forget it." Frantic, she tried to gather a shred of sanity, and as she shifted to get off his lap, she felt his arousal beneath her thigh. Her gaze widened and sought his.

Masculine assurance burned in his eyes, and one corner of his mouth quirked. "It seems my…uhmmm…problem…was only temporary."

More flashes of memory ripped through her mind, memories of him buried deep within her, carrying her to the brink of fulfillment only to tease her to greater heights before allowing their world to shatter in blinding flashes of ecstasy.

"When did you notice the impotence was fading?" Her trembling worsened as she fought the hormonal overload and tried to have a rational conversation. Garrett's range of motion was extremely limited, but they could still indulge in a lot of experimenting on that floor.

"It's been getting better over the past week. This morning when I woke up, I knew for sure." A predatory light mingled with relief and confidence. In his mind, he was a man again. "I take it this is part of the overall healing?"

A lump formed in her throat. Swallowing hard, she nodded then forced her thoughts in other directions. "I hate to ruin the moment, but the door doesn't lock."

He frowned in censure, and she blushed.

"Seriously, Garrett, if anyone catches us, I'll get fired. Even if I don't, my staff would never let me live it down."

His jaw clenched in a combination of sexual frustration and dark suspicion. "Are you sure that's the only reason?"

Understanding dawned, and without conscious decision she cradled his beloved face in her hands. "I don't see you as a charity case, Garrett. What we feel is real." She wilted. "It's just not very bright."

He digested that a moment, then nodded, pacified.

Maggie looked down at herself. Her blouse gaped open and her bra hung loosely from her shoulders. "Talk about making unauthorized use of a therapy room."

Looking torn between swearing and smiling, Garrett reached out for one final touch. She shuddered with want, but clutched the front of her blouse together. He chuckled in pure male self-satisfaction. Glaring at him, she slid off his lap, her pulse still throbbing with the echoes of unfulfilled desire.

"Mom! What are you doing!"

As one, Maggie and Garrett jerked their attention to Rick, standing in the doorway, his face a study of horrified betrayal.

Mortified, Maggie turned away. "Not again," she moaned low.

Garrett muttered something about Rick and psychic timing. Louder, he said, "Come in and sit down."

Maggie strained to hear the soft swish of the door closing or the tread of footsteps, the slightest sound to indicate Rick had complied, but there was nothing but silent condemnation. Worse, she could feel his eyes on her. There was no changing room in here, not even a closet she could slink away to, so she stood with her back to her son and fumbled with her bra, feeling like a teenager whose father had caught her with a boyfriend.

Her fingers seemed glued together, and smoothing her bra over her breasts and fastening the hooks took nightmarishly long.

"Rick, stop glaring at your mother. You were raised better than that." Garrett's low voice was edged in iron.

"I thought it was over," Rick said, accusation sharp in his voice. "You told me it was over."

Maggie flinched.

"And you're always looking for an excuse to prove me a

liar, aren't you?" The iron took a sharper edge. "I said, sit down."

Maggie fumbled with the last button and turned back around as Rick flopped, rebellious, into the chair she'd vacated when Garrett's therapy took such a heated side trip.

"Okay, I'm sitting," he snapped. "Now what? Is this where you tell me casual sex is off-limits for me, but it's okay for you?" The moment the last slipped out, Rick clamped his mouth shut, eyes huge as saucers. He'd gone too far and knew it.

Raw fury radiated from Garrett as he sat unnaturally still in his wheelchair. Other than the occasional swat on the bottom for extreme offenses when Rick was little, Garrett had never struck their son, but Maggie knew beyond all doubt that he was dangerously close to physical violence.

Drawing on his tremendous store of self-discipline, Garrett took a slow shallow breath and rested an elbow on the armrest. "Don't stop now, son. What's the rest of it?"

"What do you mean?" Rick asked, seeming to shrink further into himself.

"I've heard about how I deserted you. How you and your mother mean nothing to me, et cetera. Now out with the rest of it. What else?"

Rick sputtered incoherently, words beyond him. Garrett waited him out, motioning to Maggie to pull up a chair from the other therapy station. Numbly, she complied. As she sat down, she caught a glimpse of her blouse. Sick mortification swept through her. The buttons were one hole off. Worse, Rick noticed it, too.

"What about what I interrupted?" Rick's voice wobbled.

Garrett gave a one-shouldered shrug. "What about it? You're too old to believe the stork brought you."

Maggie's face crimsoned.

"Dad, you two were acting like a couple of...of—"

"Sex-starved teenagers?"

"Garrett!" Maggie wheezed.

He gave her a bland look. "Since it's obviously a problem

for him, let's get it out in the open and be done with it.'' His gaze swiveled back to his son.

Rick stared at him, haunted and looking very much alone.

"No one is immune to getting carried away," Garrett said softly. "Your mother and I were married a long time, and that complicates normal boundaries."

"Then you're coming back home?" Naked longing mixed with pain flashed in Rick's eyes. He clutched his uncaring facade to him like a coat four sizes too small.

Not so much as a muscle twitched on Garrett's face. "Would that be so bad?"

The quarrel had erupted so quickly then changed to yet something else that Maggie felt like Alice falling down the rabbit's hole.

"I love you, Rick," he said quietly, "whether you want to talk or not. And regardless of where I live when I get out of here, I'm in San Francisco to stay."

"Whatever." Rick twitched like a starving animal confronted with an offering of food, too skittish to reach out and take what he so desperately craved. "Can I go now?"

Garrett nodded placidly, and Rick bolted out the door.

Despair swamped her. "I thought you two were doing better."

"We are." He sounded so cheerful, her head snapped up. His expression matched his voice.

"How can you say that?"

He gazed at her tenderly. "Rick is still convinced I'm going to leave, and he can't bring himself to take any emotional risks."

"Are you saying he wants to?"

"Not that he can admit, but yes."

Maggie groaned and buried her face in her hands, wishing she had a fraction of his confidence.

"Babe, the root of the problem is that Rick will never be able to recover from the divorce. It's not in his emotional makeup. He needed a forever family and got us instead."

"You mean me." Her voice was very small.

Garrett rolled his wheelchair to where she sat. Maggie hadn't noticed the tear that had dripped down her cheek until he brushed it away.

"Look at me, babe."

Compelled, she did. His expression was achingly tender. "When are you going to stop seeing yourself as a coward? You're the most courageous woman I know."

Maggie made a rude noise. "You've been comparing notes with Blake."

That seemed to startle him. "No, but if we've drawn the same conclusions, it's because we both know you so well. You doubt yourself sometimes and carry more than your share of guilt, but you're always strong when you need to be. The rest is just baggage you don't need to carry around."

It wasn't like him to be so eloquent, and she was both touched and uncomfortable. "Oh, come on, Garrett, I was the one who bailed out of the marriage. I'm the reason Rick is—"

"Stop it," he snapped. "I made mistakes, too. I could have fought the divorce, demanded marriage counseling, but I didn't. Instead—in my infinite wisdom—I decided to let you rattle around in the empty house for a while. I thought the loneliness would get to you, and you'd ask me to come home."

She took his hand. "But that didn't happen, and you got assigned to Washington."

"Bingo."

So many regrets. So many mistakes. Maggie wiped at her face then sniffed. "So where does that leave us?"

He stared down at his legs. "No place, I'm afraid."

On top of her regular workload, Maggie spent hours each day on Garrett's therapy. The pace he set drove them both to exhaustion. Never in all her years in rehabilitative medicine had she ever admonished a patient to ease off. He'd made his decision to be released ahead of expectations, and arguing with him about overexertion proved futile.

Garrett sighed and leaned back on the treatment table. Involuntarily, Maggie took his hand in hers, relishing the tingle of pleasure that raced through her. Each time they touched, she felt the magic of a new love's first glow. She knew Garrett never allowed himself to succumb to something he'd deemed unwise—such as a reconciliation. He'd made up his mind, and no matter how intense the chemistry between them, whenever he left RPI, their lives would take separate paths, crossing only occasionally because of their son. She didn't think she could bear it. So she ached for him in silence, trying to ignore the way his eyes darkened with the same need she knew was reflected in her own. Pulling her hand away, she gestured for him to roll over.

Once he lay comfortably on his stomach, Maggie braced herself to endure the bittersweet torture of running her hands over his satin skin. The muscles needed to be worked to stimulate circulation and retain muscle tone. He needed her skills, and Maggie would be there, no matter the cost.

A grinning Blake sauntered into the treatment room. "How are Grumpy Bear and friend today?" he asked.

Grateful for the interruption, Maggie chuckled. Garrett glared.

"It's true, big brother," he chirped, giving Maggie an affectionate hug. "Ever since you two decided not to get back together, your disposition—"

"That's enough," Garrett growled.

Blake shook his head and pointedly turned away from him. "Well, Mag, he won't be underfoot Saturday."

An irrational sense of panic seized her. "Oh?"

Casting a mischievous look at his brother, he said, "How does a furlough sound?"

"A what?" Garrett frowned.

"It's a day pass out of this chicken outfit. Sort of a test run before we spring you for good. How does Saturday sound? I'm not on call, and I plan to unplug the phone and flush my pager."

Garrett looked thunderstruck.

"You with me, big brother?" Blake flopped into Garrett's wheelchair, tilted it back on the rear wheels and grinned as if having just delivered a plum of a Christmas present.

"Out?" Garrett breathed, sitting up. "When am I being discharged?"

"In a week if Saturday goes well and your living arrangements are approved. Which I happen to know they are."

Maggie stood rooted in place, torn between pleasure and pain. *He can get on with his life, but I won't see him every day.* She rejoiced yet grieved.

The conversation between the two men continued without her, and she suddenly realized that Blake was singing the virtues of the remodeling he'd done in preparation for Garrett coming to live with him.

"The ramp at the front and back doors plus some gunk in the guest bath were really the only big things it needed." Blake dropped the chair back down on all four wheels. "The doorways are plenty wide for you to get through without bashing your knuckles."

A disquieting surge of competitiveness flooded her. Her own home needed no more than minor modifications, too, but Blake could offer Garrett so much more. Unlike the wealthy neurosurgeon, she didn't have a home gym conveniently located across the hall from a downstairs guest room or a backyard swimming pool.

"What about therapy?" Garrett asked.

Blake idly pivoted in place and shrugged. "Your slot in RPI's outpatient program is in the bag. Oh, by the way, since your last visit, I built a solarium around the spa. We use it all winter."

Memory flashed of another spa, and Maggie swallowed hard. *Bodega Bay. Does he remember?*

"We're ready whenever you are." Blake crossed his arms over his chest, insufferably smug.

"I still don't know what to say," Garrett breathed.

Eyes sparkling, Blake stared at him with theatrical intensity. "Say, 'thank you, oh, wise and generous sibling.'"

"Not on a bet." Garrett's lips twitched. "Is it safe to assume you'll bill me?"

Blake burst out laughing. "You got that right. The coming settlement from the airline ought to set you up for life. I want a chunk."

The sophomoric heckling deteriorated from there, but Maggie couldn't help noticing the vague discontent in Garrett's eyes.

"Are we running your life again?" she asked bluntly.

The humor faded. "Not more than a lot," he answered dryly. "But I don't have many alternatives."

She clamped her jaws shut to keep from offering him one. Their home. Their bed. Arousal coursed through her veins, settling low in her stomach. Firmly, she squashed it.

"Hey, bro," Blake broke in, "if you want to live someplace else..." His gaze cut blatantly to Maggie, who glared at him.

"It's not that." Garrett looked at her, a brief shadow of longing in his eyes. "I've just got some mixed emotions."

Second thoughts? Would you come home if I asked? She gathered her courage, but the shadow vanished and he deliberately turned the conversation toward lighter subjects. The three went to the cafeteria for lunch. On the surface Garrett appeared relaxed, but she sensed a deep turmoil eating at him.

Over the next few days, Garrett couldn't focus. After spending just over half a year in hospitals, he craved wide-open spaces. But life on the outside held a set of unknowns that unnerved him. Maggie dealt with this all the time. It was her job to know the answers. Yet how could he ask without risking her developing an exaggerated sense of obligation toward him?

"Are you looking forward to the furlough tomorrow?" she asked, beginning a deep massage of his back after a particularly tiring workout.

As usual, his muscles constricted involuntarily beneath her hands. Sexual tension arced between them, hot and undeniable.

He concentrated on the pain instead. "It ought to be interesting, a regular three-ring circus."

"With you as head clown?" she probed gently.

Garrett tensed. Maggie was far too perceptive for his peace of mind. He rested his forehead on crossed arms and debated how candid to be. "I was thinking more along the lines of freak on display." *There. It was out.*

"Come on." She tweaked the skin at the base of his neck. "At Blake's? I wouldn't put it past him to swipe a wheelchair from his office and challenge you to a street race."

His brother's Oakland Hills neighborhood was known for its steep streets, and a mental picture formed of a suicide run down the winding road. Despite himself, he smiled. Maggie had a gift for chasing away gloom. He wondered how well he'd be able to survive without it in the difficult months ahead.

Her next pass over his lower back felt more like a caress than a therapeutic attempt to ease overworked, knotted muscles, and brought far more erotic temptations to mind than his body was comfortable handling. *At least I have the problem. Beats the alternative.*

"I think moving in with Blake is a great idea."

An odd note in her voice didn't ring true, and his attention locked onto it. "What's bothering you, babe?"

She hesitated, and he waited her out. "Nothing."

"Liar."

Her breath puffed out in a chagrined laugh. "Okay," she admitted tentatively. "I kind of hoped you'd come back home. I've gotten used to having you around again."

I knew talking about my problems was a mistake! Fool! Better stop this right now for her own good. He half turned on the table. Her expression was tortured, but he hardened himself against it. "You don't owe me anything."

With an outward calm she couldn't have been feeling under his calculated glare, she dried the lubricating oil from her hands on a towel. He sensed it was more of a mindless activity to give herself time to think rather than something she really needed to do. For a moment, he wished he were back in the coma. *Back then, I didn't have to guess what you felt. I knew.*

"You coming home feels right." Her voice was none too steady.

"Liar." Garrett sighed. "What's the real reason?"

She looked away. "I love you. Isn't that enough?"

The need to wrap his arms around her nearly unmanned him. It would be so easy, so very easy to succumb to the cowardice. Common sense won out, barely. "Look, babe, you said it yourself. We loved each other before, and look what happened." It came out softer than he'd intended. He needed to push her away once and for all. The conflict between what he knew was right and what he wanted tore him in two.

"That was then," she answered slowly. "A lot has changed."

"God, what an understatement," he said with a snort. He maneuvered into a sitting position and carefully draped the sheet over his lap. The state of his hormones didn't exactly lend credibility to the cold-blooded rejection he was trying to carry off.

"You won't even talk about it?"

Her green eyes swam with vulnerability and hurt, and he hated himself for it. His mother's whole life revolved around taking care of his father. He couldn't—wouldn't—reduce Maggie's life to the same. She deserved so much better and, unlike his mother, Maggie had a choice. "Coming home is not a good idea."

"Why?"

Stop! He howled in soundless misery but plowed on. "How do you plan to handle Rick if it doesn't work? I can see it now. He finally gets his head screwed on straight. Then I move out again. He'll take that as another desertion."

Her gaze became piercing, and she tossed the towel into a laundry hamper. "What's eating you, Garrett?"

You! I love you more than my own life. But I won't let you harness yourself to endless years of virtual slavery.

"Are you going to answer me?"

"Nothing more to say." His decision was right. She'd sacrifice her happiness for him. He couldn't live with that. He forced a gentle smile. "Thanks for the offer, but no thanks."

She frowned suspiciously at him. "What are you trying to pull? You're wearing your testosterone-knows-best face."

The barb startled him, and he nearly smiled. "Stop imagining things." The note of censure sounded harsher than he'd intended, and he fought the impulse to apologize.

"Imagining?" she challenged. "Not likely."

Frustration lit a short fuse on his temper. "Maggie, I appreciate the offer," he ground out, "but we're not married anymore. Your suggestion is awkward enough without you pushing it. Now, drop it." He swore he felt her flinch under each blow, but it was better to hurt her cleanly and be done with it.

Maggie stepped away and put her hands on her hips. "Fine. I haven't thrown myself at you since I was a kid. Sorry for the lapse." Her voice cracked on the last, spoiling the effect.

Forgive me, babe, he pleaded silently. *This way is best. Trust me—just once more.*

She grabbed the bottle of oil and squirted a generous amount onto her hand. "Now roll back over so we can finish this. I've got a tight schedule today."

Chapter 7

Sunlight streamed into the Mercedes convertible as Blake negotiated the twisting turns of his Oakland Hills neighborhood, and Garrett drank in the fresh air as if he could never get enough. For the first time since the crash, he felt alive, every muscle alert. The confines of RPI had been left behind, even if only for a few hours.

"Once the settlement from the airline comes in I plan to get one of those special vans."

Blake chuckled. "Want to burn up a little road?"

"Something like that. Staring at the same four walls month after month really got to me."

Blake's expression transmuted into something twenty years younger and decidedly reckless. "No reason we can't do a little burning now. Speed limit optional?"

Garrett's craving for raw motion warred with twenty years of ingrained law enforcement. It was a short war. "Do it."

Blake flipped a U-turn in the middle of the block. A couple of freeway changes later, the Mercedes sped north up the coast. Wind blasted Garrett's face and hair, and adrenaline roared through his veins. The morning slipped by, and they laughed over childhood stunts. By the time they got back to Blake's, it was just after one o'clock, and he was more tired than he cared to admit. They pulled into the driveway behind their parents' Oldsmobile, a caterer's van and a beat-up, rusted green Chevy.

"Are clunkers a new hobby, little brother?" he quipped.

"The rolling wreck belongs to your son," Blake chortled. "Looks almost as bad as that thing Dad bought us."

Cold shock iced Garrett's veins. He opened his mouth to demand what Rick was doing here, but it was a little obvious. This was a family thing, and the family had been called together.

Faith swept out onto the front porch of the elegant three-story Victorian-style home, her ivory complexion suffused with pleasure. As usual, her makeup and shoulder-length blond hair looked as if she'd stepped from a fashion magazine. A wrinkle wouldn't dare show itself on her designer clothing or on her face.

"Welcome home." She offered Garrett a brotherly kiss on his cheek, but the look she cast Blake was barely suppressed lust. Even after fourteen years of marriage those two still lit sparks off each other. "I expected you hours ago. Did you get lost?"

Blake grabbed his wife around the waist, swept her over backward and planted a kiss on her that was only half-theatrical in intensity. Garrett tactfully looked away and worked the wheelchair from the back seat. "I'm going inside so you two can neck in peace."

Faith crimsoned, and Blake laughed. Then Garrett wheeled himself into the house. The flawlessly decorated living room had always struck him as sterile, pretentious and cold. Besides, he hated beige. He much preferred the casual comfort of Maggie's tastes. The warm green and gold living room had been a place for friends to drop by and relax, a welcoming haven at the end of a long shift. But it wasn't home to him anymore, and comparisons were pointless, not to mention painful.

"I assumed you'd like some fresh air, so everyone is outside," Faith explained from behind him, trying to talk around Blake nibbling at her neck.

The distinct splash of a body hitting the water in a swimming pool drew him to the backyard. Rick pulled himself out of the water, then executed a flawless cannonball, showering his delighted cousins, ten-year-old Desiree and eight-year-old Ashleigh. On the patio, white linen adorned two long tables. One was set for dining, complete with china and crystal. The other was decked out with enough food for a small army.

Garrett caught a movement to his left. Maggie! His gut twisted. How could she be here, too? He'd needed today to start regaining control of his life, his first day without her.

She rose from a lawn chair by the pool, an uncertain smile on her lips. He looked away, fighting a scowl. She poured a glass of iced tea and handed it to him. His wide fingers brushed her slender ones, and his senses screamed awareness of the contrast between her sensual warmth and the chill of the glass.

"What took you so long?" she asked.

Babe, why are you doing this? Get back to your life and leave me to sort through mine! "We took the scenic route."

Her expression closed. "Why are you glaring at me?"

Disgusted by his failure to keep his feelings private, he schooled his face to bland neutrality. "Sorry, the drive took more out of me than I expected." Then he gestured with the tea glass in the general direction of the bored caterer, who made unnecessary adjustments to the salad. "And this is a bit more than I bargained for."

Her face opened in a relieved smile. "I talked Faith out of inviting half the police officers in northern California."

Garrett recoiled, appalled. The last thing he needed today was the pity of his friends and a reminder of all he'd lost. When cops got together, they talked shop. Period. "Thanks."

The pool house door opened and his parents strolled out onto the patio. His mother's face blossomed when she saw him, but his father's transmuted into dazed horror.

"What did you do to yourself, boy?" he thundered. The older man frowned as if struggling for memories that couldn't be found.

A familiar dull ache lodged in Garrett's throat at his father's condition. "I'm fine, Dad," he returned softly, casting a reassuring look at his mother. "Grab a seat."

As the older couple sat down, he studied his mother. What he saw again grieved him just as much as the first time he'd seen it. She was killing herself caring for the man she loved. In the four years since a stroke had started Dad's downhill slide, she'd aged ten, and Dad didn't have a clue. He cast a discreet look at Maggie, his beautiful Maggie, willing to put herself through the same hell as his mother. The knot of resolve hardened.

At that moment, Ashleigh spotted Garrett, pulled herself from the water and flung wet arms around his neck. "Uncle Garrett! Now we can eat. I'm starving."

A soggy eight-year-old was exactly what the moment needed, and Garrett's laugh was heartfelt. It was then that Rick noticed him. The boy's smile was more relief than pleasure. After a moment's reflection, he forced a wave. Garrett nodded in return.

So much for a one-day reprieve. He tried to recapture the sense of freedom and peace he'd found as he and Blake had raced up the highway. But it was gone, and he feared the day could only go downhill from there.

Faith gave him the place at the table between Rick and Maggie. He wanted to slide into the easy camaraderie that used to be so normal for them. But those days were gone. So was the casual affection. As the caterer served their plates, Garrett remembered countless other backyard parties. The adults had sat around, watching the kids and swapping small talk. Maggie often leaned her head against his shoulder, and he'd occasionally nuzzle her hair.

Today, in sullen silence, Rick swallowed his displeasure at his father's proximity. Maggie tried to avoid talking directly to Garrett, but the obvious effort to give him space only irritated him more. She shouldn't have to walk a tightrope like that. On the other hand, she knew he needed to be alone, so why had she accepted Faith's invitation in the first place?

The moment the caterer cleared away the meal, Desiree turned to her older cousin. "Rick, I bet I can swim under the water longer than you."

Rick grinned at her. "Since when?"

"Since I've been practicing." Her perky little face glowed with confidence.

"Prove it." He shot from the table, both girls on his heels.

"Give your food time to settle first," Maggie called out. Three disgusted faces turned toward her. "Find a board game or something."

Muttering, the trio trudged into the house.

To Garrett, this was too much like tormenting him with the past, taunting him with a life he could no longer live. He couldn't deal with it, not today. Blake and Faith went to check a weird noise coming from the pool pump, and his mother took Dad into the house.

"Maggie, I need to ask a favor," he said when they were alone.

"What kind?"

"Could you and Rick go home early today? I need time to get used to the new order of things. You two being here isn't helping."

Maggie's expression congealed into one of shocked pain. "How do you expect me to explain leaving to the rest of the family?"

Without intending to, Garrett had cast himself in the role of the bad guy. It embarrassed him, and temper opened his mouth. "Knowing how things stand between us, what were you thinking of coming here at all?"

"You can't talk to Mom like that," Rick snapped, slamming a board game onto the table. Green eyes burned.

"Your mother and I are having a private conversation."

"Yeah, right." He snorted, cutting his gaze to Maggie and blatantly dismissing his father. "Come on, Mom. Let's go."

"What about swimming?" Ashleigh asked.

"I'll come back tomorrow, and you can show me your stuff. It'll give you two another day to practice."

Distantly, Garrett noticed how good Rick was with his younger cousins. No wonder they doted on him.

Faith and Blake wandered back to the table. "What's up?" Blake asked, his arm draped around his wife's waist.

"Dad told us to get out, so we're leaving."

Maggie shook her head in disbelief. "Don't exaggerate." She turned to her in-laws. "All this is a bit much for a furlough, so I think we'll disappear. That'll make for two less bodies to complicate things."

"Stop compensating for me!"

Maggie gave Garrett an acid look over her shoulder as she steered Rick toward the house. "Someone needs to."

Faith followed, trying to talk them into staying. Blake just looked at his brother, apology in his eyes.

"Sorry, bro. I should have thought this through better."

On Monday, Maggie turned Garrett's care back over to a reluctant Carl Sapperstein and avoided Garrett completely. If that was what he wanted, fine.

On Wednesday, the morning fog burned off early, leaving a perfect Bay Area summer day. Half the staff, including Maggie, took their lunches to the inner courtyard, and she snagged her favorite spot by the rose arbor.

"You reassigned him to me for punishment, right?" Sapperstein dropped his overtall, underfat frame into the lawn chair opposite her own.

She had no intention of discussing the real reason with an employee—friend or not—so she blinked at him with exaggerated innocence. "Would I do that to you?"

Sapperstein whimpered dramatically. "Boss, if I promise to do my charting like a good little boy, will you let me out of the lion's den?"

Maggie covered her worry with a fat-chance-buddy grin.

Every shift since Garrett returned Saturday night had reported a serious change in his attitude. "How bad has he been?"

Sapperstein snorted deep in his throat. "Monday, he took my head off. Tuesday, he told me where I could go and what body orifice it involved. We won't talk about today."

She took a bite of her sandwich. The bitter tang of too much mustard grabbed a disproportionate amount of her attention. Saturday's fiasco had renewed Rick's self-imposed penance, and he'd made lunch for her every day this week.

"Is he still being discharged Friday?"

"Blake's orders," she said, forcing the bite down her throat.

Sapperstein hooked a leg over the chair arm and swung his foot. "The outside world can be a scary place. Odd, though, he doesn't strike me as a baby bird having trouble leaving the RPI nest. But is that part of it?"

The concept of Garrett being insecure about anything was still somewhat alien to her; then again so was this whole situation. Dubiously, she eyed the other half of her sandwich, then offered it to Sapperstein.

"Oh, wow," he said after chomping into it with childlike glee. "I finally found someone who knows how to make a decent sandwich." He waggled his eyebrows appreciatively. Then, gazing over her shoulder, his expression became fixed in midchew.

"What's the matter?"

"I, ah, think I have some suppositories to count." He got to his feet, and Maggie turned to see what had caught his attention.

Garrett slowly made his way along the sidewalk, his jaw set.

"Thanks, *friend*," she groused as he undraped himself from the chair and started to leave. "See if I ever feed you again."

"Boss, I can see a family squabble coming a mile off, and I make every effort to not be in the middle." He winked. "See ya back at the salt mine."

Maggie took a deep breath as Garrett approached. *I am not*

a wimp. I won't run and hide. Keep telling yourself that, Hughes, and maybe one day you'll believe it.

Restrained anger churned in his eyes, and a tightness pressed his lips into a flat line.

"Did you need something?" she asked, her voice not quite as stable as she would have liked.

"Maggie, I was out of line Saturday."

Temper flared before she had a chance to swallow it back. "Well, at least you waited until Rick and I had eaten before you asked us to leave." She supposed she shouldn't be so sharp with him, but even after five days, she still hurt. He'd been polite, but the bottom line was he hadn't wanted her there. "It wouldn't have been so bad if Rick hadn't overheard and decided to do his White Knight imitation and rush to my defense," she said. "Now I'm stuck with him trying to expiate his latest sins." Grimacing at her half sandwich, she stuffed it back in the bag. "Again."

"I really am sorry. I was exhausted. I needed time alone, and I could have handled it better."

She dragged her gaze to him, the remorse on his beloved face draining away the anger. "It's okay. I shouldn't have come Saturday, and I knew that beforehand."

He sighed. "Ever since I jumped down your throat, I've tried to find an apology that didn't sound trite."

Here we are, again. Hurting each other. Apologizing. Wishing it hadn't happened. There was a certain sick humor to it, and Maggie's lips quirked uncontrollably. "How does this sound?" she suggested. "The day didn't measure up to my expectations, and I came down with a major case of testosterone poisoning."

A bark of rueful laughter erupted from Garrett's chest. "Guilty as charged, Your Honor."

The underlying problems remained, but the surface tension shimmered away like mist, leaving behind an unutterable sadness and a breach neither knew how to cross.

What do you want from me, Garrett? Don't you know it

tears me up that I won't see you every day? They sat in silence, too vulnerable to risk the pitfalls of speech.

"Aha!" Blake's sudden presence startled both of them. "My two favorite people. Together! Just like they should be." He snagged Maggie's lunch sack and gleefully rummaged through it.

"What is it about my food that people find so attractive?" She made a swipe for it, but Blake darted out of reach.

Deep lines etched his face, and his eyes looked hollow with fatigue, a picture totally incongruous with the wicked pleasure in his expression. Pulling out the half sandwich with a bite missing, he looked at it dubiously. "Another one of Rick's?"

Maggie nodded.

With a shudder, Blake stuffed it back in the sack. "Oh, well, I'd rather go out and celebrate than brown-bag anyhow. This calls for champagne."

"Oh?" Garrett asked, sharing a suspicious look with Maggie. "You're entirely too happy for a man with bags under his eyes. What gives?"

"Yep." He yawned. "Rough surgical load this week."

"Okay, Blake," she said, bracing herself. "You're either punch-drunk from exhaustion, or your sneaky little conniving mind has been working overtime again."

He pulled a face of mock hurt. "Boy, I know when I'm not loved—or appreciated. Besides, this didn't require any effort on my part at all." He burst out laughing.

Garrett looked murderous. "I'm not in the mood."

Blake sighed contentedly, determined to savor the moment despite his brother's rising fury. "Desiree woke up this morning with chicken pox. She looks like a blond leopard."

Maggie gaped in confusion. Blake was a sensitive, loving parent. She couldn't comprehend such a callous attitude over his child's suffering.

"The best part," he continued gleefully, "is that Ashleigh hasn't had them either. Nor was she exposed by the same child Desi was."

Maggie cast a confused look at Garrett, stunned to see him sitting deathly still, immobilized in horror.

"That's right, big brother. My house won't be safe for about three weeks."

The blood finished leaching from Garrett's face. He was so pale, Maggie feared he might be in danger of passing out. Slowly, he shook his head in mute denial. "I can't stay here another three weeks. I'll go insane."

"Will you two *please* clue me in here?" she demanded.

Blake laughed so hard he could barely stand. "Three weeks it is, bro. I called Mom just to make sure."

"Be sure of what!" she snapped, ready to strangle them both.

He reined in his good humor long enough to smile at her beatifically. "I'm surprised at you, Mag. How could you not know that your hero—and mine—never had chicken pox?"

Maggie sucked in her breath. Childhood diseases could be life threatening for an adult in Garrett's position.

"This isn't funny," she choked out.

"If he'd already moved in and gotten exposed, you're right." Blake rubbed his ear thoughtfully. "But since he hasn't, that means I can laugh all I want. The way I see it, he has two choices. Stay here until I'm positive Ash is safe. *Or* he can find alternate housing." He kissed Maggie on the cheek and ruffled Garrett's hair. "Gee, I wonder where?"

Garrett's face was a study in abject despair.

"You two set yourselves up as such great targets." He turned on his heel and sauntered off. "If you need any help figuring things out, let me know."

"I'll kill him," Garrett muttered under his breath.

"Not unless I get him first," she snarled. "Why does he do that to us?"

Garrett was a long time in answering. "Rubbing our noses in our problems is his way of punishing us for the divorce."

"Oh."

They shared an uncomfortable glance, then their gazes skittered away. Blake couldn't have made it harder on them if he'd tried. Then again, that had undoubtedly been the point.

"Garrett?" she asked into the silence. "Is it true? You never had chicken pox?"

He shook his head. "Not even a light case."

It felt extremely odd after all these years to suddenly discover something new about him. "What about when Rick—"

"I was gone on a sting operation for nearly a month. I missed the whole thing."

The memory erupted from the recesses of her mind. Silence descended again. If talking had been strained before, it became impossible now. Yet neither could bear to be the first to leave. When Sapperstein came out and stalked toward them looking as if he could eat somebody, she nearly kissed him.

"Sorry to intrude, boss," he said, his jaw clenched in rare annoyance, "but I've got a real whiner squawking for management."

Thank you! She fought down a smile and made herself appear professionally sober. "On my way."

On Friday, a decidedly masculine knock sounded on Maggie's office door. Her heart leaped into her throat. After twenty years, she couldn't mistake that knock.

"Come in," she rasped out.

Garrett shoved open the door and wheeled in. Tension lines marred his square features, and his hair was rumpled as if he'd been digging his fingers through it, something he only did in extreme agitation, and never if he caught himself at it. Maggie took it as a warning and braced herself.

"Are you busy?" His brow furrowed as he took in the mountain of papers in her in basket.

"Should be, but I'm not." She hadn't been able to concentrate since Blake dropped his bomb two days before. "You look like you're not sleeping well."

Fleeting surprise crossed his features. "So do you." A wildness churned in his eyes she'd never seen before.

His breath rushed out in a single groan. "Maggie, never in

my life have I felt so closed in. I feel like I'm in prison. I can't stay here any longer. I'll be a raving lunatic."

You're close to that now.

He tapped his fingers on his knees, and his eyes darted around the room.

Her heart went out to him. "Three more weeks of Club RPI won't be easy, but you'll make it."

He muttered an incoherent expletive and shot her an acid look. "Only if you sedate me for the next twenty-one days."

Discreetly, she gripped the edge of her desk to keep from throwing herself into his arms. *Garrett, come home where you belong. Give us a chance. Please? How can I live without you!*

Even if he did come home, she knew there were no guarantees. True, he wasn't a cop anymore. However, he wasn't the same person either. How well would he adjust to his limitations? He'd spent his entire adult life courting danger like a lover, unable to take a simple cross-country flight without its insistent presence. Maggie couldn't imagine him at a job empty of risk, yet what remained open to him that would satisfy that tremendous internal drive? Could she live with what he found?

But her heart kept coming back to the same point. He's not a cop anymore. No more bullet tag with drug dealers. No more waiting for the phone call that might send her rushing to his side at a hospital somewhere.

"Your disability checks have started," she said, shaking off the pointless debate. "Why don't you spend some of it on a night or two in a bed-and-breakfast I know of? It's very wheelchair friendly. Owned by a retired nurse. Not a bad place."

He looked considering a moment, then shook his head violently. "I'd never come back. I'd find an alley and live in a cardboard box first."

Laughter burst out, but she strangled it off when she saw his face. He wasn't joking.

"What about spending some time with Mom and Dad?"

"No!" He looked horrified, and she half expected him to

fling himself out of the wheelchair and pace the room. "I won't do that to her."

That made no sense. "Do what to her?"

"Nothing," he snapped. Silence spun out as it so often did now.

The depth of his despair pulverized her resolve into dust. "You could come home." It came out in a little-girl voice, not at all the strong proposal she'd wanted it to be.

He recoiled as if she'd kicked him in the stomach.

Why? Is living with me so awful? She choked back a sob.

"We've been through all that, babe," he rasped out. "The marriage is dead. It needs to stay that way."

Blood pounded in her ears, and every feminine instinct she possessed suddenly screamed that he was lying to himself, needing them both to believe. *Come on, Hughes. Everything's on the line now. Push! Push hard!*

"Garrett, you nearly got yourself killed trying to come home to us. And our relationship hasn't been exactly platonic since."

He grimaced. "I know where this is headed, Maggie, and you're only suggesting it because Blake butted in where he had no business. A reconciliation would be foolish."

She shoved her chair away from her desk, her brain kicking into high gear. If ever in her life she needed to be devious, it was now. "Reconciliation? You arrogant jerk! I only intended to invite you to stay until Blake lifted his quarantine." She turned her back on him so he couldn't see her eyes, praying her body language said "Insulted ex-wife. Handle with care."

"Garrett, when I mentioned the other stuff, I was only pointing out that we still care for each other and it wouldn't be a war zone like with many ex-spouses." *Wow, Hughes, that lie actually sounded reasonable. Maybe a good dose of desperation was what you needed all along.* Desperation or not, she knew if he wasn't an emotional disaster zone he'd never buy any of this garbage she was shoveling.

He stayed too quiet for too long, and all she could hear was the thunderous rhythm of her pulse, convinced she'd scream from the pressure. What was he doing!

"Temporary?" he asked breathless.

She cast a glance over her shoulder. He looked like a man on the rack, and she nearly fell at his feet. "Three weeks—give or take a little. We'll play it by ear."

His sapphire eyes seemed to look into her soul. "I don't know, babe," he said, hedging.

She groaned in genuine frustration, knowing he'd misinterpret the cause. "If you're not interested, fine. Stay here." She sat down and returned to her discreet desk-edge grabbing. The phone rang, and she did her best to handle the call while appearing to ignore him. Not an easy task when she could hardly talk around the lump in her throat.

"I have a patient to check on," she said afterward. "Do you want me to take you back to your room? It's on my way."

Defeat dulled his magnificent eyes. "I have no right to inflict myself on you. Not even temporarily, but I can't seem to...." He cut himself off. His shoulders sagged. "I'm a selfish man, Maggie. Blake's stunt aside, I need you." The face he lifted to her radiated a torment that burned soul deep. "I can't take three more weeks in this prison."

My poor hero. Welcome to mere mortality.

Knowing their entire future rested on her reaction, Maggie clamped down hard on the urge to fling herself at his feet. Each step she took as she moved from behind her desk was made with absolute precision to betray nothing. "Then come home."

He nodded, his expression begging forgiveness for being weak. "We may live to regret this," he said hoarsely.

She stepped behind him and took hold of the back of his chair so he couldn't see the hope and fear that had to be written all over her face. "Regret won't be a first for us, will it?"

Maggie couldn't get the house ready until Monday, and the intervening weekend was the longest two days of Garrett's life. Anticipation heated his blood while conscience condemned him as the worst kind of coward. When Blake had made his announcement, something snapped. Worse, Maggie had watched him disintegrate. Facing her at all humiliated him. A strangling politeness crippled each conversation. *His* problem he understood. But why was *she* uptight? Did she regret her kindness already?

In the old days, he would have demanded that they talk it out. In the old days, he wouldn't have let her hide behind overly bright smiles and trivia. But the old days were gone and trivia was all either of them could manage. By the time they reached the house on Monday morning, they hardly spoke at all.

It had been a long time since Garrett last saw the house he and Maggie bought fifteen years ago. He'd practically sweated blood to come up with the down payment. She had still been in school and Rick wasn't walking yet, not the most ideal time to buy their first house. But the two-story, white stucco had been too good a bargain to pass up. The neighborhood was solid and unpretentious, the kind where people kept their yards up and their noise down, the kind where he wanted his family to put down roots.

As Maggie pulled into the driveway and killed the engine, he drank in years' worth of memories. The water fights on the front lawn, the day he and two-year-old Rick planted the sycamore tree out front. He looked up into the towering branches and smiled. So many good times, so many bad. His mind played through them like an unending movie, and he didn't immediately notice Maggie beside the open passenger door, his wheelchair at the ready.

"Sorry," he mumbled. "I kind of zoned out."

Maggie puffed out her breath in a nervous laugh and glanced at the house. "This place will do that to you."

"Does the front door still squeak?" he asked.

Her smile relaxed a little, apparently relieved that he hadn't asked anything serious. "Loud as ever. I defy any burglar to get through it without waking me up."

He cast her a reassuring smile and opened his mouth to tell

her everything was going to work out just fine, but he couldn't bring himself to lie. He was here for one reason. He was a helpless cripple who'd wimped out. He disgusted himself.

Involuntarily, his gaze traveled to the sloped, concrete driveway. The incline wasn't much worse than many of the ramps at RPI, but getting out of a car at that angle wouldn't exactly be a piece of cake. The sidewalk connecting the driveway to the house was nice and flat. No problems there. But getting into the house meant three steps up to the porch and a half step over the doorsill.

Several times during his years as a police officer, he'd stared down the barrel of a suspect's gun. Each time, he'd stood firm. But the sudden wrenching terror of not being able to get into his own home made his blood run cold in a way he had never imagined. A taunting voice reminded him that it wasn't even his home anymore. "I think we have a problem."

Her eyes clouded with sympathy. "Don't worry. Getting in and out of a car is something you've practiced."

His old enemies—helplessness and frustrated anger— slammed into him. "I meant the porch, damn it!"

She started to reach out a reassuring hand, then withdrew it, no longer the woman who loved him but a professional doing her job. That made it a lot easier.

"We'll go in through the back," she said coolly. "There's only one step between the ground and the sliding glass door leading into the dining room."

"One or ten hardly matter," he snapped.

"I put in a temporary ramp back there."

"Oh." Embarrassment climbed aboard with all the other garbage, and Garrett levered himself from the car into the wheelchair without falling on his face. A little victory.

They went through the side gate to the backyard. A forty-pound canine ball of steel-gray fur gave Garrett a stunned look, then raced to his side. Between the whimpering and wiggling, the dog could hardly stand.

"Hairy?" Garrett sputtered, then gazed up at Maggie.

"He's got to be fifteen years old. I thought he'd be gone by now."

Maggie shook her head. "I guess he's like the rest of the Hughes family. We're all pretty tough."

Garrett only half listened as she described the aging dog's antics. The rest of him was absorbed in Hairy's total acceptance. The animal didn't care if Garrett was paralyzed or not. He was home and, to Hairy at least, that was all that mattered.

The dog dashed off to retrieve his prized possession, a well-chewed, faded blue Frisbee. He plopped it in Garrett's lap, sat back on his haunches and barked once.

"You're kidding." Garrett stared.

"Nope," Maggie answered. "He doesn't do the heroic leaps he used to, but he likes to think he can. Throw it low, and he acts like he's king of the world when he catches it."

A ribbon of panic sliced through Garrett. Throwing a Frisbee. Simple. Anyone can do it, right? Not him, not anymore. Garrett was left-handed now, and throwing plastic disks wasn't a life skill that RPI taught. This was just the first of a thousand things guaranteed to frustrate and torment him.

"Uhmmm, maybe later."

Maggie gave him a probing stare. "You stiffened up."

"It's nothing." It came out more harsh than he intended. "I just want to get into the house."

"Tired?"

He wasn't, but he shrugged noncommittally. It beat admitting the truth. He tossed the Frisbee onto the grass by the dog's front paws, and Maggie pushed the wheelchair toward the covered patio. He deliberately looked away from Hairy's disappointed face and tried to find something to think about other than this unexpected challenge, one he'd failed because he hadn't found the guts to try. And that bought him the greatest defeat of all.

He caught sight of the new flower bed to the left of the patio and nearly groaned out loud in relief. Here was a subject he could talk about.

"You're right," he said with forced cheer. "Those roses

look good there. Did you really reroute the sprinkler system
yourself?''

Maggie froze. Her voice came out choked and uncertain.
"How did you know about the roses and the sprinklers?"

*Idiot! The only time she mentioned that was while you were
in a coma.* "You told me, babe," he said softly.

She was quiet, too quiet. "How much *do* you remember?"

He shrugged, then mentally groped for a way out. She'd
asked him a point-blank question, and by rights, he needed to
give her a straight answer. He'd never lied to her, and he
refused to start now. Hairy chose that moment to land in the
middle of his lap, and Garrett had his hands full with wiggling
dog and blue Frisbee.

Her attention diverted, Maggie shrieked at the dog.

Thanks, boy, Garrett breathed inwardly. *I owe you.*

Hairy offered only token protest as Maggie grabbed him by
the collar and hauled him to the ground. He gave her a soulful
look—plastic disk still in his mouth—and wagged his tail.

"Oh, for Pete's sake," she muttered. In one fluid motion,
she sailed the disk across the yard in a clean arc. It bounced
off the wooden fence, and Hairy snatched it out of the air.

Garrett looked away. This whole scenario was too much like
the young father at RPI who tried to throw a ball for his son
but couldn't. *Helpless. Useless. A burden to family and society.* The accusations pounded his mind and soul. To banish
the debilitating fear, he riveted his attention on the beat-up
steel ramp resting on the sliding glass door's sill. Gouges,
scrapes and stains marred the textured surface. The thing
looked grotesque against the carefully tended yard and house.

"Where did you get that?" he asked

"I rented it from a moving company," she said, apparently
oblivious to his spiraling depression. "A contractor will be
here next week."

She opened the sliding glass door and Garrett wheeled himself into the dining room. Once inside, he gritted his teeth
against the bittersweet sense of homecoming. The same hint
of flowers so uniquely Maggie hung in the air, just as it had

when they'd lived together as man and wife. He glanced at the cherry-wood table shoved toward the wall to make a path wide enough to accommodate his wheelchair. A generous bouquet of flowers sat atop it. Flowers were Maggie's one frivolous expenditure, and they had figured prominently in his original plans to win her back.

This was a mistake. A horrendous mistake. His jaw muscles clenched to the point of pain. *Living here, even for a short time...* He swallowed hard. *I only thought staying at RPI would kill me. This really will.*

"I don't like that look, Garrett," she said. From her tone, she wasn't in any better shape than he. "What are you thinking?"

He snorted in self-derision. "Same old stuff."

She moved in front of him, and he glanced up into her tight, fierce smile.

"Want some coffee?" she asked.

His pent-up breath eased out in relief. She hadn't pursued it. "Please."

She wheeled him into the living room, then spoke over her shoulder on her way to the kitchen, "Has the house changed much?"

He looked around the room. Their old nineteen-inch color TV had been replaced by a thirty-six-inch big screen with a built-in VCR. A huge tape cabinet stood beside it. *You always were a movie nut, babe. But what has changed that I don't know about?*

His gaze raked the room, desperate for familiarity. The maple coffee table was the same. So was the L-shaped sectional, except reupholstered. Buying new would have been cheaper. Why had she gone to the expense? They were functional, solid pieces of furniture, but hardly anything that couldn't have been discarded. Sentiment?

For that matter, why did she still live here? This was little more than a starter house. Her income had ballooned dramatically after her promotion to assistant director. Why hadn't she sold this place and bought something better? Memories of the

good times? Or had it been because she'd lived such an insecure life as a kid that once she put down roots, they stayed
down?

The photo collection on the far wall was about what he
remembered. It had some new additions, but one photo was
conspicuously missing—their wedding portrait. Not surprising,
he decided, but its absence did nothing to keep him from seeing it in his mind's eye.

He had wanted to give her the ultimate fairy-tale wedding,
not realistic on a rookie cop's salary, but with the family's
help he'd made it happen. Maggie and his mother sewed for
weeks on the gown that had swirled around her feet like a
river of satin. The flowers alone had cost half a month's pay,
but when she'd walked down the aisle toward him that afternoon, bouquets lined every pew, and she'd stepped on a carpet
of rose petals.

Garrett gripped the wheelchair's hand rims and shook off
the memories. Seventeen years ago he would have killed anyone who'd even hinted that their lives would come to this.

Wheeling himself across the new plush carpet required more
effort than he expected, but he managed to get closer to the
wall to inspect the new photos. There were assorted enlarged
snapshots of his parents, of Blake's family, yearly photos of
Rick's soccer teams, eight-by-ten school portraits, and one of
Rick and Maggie perched on a granite boulder the size of a
barn.

"Donner Lake," Maggie explained from behind him. He
hadn't heard her return. "It wasn't the same without you.

As a family, they'd hiked all over the Sierra Nevada, the
Donner area one of their favorites.

"I've missed a lot, haven't I?" He hadn't meant to sound
so grieved, but he could never join them again and his voice
betrayed that pain.

Tentatively, she touched his shoulder. There had been a time
when touch had been as natural as their love. Both had suffered grave blows. She smiled self-consciously, and he covered her hand with his own. In silence, they turned their at-

tention toward the other photos, old and new. Rather than soothe, the memories of the times shared scraped open old wounds, and Maggie withdrew her hand.

"I think I'd better check on the coffee."

He nodded, not trusting his voice, and watched her walk away. Maggie's figure had matured over the years, and he found her vastly more erotic than the sixteen-year-old he'd fallen in love with. She was trim and supple, yes, but she also radiated the aura of a woman who'd lived life. The faint lines around her eyes and the scars of old stretch marks from pregnancy were badges of honor, not flaws to be hidden or corrected. She was a woman who had worked hard to get what she wanted, and success had its own sexuality that youth couldn't hope to compete with.

"I need her," he said in a low, desperate whisper. "And the last thing she needs is me."

Chapter 8

Rick worked the noon to nine shift that night, so Garrett and Maggie sat down to dinner alone. He didn't call attention to the fact that they hadn't shared a meal in this house since the night before they separated. From her overly self-conscious body language, she was just as aware of it as he and just as reluctant to bring it up. The last time she'd cooked for him, he was convinced she wouldn't really go through with the divorce. So much had happened since then.

He'd had such plans when he'd boarded that plane in Washington. The intimate dinners they'd share. The quiet walks. The way she'd feel in his arms again. Instead, she stood beside him, both of them as tongue-tied as teenagers on a blind date.

"Seems to me you used to like this." Shyly, she set a plate in front of him.

For four years, Garrett had gotten few home-cooked meals, and none compared to Maggie's. Tonight she'd fixed his favorite: plain, no-frills roast beef, roasted carrots, mashed potatoes and gravy. The aroma had teased him unmercifully while dinner cooked. "It's perfect, babe."

He could have sworn he detected a soft sigh of relief. She sat across from him, the same places at the same table they'd shared for years.

At RPI he'd become rather adept at getting food to his mouth left-handed, but cutting meat required two functioning hands. He laid the adapted knife across his right palm and strapped it in place with two sets of Velcro strips.

Conversation was limited to aborted starts, stops and covert glances over the rims of their glasses. *What am I doing here?* He groped in the darkness of his mind for an answer he could live with, but it remained unchanged, soft and simple, painful in its simplicity. *Because, like any wounded animal, you crawled back to your den. You came home.*

After dinner, they loaded the dishwasher together in virtual silence. Maggie scraped plates and handed them to him to put in the rack. *My kind of job*, he observed acidly. *The dishwasher is on my level—the ground.*

The tension between them continued to build over the course of the evening. They sat through a movie, he on one side of the room in his wheelchair, she in the corner of the L-shaped sectional couch, feet tucked up beneath her, a glass of orange juice on the coffee table in front of her.

There was a time when we watched movies curled in each other's arms, feeding each other popcorn, licking the butter and salt from each other's fingers, he remembered morosely. *Occasionally, we even saw the ending before I carried you off to bed. You never complained.* He turned back to the TV, not that he had any idea what they were watching.

The torture ended with the late-night news, and neither moved or looked at each other. It was as if they feared making a fatal misstep. That made him furious. Maybe the nerves in his spine hadn't been the only ones damaged in the crash.

"Do you want to watch a video, or are we going to call it a night?" he asked bluntly. He could feel the set cast to his expression, but smiling was more than he could muster.

She ran her fingers through her rumpled auburn hair, easing

it back over her shoulders. Then she turned apprehensive green eyes toward him. "Bed sounds pretty good."

Bed. The one word he hadn't wanted to voice out loud. Hearing it made their problems all the more immediate. Earlier, she'd put his clothes in the master bedroom closet, sparing him the indignity of asking where he was to sleep. Yet, as badly as he wanted her, he knew better. Once he tasted of her again, how could he ever leave again in three weeks? It was enough to make him wish she'd banished him to the couch.

Maggie still looked at him, waiting for his answer, her own nervousness apparent in the way she needlessly adjusted the couch cushions.

"I'm tired." *Sure you are. You're wired enough to swear off sleep for a week.*

Maggie knew it too from the flash of skepticism that crossed her face. "Okay."

Sexual awareness charged the room, and a tightness gripped his chest.

"I'll get the lights," she whispered, turning away.

He nodded without comment and headed down the hall. If they were any more polite, they might rupture something.

Negotiating the tight, right-angle turn into the master bedroom proved a bit tricky but not impossible. The king-size bed was the same, as was the Oriental spread that covered it. The dresser and bedside tables had a few more nicks and dings than before but were where he remembered them. A quick glance at the far wall told him where their old TV and VCR had gone.

Then he caught sight of his reflection in the mirrored doors of the walk-in closet and sucked in his breath. How many mornings had he stood tall before that mirror, making sure his uniform measured up to department standards before he kissed Maggie and Rick goodbye for the day? Now, he stared at the man he was today, for the first time since the accident able to see the total picture. His eye was brutal as it scoured the gaunt figure glaring back at him. In the soft light, the chrome wheel spokes and chair frame shone with stark brilliance.

* * *

In the living room, Maggie clicked off lamps and pulled the drapes closed. Garrett was home. Yet he seemed farther away than when they had lived a continent apart. Feeling more unsure of herself than on their wedding night, she slipped into the bedroom.

She watched Garrett study his reflection, his deep-set sapphire eyes taking in every detail, his chiseled features rigid with harsh appraisal. Even in a wheelchair, he radiated a power and authority few men could hope to attain. His ordeal had taxed his strength to its limits, yet he'd survived. The pain had aged him, frosting his temples with a light touch of gray, but the overall effect doubled the impact this darkly handsome man had on her senses.

But what do you *see, my love?* she wondered, wishing— not for the first time—that she had his uncanny ability to read people.

Abruptly, he turned away, his face ravaged with hatred and self-doubt.

Maggie sucked in her breath. "Let it go, Garrett." Her voice came out no more than a choked whisper. "The past is where it belongs. Today and tomorrow are all that matter."

He jumped but made no reply. Apparently, he had been so lost in thought he hadn't noticed her presence, something that was no longer a rare occurrence, but one that emphasized the changes in him.

The bed loomed monstrously in the room. Garrett wasn't home because he wanted her. He was home because she'd taken advantage of him in a weak moment. Should she have asked before she'd put his clothes in the closet they'd once shared? On the other hand, this was the only downstairs bedroom.

Was he feeling trapped? Did he feel he had to perform? The spontaneity of their raging hormones in the pool and therapy room at RPI was far different from calmly, deliberately climbing between the sheets. Besides, if she pushed too hard too fast, he'd realize he'd been had and she'd never get him to stay.

Maybe it would be best to give him an out. Unable to voice it while looking at him, her gaze drifted to the ceiling. "Would you...uhmmm...prefer if I slept in the spare bedroom? You might rest better without me tossing and turning next to you all night."

Her rejection sliced deep, taking Garrett's breath away. *So the truth comes out at last.* He laughed bitterly at the irony of the situation. "Here I've been worried about whether or not we should make love at all, and you're not even interested in sharing bed space."

"That's not true!" she snapped back. "I just thought—"

"Sorry. I assumed we'd be sleeping together. After thirteen years, sleeping chastely in separate beds seemed rather foolish to me. I guess it doesn't to you."

She gasped.

"I'm only here temporarily, and I should have asked about the sleeping arrangements rather than assuming."

She felt her face heat in embarrassed fury. Her breath rushed out, and she clenched her fists at her sides. "The first day home is often rough, and we're not communicating very—"

"When you suggested I stay here, I thought you might be trying to pull something. What you said didn't quite fit. But I was wrong about that, too. You don't need to rub my nose in it."

Maggie sputtered incoherently, then clamped her jaws shut. After a long brittle silence, she put her hands on her hips. "Garrett, I'm not going to get into a shouting match with you." She bit out each syllable. "Good night."

She snatched her lavender pajamas from the hook in the bathroom and stormed to the door, her back ramrod straight. An annoying sense of responsibility stopped her. Despite all, it was his first night out of the hospital. "Before I go, is there anything you need?"

"No," he drawled. "Thanks to you and your devoted minions, I can get in and out of the damn chair alone, get dressed alone, I can even go the bathroom alone just like a big boy.''

She grimaced at the biting sarcasm and left.

Furious with Maggie, with himself and with the world at large, Garrett whipped back the blankets, took one look at the sheets and groaned. They had faded a little after years of laundering, but he remembered them well. More to the point, he remembered Maggie's creamy skin a sensuous contrast against the royal blue satin.

Shaking off the tormenting memories, he snapped off the light and attempted to get himself from the chair to the bed. The edge of the mattress—softer than he remembered— sagged, dumping him on the floor. He landed hard between the bed and wheelchair. Unhurt but livid, his frustration and rage poured out in a string of obscenities wholly inadequate to the occasion.

Blitzing through the living room, Maggie heard the crash and froze. Too furious to go back in there without good reason, she called out, ''Are you hurt?''

There was more swearing. ''I'm just fine.''

Sure you are. Fine explains why you're such a crabby, potty mouth. ''I take it you fell. Do you need any help?''

The momentary silence sounded more obscene than his vocabulary. ''Good night, Maggie Jean.''

Maggie crept down the hallway just far enough to hear the sounds of him painstakingly getting from the floor to the bed. Then she stormed upstairs. ''Why do I love that man? Why! Why! Why!'' She swallowed hard and sniffed back threatening tears.

Patience, Hughes. He's not himself, came a softer, more rational voice. *He still needs months more—if not years—to adjust. You're lucky the pressure hasn't sent him exploding off on a tangent over something really crazy.* Her anger melted into sadness.

''It's not fair,'' she moaned. ''We've been through so much. Why can't we make it the rest of the way?''

She flipped on the light and stopped dead. On the far wall hung their wedding portrait. After the divorce, she hadn't been able to stand it in the living room, but she couldn't bring herself to get rid of it either. So she'd compromised, putting it in a room she rarely entered, knowing it was there, but not having to look at it every day.

A mournful laugh whispered from her throat. She and Garrett had been so young—her nineteen to his twenty-five. Studying the confident set to his square features, she smiled at the bittersweet memories. Back then, she'd believed he could do wrong, no task too great. All that and more showed so clearly in the way she had adoringly gazed up at him, the photographer capturing their love forever.

With a slow shake of her head, she changed into pajamas she hadn't thought she'd be needing tonight and turned toward the lonely twin bed. Pulling back the covers, she stared for a moment at the floral print percale. She'd put the royal blue satin sheets on downstairs, believing Garrett would be beside her in their bed. Did the old sheets mean anything to him? Or were such memories a woman thing?

Looking distastefully at the bed again, she scowled in hurt and frustration and flipped out the light.

The mattress was comfortable, the sheets crisp and clean. She knew she should fall asleep instantly, but she lay staring at the ceiling, her mind torturing her with what she and Garrett once had, and all they'd lost.

The master bedroom and its big bed were directly below her. Did Garrett also lie staring at the ceiling? Did he wonder if she was awake? The endless loop of tormenting possibilities raced faster and faster, until she thought she'd go crazy.

"Stop it, Hughes," she groused, struggling for a little professional detachment. "Our first day was a disaster. Keep it in perspective. You got him here. That's a big first step. Tomorrow will be better." *Sure. And pigs fly.*

Time snailed by, and she fidgeted until she found herself tangled in the blankets. The front door squeaked open and shut. Then she heard the soft tread of footsteps on the stairs.

Bolting out of bed, she met Rick in the hallway as he turned toward his room in the dark.

"Richard Patrick Hughes, where have you been?"

With a wordless shriek, Rick whirled around. "Mom, you scared me to death!"

"Where have you been?" Her hands dropped to her hips. A distant part of her mind told her to back off, that the missed curfew was only an excuse to explode.

"What are you doing up here?" he asked, still breathless.

"Rick, this was your father's first day home. The least you could have done was come straight—"

"Dad's here? He didn't change his mind?" Green eyes sparkled in a hungry hope.

"You got off work almost four hours ago. There's no excuse for your behavior this time."

He took a defensive step backward and raised his hands placatingly. "Mom, my car broke down."

A thread of sanity breached the storm. "It what?"

"It wouldn't start after work, so my friend John called his dad, and we towed it to their place. We've been working on it for hours. As soon as we got it going, I came straight home." His expression became sheepish. "I guess I should have called anyway, huh?"

Only then did Maggie notice the grease smears on his hands, forearms and one cheek. She groaned. "I'm sorry, honey. I just assumed."

Rick didn't answer at first, then gave his trademark shrug. "I guess you figured you had a right to shoot first and ask questions later."

Maggie nearly whimpered out loud with remorse. "I feel like an idiot."

"Is Dad really here?" The light shining in his eyes was one she had never thought to see again. Garrett had been right. There was progress.

"Yes, he really is." Her smile came easily.

"Is he...I mean is he staying?"

"Until Blake says Desi and Ash are okay."

"Chicken pox." He chuckled. She didn't need Garrett's gift of reading people to discern her son's thoughts. A simple childhood disease had brought his father *home* and, despite himself, he couldn't be happier about it.

"He may be asleep already," she said, "but you can go check if you want."

Rick smiled tentatively, then lowered his face to hide his sudden shyness. "I'll wait till morning." A moment later, he frowned a question at her. "Mom...uhmm...if he's down there, what are you doing up here?"

Maggie, embarrassed that he'd zeroed in on the sleeping arrangements, had a hard time meeting his puzzled gaze. *He's sixteen, Hughes. His whole world revolves around hormones. You should have expected that.* "Today was a little stressful and—"

"You had a fight?!" His expression twisted into a mute accusation of betrayal. "I knew it wouldn't work. I knew it!"

He turned away, and Maggie grabbed his arm. "We told you this was temporary. I need your support for the next three weeks, Rick, and so does he! We're treading water as fast as we can, and I *expect* you to tread right beside us. Is that clear?"

"What good will it do?" The wary skepticism that clouded his expression wasn't much better than the anger, but it was the best she could hope for. "He's leaving again."

His obvious distress cooled her temper. "If you won't try for yourself or him, then do it for me."

He nodded, but she sensed his reservations and fears. Garrett had been right. Rick couldn't handle anything less than an intact family. The emotional price tag for risking his heart again was higher than he could pay. She understood exactly how he felt. Only she wasn't an insecure sixteen-year-old, and she had no choice but to find the courage to try.

"Good morning, son," Garrett said in a deliberately conversational tone as the boy entered the kitchen.

Rick stopped in the doorway, scrutinizing him as if he

didn't quite trust his senses. "Hi, Dad." His voice sounded years younger than it should have.

He's nervous! At the realization, Garrett flattened the urge to grin like an ape.

"I'm...uhmmm...sorry I came in so late last night."

"No problem." *I don't know where you stuffed your hostility, but I'm not complaining.* "What happened?"

Rick reached for the cereal in the cupboard above the refrigerator and explained.

"Sounds like the carburetor needs rebuilding, too," Garrett said. "I can't do the work—" he indicated his right hand "—but I can talk you through it if you're interested."

Rick looked eager, like years ago, before the divorce. Then the eagerness vanished behind a defensive mask. "Thanks, but John's dad is picking up a rebuild kit. He's a professional mechanic."

If Rick had stabbed a knife into Garrett's heart it wouldn't have hurt worse. His son preferred an outsider to help with his car. Garrett took another sip of his coffee, a ploy to give him a moment to recover.

At least his son hadn't come down a few minutes earlier to witness his struggles with the simple task of making coffee. Maggie had left a clean mug and the coffee can on the counter. Filling the pot with water from the sink was no problem, but pouring it into the reservoir required a reach and dexterity that had almost proved disastrous.

This was his first full day out of the hospital, and it hadn't begun at all well. Maggie woke him just as she was ready to leave for work, effectively blocking out any possibility of conversation other than a terse quarrel about her sending someone to check on him. Now his son threw him some new curves.

Rick filled a cereal bowl and took it into the dining room. Garrett wanted to follow, but he couldn't handle the wheelchair and hot coffee at the same time. He took another swallow, set the cup on the counter and went into the dining room.

"What are your plans for the day?" he asked.

"Work. The manager is giving me all the extra hours he

can until school starts.'' He looked as if he wanted to say more, but focused on eating instead.

Garrett pushed on. "Are you playing soccer this year? Seems to me that the team gets back together about now."

Rick shot him a look of terrified vulnerability, then walled it off behind a diffident shrug. "Yeah, I still play. First practice is tomorrow."

He's hiding, Garrett realized. What had happened? Had he somehow figured out things weren't going smoothly between his parents? *Swell.* "What position?"

Rick froze, spoon halfway to his mouth. Deliberately, he concentrated on his meal.

"What position?" he repeated.

Rick glared into his bowl, his breathing too even, too controlled. "Offense."

Garrett clamped his jaws shut to keep from making the obvious comment about being offensive, then took a couple of controlling breaths of his own. "You've been playing how many years now? Seven?"

Rick stabbed his spoon into the cornflakes and stuffed another bite into his mouth. "Yeah." He gave Garrett a haunted glance, then went to the kitchen. From where Garrett sat, he watched Rick dump the half-eaten breakfast down the garbage disposal, then put the bowl and spoon in the dishwasher.

"Well, even if I can't figure you out," Garrett muttered to himself, "you're at least neater than you used to be."

Rick spun around. "What's that supposed to mean?"

Garrett hadn't intended to be heard. He sighed heavily. "What's wrong? Soccer used to be one of your favorite subjects."

"Nothing. I'm...I'm kind of burned out."

A bomb went off inside him. "Don't lie to me." *Don't make things worse, you idiot. Calm. Control. You're the parent. Act like it.* "What time is your practice tomorrow?"

Rick's body tensed, and his face flushed with longing, both obvious signs of a battle between keeping up his defense mechanisms and the need to spill his guts. Garrett held his breath.

"Why?"

"Because I'm going to be there."

Rick's mouth gaped open. "Why?"

"We have a lot of missed time to make up for."

For a timeless moment, Rick's face opened and Garrett saw the trusting, secure kid he'd left four years ago. But the boy's scars were stronger, and the wall came down again.

"Two o'clock," he muttered, leaving the room.

When the front door squeaked open then banged shut, Garrett smiled. The school where the team practiced was only four blocks away. He'd get there if he had to drag himself hand over hand down the sidewalk.

Slightly after midmorning, a delivery crew arrived with the rehab equipment that had been purchased and originally taken to Blake's house. The driver stood in the doorway, clipboard in hand and a beer gut hanging over his belt. He looked as if he hadn't bathed in days.

But at least he can walk, an inner voice taunted.

"We were told to set up this stuff in the garage. Is there someone here with a key?" The man didn't even look directly at Garrett, more like over him as if he were a piece of furniture.

Disbelief held Garrett's fury in a state of frozen control. With his jaws clenched, he retrieved the spare set of keys from a drawer in the china hutch then maneuvered his wheelchair through the dining room, through the backyard and out the gate to the front. It made him feel like a rat running a maze, but *no one* was going to unlock that garage door but *him.*

As the crew unloaded boxes and crates of exercise equipment, they also unloaded equipment that Garrett recognized as refugees from Blake's gym. The men ignored his presence as they worked. Not ignored, he decided, more like going overboard not to stare.

Once they had the machines set up to their satisfaction, the beer-bellied wonder turned to him. "Is there someone here who can sign for this?"

Garrett's temper flared. He ached to leap from the chair, grab the jerk by the throat and pound him into a bloody pulp. "Is there a problem with *me* signing the work order?"

Beer Belly's face suffused with color, and his eyes darted from side to side, looking anywhere but at Garrett. "Well, no," he said lamely. "I just sort of thought that...well, you know."

Impaling him with an arctic glare, one that had served him well as a cop, Garrett then held out his hand for the clipboard. Squirming with humiliation, the man handed it over as if he couldn't get rid of it fast enough.

Garrett picked up the pen. It felt alien in his left hand. He'd dismissed Maggie's pleas that he learn to write left-handed. At the time, working on regaining the use of his right hand seemed like a more efficient use of his time. *The price one pays for overconfidence.*

Pride wouldn't allow him to let on that anything was wrong, but the final result of his efforts was an illegible scrawl.

"Have a nice day," Beer Belly said, his smile strained.

Garrett gave a curt nod, but didn't reply.

For more than an hour, he sat in the garage, inspecting the equipment that would be a part of his life for years to come— if not forever. An all-consuming sense of isolation engulfed him. Facing the machinery in the hospital had been so much different than having it in his own garage. This was too close, too personal, like an umbilical cord that tied him to the conglomeration of lead weights, steel pipes and assorted molded plastic parts.

"When I chose to live, I never dreamed it would be like this."

He sat in the silence for a while, then systematically worked through the exercise regimen until pain and fatigue drained away all of his strength. The workout didn't cause the blinding agony it used to, but bad enough for him to be sweat-soaked by the time he went back into the house.

Preparing a meal proved to be another experience he would have preferred to avoid. The lunch meat and bread weren't a problem. However, opening the mustard jar one-handed turned into a demeaning, impossible task. He finally tried bracing it between the wheelchair arm and his leg. The jar shot out from its precarious spot and hit the floor. The muted crack of fracturing glass sounded a full second before his temper exploded.

"Why the hell can't Maggie buy mustard in squeeze bottles like everyone else!" The fact that it was a brand-new jar of the deli variety that he enjoyed—and she hated—barely registered.

He scrounged through the drawers until he found the kitchen towels—apparently, she'd rearranged the kitchen since the divorce—then bent carefully to pick up the sharp-edged mess. Bending over wasn't a problem. Coming up got tricky.

"Consider it exercise," he muttered.

When he was through, a dull yellow stain stood out in glaring relief on the floor like a banner proclaiming his ineptitude. His appetite disappeared, and he left the kitchen, his half-made sandwich untouched on the counter.

For months his focus had been to get out of the hospital. Now that he was out, it felt almost anticlimactic. Nothing had fundamentally changed. He was still a forty-two-year-old cripple occupying space with nothing meaningful to contribute.

Career counseling had been part of the RPI's services, but none of the options held any appeal. Some idiot had even suggested that he go back to college and become a pencil pusher!

From the backyard, Hairy barked at an undoubtedly imaginary threat to his domain, and Garrett remembered the Frisbee. He didn't have an audience now. No pressure except what he placed on himself. Fighting a staggering sense of insecurity, he returned to the backyard, where Hairy greeted him with an enthusiasm reserved for long-lost royalty.

Garrett ruffled his fur and scratched that special spot behind Hairy's left ear that sent the old dog into groaning whines of ecstasy. "I never gave the expression 'dogs are man's best friend' much thought till now." He smiled fondly at the ball of long, gray fur. "How patient are you feeling today?"

Hairy cocked his head and wagged his bushy tail.

Garrett gave himself one last internal push to gather his courage. *This shouldn't be so hard.* But it was. "Frisbee, Hairy. Frisbee."

Joy flared in the animal's brown eyes, and he bounded across the yard, trotting back with the chewed-up, blue treasure.

Garrett focused on transposing a right-handed skill to his left, then curled his wrist and let the disk fly. Launch and plummet best described the way it soared virtually straight up, then slammed into the lawn. Hairy gave Garrett a you've-gotta-be-kidding look, and Garrett felt his face heat. Embarrassment over what a dog might or might not think had to be a new low.

Hairy dutifully pounced on the disk, then trotted over and laid it in his master's lap. Garrett was glad dogs couldn't talk. He didn't really want to hear it. Over and over he struggled to get the child's toy to soar in a straight line. Again and again, it flew with the erratic pattern one would expect from a two-year-old, not a grown man.

One last time, he gave his wrist a hard snap. The Frisbee sailed in a perfect trajectory—right over the back fence. Garrett closed his eyes and swore.

An illegible scrawl was all Maggie could produce, thanks to her shaking hands, but she managed to place her signature on the line the police officer indicated.

"What do we do now?" she asked. For the first time in her life, she wished Garrett was still a cop. She needed *him* here, needed his steadying voice, not a herd of uniformed strangers.

"We're going to search the ground floor and courtyard first. Then we'll work up." He pointed a thumb at the ceiling. "Is there a chance that he's hiding?"

Maggie didn't know if the urge to pull out her hair or scream was the more irresistible. "For the last time, *yes,* it's possible," she gritted out, determined to smile at the idiot, even if it killed her. "He's a head injury patient. Anything's possible—combativeness, paranoia, radical personality change without warning. I won't know what we're dealing with today until we find him." Her boss was power-lunching with the other bigwigs and RPI's investors. She didn't have a clue where. Which meant the responsibility for a patient wandering off—and finding him—rested squarely on her shoulders.

She glanced up just as the patient's wife and father stormed through the front door, looking ready to devour the first piece of management meat they ran across. She swallowed hard, excused herself and went to greet them.

Promptly at two o'clock, a burly man in his late twenties arrived at the house, a folding massage table under one arm and a duffel bag slung over his shoulder.

"Hi, I'm Mike, your physical therapist." He invited himself in, leaving Garrett sitting by the door with his jaws clenched.

Mike snapped open the table with crisp efficiency.

"No one told me you were coming," Garrett said acidly.

Mike looked up, clearly surprised. "Oh, yeah? That's weird." He shrugged. "Well, Doctors Hughes and Kelly want the same program going that was set up at RPI. So I'll be here five afternoons a week." He flipped through a stack of papers in a folder that he pulled from the duffel bag. "Hughes," he said contemplatively. "Any relation?"

"My brother. Maggie is my ex-wife."

"The assistant director?" Mike raised a brow. "No wonder my supervisor said you were to get the VIP treatment."

Garrett ground his teeth. "Define VIP treatment."

"You mean nobody told you?"

Garrett held his breath until his temper subsided. "If they had, I wouldn't have asked."

"Oh, yeah. Right."

Mind like a steel trap.

"Well, in addition to me coming out every afternoon, you've got outpatient water therapy three days a week." He flipped through the papers again. "You're probably scheduled with the same therapist." His eyes widened fractionally when he found the name. "She does get around, doesn't she?"

Garrett despised being so out of his element. "Get on with your job, and let me worry about my family."

"No sweat." Mike closed the folder with a snap. "What shall we torture first, your legs or that hand?"

Chapter 9

At six-thirty, Maggie finally made it home, a bag of groceries under each arm, her purse strap between her teeth and car keys dangling precariously from her little finger. The moment she cleared the door, the simple tranquillity of just being home washed over her. Garrett was here. He'd make her feel like she conquered the world, not just found a patient hiding in the ductwork between the second and third floor. Soon she could change into comfy sweats and unwind.

The soft squeak of Garrett's wheelchair sounded behind her as he came into the room, but her smile of pleasure froze at the expression on his face. Tension lines tightened his strong features, and his olive skin was slightly flushed.

"How was your day?" she said, continuing on into the kitchen and setting the groceries on the counter. *Please, tell me it was wonderful. Please?*

"Just terrific."

The sarcasm made her wince. "Did it go all right with Mike this afternoon?" She was going to be pleasant even if it meant rupturing something. Just because she'd come home with expectations didn't mean he'd indulge them.

"About like you set up."

Now what's that supposed to mean? You really should ask, you know, the inner voice chastised. *But I'd rather be a coward, thank you very much.* "I talked to Dr. Kelly, your orthopedic surgeon, when he made rounds. Apparently, he's done some brainstorming with a colleague about you, and he thinks he's found a way to tighten up those tendons. That'll increase mobility in your hand a lot, if it works. Once he sees you tomorrow, he'll know if it's a go."

"Tomorrow?" Garrett growled.

Maggie turned to face him. He looked like Mount St. Helens just before it blew. "Yeah. When I had a minute I called his office. I got you in at one-fifteen."

"Don't you think that might interfere with my therapy schedule? Or did you take care of that, too?"

Maggie was too confused and too emotionally drained to try to figure out why he was so angry. "As a matter of fact, yes, I did. Mike will switch you with his last patient of the day and be here about four. Is there a problem with that?"

Garrett's eyes spit sapphire-blue flames, his silent rage heating the room. Without a word, he turned the chair around and went to the garage.

After a moment's struggle to find her mental balance, Maggie followed. By the time she got there, he was already seated at one of the exercise machines. His intense concentration added to her confusion, creating another burden she didn't need today.

She pulled up a folding lawn chair and sat down to watch. She needed him to lean on, but he'd locked her out. In the old days, he'd have picked up instantly that she'd had a rough day and needed some TLC.

He switched machines to work on his legs. Pain flared in his eyes as he fought for even minimal response, but as usual that was the only outward sign of the price he paid for forcing his legs to relearn how to move. Several times Maggie was tempted to suggest ways to optimize benefits from energy spent, but she kept her professional opinion to herself. Therapy didn't seem to be as much the point as did working through his temper. So they sat side by side in isolated silence.

By the time sweat ran in rivulets down Garrett's face and body, he had completed the full exercise regimen and then some. Yet whatever bothered him hadn't abated any. He had merely worn himself out.

His movements as he maneuvered back into his wheelchair lacked his usual level of coordination, emphasizing his fatigue.

"Would you like some help?" Odd how such a simple question was so hard to get out of her mouth after the long silence.

He shot her a damning glare. "No thanks. You've done more than enough today."

The remark couldn't have been more incendiary if he'd doused her with gasoline and lit a match. Her temper erupted. "What's wrong with you? I've had the day from hell. Then I get stuck with Mr. Attitude."

A twisted, sneering smile distorted his features. "There's not a thing wrong that you can't take care of, believe me. Until recently, I had no idea how competent you really are."

"Now what's *that* supposed to mean?"

He gave a dismissive wave of one hand and returned to the house. "Nothing."

She followed him into the kitchen as he got a drink of water from the refrigerator door dispenser, actively ignoring her presence. Then her eye caught the half-rinsed, mustard-stained kitchen towel in the sink.

In the course of her life it was nothing, but in her frazzled state, it pushed her over the edge. "My best towel!" The strident screech wasn't like her, but at that moment, she didn't care if she sounded like the Wicked Witch herself.

With thumb and forefinger, she pulled the sodden mess from the sink. Watered-down mustard oozed and dripped. The stains on the brand-new terry were unmistakable, as were the stains to the porcelain sink. Then she noticed the floor. "This mess rivals some of Rick's more notable accomplishments. If that's what you were trying for, you succeeded.''

"Well, pardon me. I had no idea cripples couldn't fix lunch all by themselves." His biting sarcasm dumped fuel on her already blazing temper.

Maggie spun around. Garrett obviously itched for a fight, and heaven help her, but a good screaming match was exactly what she needed. "What's your problem?"

"You've organized my life down to the last detail. Except you overlooked one little thing. I can't open a glass jar with one working hand."

"Organized your life? Since when!"

"Since the equipment arrived. Since Mike the Wonder Boy showed up. Since I discovered my appointments with RPI and Kelly. You're doing a great job."

"You're mad because I took care of things that needed doing?"

"Helping is fine, Maggie Jean. Treating me like a small child *isn't*."

"Look, Garrett. Blake and I work with these people all the time. I could get things done faster than—"

"I'm not saying you couldn't. What I object to is not being consulted. You could have warned me about the program you'd set up. It was a little demeaning to find out about it as it happened."

"You're mad because I didn't ask your approval first!"

"Wouldn't you be?"

Despite a foolish desire to cling to being the wounded party, Maggie could see his point. As well-intentioned as she'd been, she'd overlooked the basic tenet of rehabilitative medicine. People coping with a recent onset of paralysis—whether due to illness or accident—had tremendous chunks of their personal dignity stripped away. It was essential to reinforce the fact that they weren't helpless, that their lives were still their own—if somewhat altered. She'd blown it, and not for the first time, either.

The day's stress tally came due and, to her horror, tears

streamed over her lower lids. She whirled around to the sink, and picked tiny shards of glass from her favorite kitchen towel. Tears dripped onto her hands as she worked, while Garrett's stunned gaze burned a hole in her back.

He moved his wheelchair alongside her and gently turned her to face him. "Babe? What is it? We've had some knock down, drag-outs over the years, but falling apart isn't like you."

Other than standing there trembling, she couldn't seem to move. His tenderness only made it worse. She desperately needed his strength but pride wouldn't let her cross enemy lines.

"Babe?" He took her hand and squeezed.

The skin-to-skin contact turned her heart over, and without conscious intent, Maggie folded into his lap. He wrapped her into a tight embrace, and she buried her face into the warmth of his neck. "I'm sorry I made such a big deal out of a stupid towel."

"I wasn't being any great prize either." He kissed her hair. "What's wrong? Talk to me."

She sniffed loudly, then told him about her day. "The family is threatening to sue. My bosses may get them to calm down, but I doubt it."

"Then I hit you with being an ingrate," he muttered.

"Not your fault. I can't seem to stop making the same mistakes I warn other people about."

He stroked her shoulder-length tresses, then held her from him and wiped away her tears. She felt the barriers between them slip away, and her heart trembled in her chest as if afraid to beat for fear it would destroy the moment.

The sensation of his fingers against her face sent pleasurable tingles throughout her body. His breath fanned her cheek as he drew her close for a kiss. His lips were warm, firm, commanding, and they both drank deeply of their love. He made forays across her jaw and throat, and she rolled her head back to give him greater access, and her heart thundered.

This is really dumb, Hughes, her common sense groaned. *Sex never solves anything. But I need him.*

His lips trailed feather-soft kisses along her cheek, slowly working back toward her lips. She remembered the games he played to heighten their pleasure, knew what was to come, and that knowledge alone set her body on fire. Garrett had always set the pace, always been the one in command, not out of arrogance, but as a habit started when they were young. Truthfully, she hadn't given the poor man any choice. In her innocence, she'd handed him her body on a plate every time he'd turned around, and only his honor had held him in check. But this was now. She claimed his lips. A startled, but approving groan rumbled from his chest, and he locked her into a tight one-armed embrace while he caressed her back.

When they came up for air, they were both slightly breathless. Surely tonight would be the night that ended four-and-a-half years of sexual frustration. She communicated that hope in the seductive smile she gave him, but the sudden reserve in Garrett's eyes sent a chill through her.

"What's wrong?"

He looked intensely uncomfortable, and she felt him mentally retreat until an icy chasm yawned between them.

"This wasn't a good idea," he muttered.

"Why not?" she rasped. The sting of rejection hurt all the more for the expectations of a moment ago. "Rick's working on his car at John's house tonight. He won't be home for hours yet."

She could have sworn fury and hurt flared in his eyes, but he masked his emotions so quickly, she couldn't be certain. Why would Rick fixing his car upset him? Or was it something else? With the fire raging in her veins, she couldn't think.

Garrett shifted in the chair, a silent request for her to get off his lap. Stunned, she complied, staring at him in disbelief. The muscles along his jaw were flexed hard. "Maggie, this really wasn't a good idea. I'm sorry I started it."

Her breath let out in a pain-filled rush. "You haven't apologized for 'starting it' since I was a teenager. What's wrong?"

"Nothing," he spit out. Then he fixed her with a frozen stare. "Do you want help with dinner, or do you want take-out?"

Furious, she turned her back on him and yanked groceries from the bags. "Go ahead. Shut me out. See if I care." *Wow, Hughes, that was really constructive.* Inwardly, she cringed, but pride refused to let her apologize. Besides, he owed her an explanation.

Garrett was never without a suitable retort, and she expected him to pick up his end of the renewed quarrel. Instead, he merely left the room.

Garrett went into the backyard, shaking from the devastation to his ego. He hadn't been able to get it up. Not even a twinge of a response. What was going on? He hadn't had any trouble for weeks.

Hairy bounded toward him, Frisbee firmly between his teeth. The neighbors must have thrown the toy back over the fence. Today's emotional roller coaster was too much, and Garrett couldn't face another failure. Hairy was just going to have to settle for a scratch behind the ears. The disappointment on the dog's face lasted only a moment before he leaned into Garrett's hand and groaned with unabashed pleasure.

"Well, at least you don't care that I'm less than human. I can't handle a simple jar of mustard, and I can't make love to my wife." *Ex-wife,* he amended silently. *There's nothing tying her to me.* After a moment's thought he added, *Thank God. The sooner I can get out of her life, the better off she'll be.*

Self-pity disgusted him, but as he found himself on a down-hill slide toward bitterness, he didn't have the faintest clue how to find his center of gravity.

Nearby, the squeak and thunk of a rusted car door slamming shut sounded. It was just the sound he'd expect from Rick's car. That suspicion was confirmed a moment later when the teenager opened the sliding glass door and stepped onto the ramp.

Your timing's off for once, Garrett observed darkly. *You're about five minutes too late to interrupt us.*

"Mom said you were outside."

It sounded accusatory, but Garrett didn't dare call him on it. There was too great a danger that he'd overreact. He still hadn't worked through his hurt and irritation that his only son preferred a stranger to teach him how to rebuild that carburetor.

"I thought you were working on your car tonight."

"John's dad had to work late. He'll help me with it this weekend." Rick fidgeted. Garrett recognized the agitation as part of the kid's bulldog puppy stance. "Dad, how come you're in the back?"

"I was cooped up a long time. Fresh air beats the alternative." He pivoted around to face his son. "Why don't you go ahead and buy that carburetor kit. We'll put it in tomorrow."

"I told you. John's dad is helping me with that."

Jealousy, not common sense opened Garrett's mouth. "I don't think so. As soon as we're finished with dinner, you're going to the parts house and pick it up."

Rick's jaw worked as his agitation increased. "But I—"

"Argue with me some more, Richard, and you'll find yourself grounded for a week."

Rick stared, dumbfounded, and Garrett braced himself for open rebellion. The boy turned away, but not before Garrett saw the twinkle of contentment in his eyes.

"If that's what you want, Dad. Okay."

As he went back into the house, Garrett sat, shocked and trying to evaluate what had happened. When it hit him, he had to laugh. Without thinking first, they'd fallen into the familiar role of parent and child. With luck, one day, it might even be comfortable. But in the meantime, he didn't delude himself that he wouldn't stumble onto another can of worms before it was through.

Once they got the meal finished and the kitchen cleaned, Maggie turned to Garrett, grim. "Time for the night shift."

"What are you talking about?" He frowned.

"From the way you're moving, you overdid today, and if I don't give you a thorough rubdown, those muscles will be locked up tight tomorrow."

After his failure earlier, the idea of her putting her hands all over his body appalled him. His blood heated at the prospect of her touch, and he doubted his self esteem could handle another blow. "Maggie, that isn't a good idea—for several reasons."

"Name one," she retorted indignant.

"You put in a full day today. You need to relax."

She snorted. "And you need those muscles worked."

"No." It was flat, unequivocal.

She frowned in confusion. "What do you mean, no?"

Rick seemed to materialize from nowhere, barely restrained panic in his eyes. Garrett gave him a calm-down gesture and kept his attention on Maggie. "It's not a tough concept, babe. You're not going to destroy yourself taking care of me. You're tired. Your workday's over. Period."

He turned to wheel himself into the living room, but she grabbed the chair's back to stop him. Garrett bristled. Having his wheelchair held on to was like being on a leash. He opened his mouth to remind her whose body it was and exactly how things were going to work from now on, but Rick cut him off.

"He's right, Mom," he said softly. "You look dead. Why don't you change into your sweats, and I'll make some popcorn?"

Rick had sided with him! They were working together. Garret didn't even try to keep the smile off his face.

The boy shrugged at his mother. "You've been sort of outvoted, Mom."

At first, she scowled as if wanting to forcibly remove their heads, but Garrett sensed the moment she drew the same conclusion about the situation as he had.

"Sweat suit it is," she conceded, then shot a look over her shoulder as she left the room. "But, Garrett, if you need help getting out of bed tomorrow, don't blame me."

* * *

Maggie knew Garrett would rather cut out his tongue than admit she'd been right about his muscles locking up, but she could see his pain in the overly cautious way he moved.

At water therapy, she drank in the sight of his magnificent body, naked except for swim trunks. He had regained much of the lost muscle mass, and she ached for him. How many years had it been since she'd played with the light dusting of dark hair across his chest? Far too long if the clawing need radiating from the pit of her stomach was any indication.

With an almost imperceptible grimace, Garrett began the stretching exercises.

Testosterone, she muttered silently.

"I don't want to hear it, babe." He glowered at her.

Despite herself, she laughed. "Mind reading again, are we?"

"Wasn't hard. It was written all over your face."

She chuckled under her breath, but he ignored her. From all appearances, he was sexually oblivious to her as he worked. Then the time came that she dreaded and longed for, the part of the routine that he lay flat in her arms while he worked his legs.

In the cool water, his skin burned hot against her forearms, and she fought down a shudder of pure physical need. He stared in the general direction of the rafters, his expression betraying nothing other than absolute concentration on the task at hand. Slowly, he brought his left leg out straight.

"Your mobility is coming up," she said, sparing a quick glance at his swim trunks and wishing something else was coming up, too. *What's wrong? Don't you want me anymore?*

"The water does most of it," he grumbled. "Could be better."

No kidding. Maggie gritted her teeth.

Garrett swore nothing could have been worse than water therapy that morning, but as Maggie gave him a rubdown that night—a *thorough* rubdown—he knew he'd been wrong. Her strong fingers kneaded deep into his flesh, and he broke out in a cold sweat. Was she made of stone? Couldn't she tell what this did to him? From her look of total concentration, she was totally aware of his body, yet knew nothing at all. He shuddered.

She jerked her hands back. "Did I hurt you?"

Not more than a lot, babe. "I'm fine." It came out harsher than intended. "I think we've done enough today."

"But I'm not finished," she protested. "Those lower back muscles are still too tight. They'll hurt even worse tomorrow."

I'll live with it! "Let's call it a night." He pointedly rolled over and sat up on the bed. "By the way, where's Rick?"

From the glare she gave him, she knew full well he'd ended the subject and she wasn't at all happy about it. "He's upstairs trying to give us some privacy. His version of matchmaking." She reached toward him to wipe off the oil from his skin.

Too quickly, he grabbed her wrist and took the towel. "I'll do that." If she touched him again, he'd go out of his mind.

Disappointment? Was that what flashed through her emerald eyes? Or had it been relief?

"Suit yourself." She shrugged.

Definitely relief, he decided. Despite the way she'd occasionally responded to him, he still believed his condition repelled her. Even if he got an erection, what good would it do? He could barely move. Worse, making love would bind her more closely to him, the last thing he wanted for her.

Saturday showed him a new set of pitfalls that drove his confidence deeper into the ground. None of his clothes fit anymore, and he was tired of the baggy look. Fixing it meant a trip to the mall—the outside world.

On the way, they didn't speak much. That was for the best. Even casual subjects ended up with him biting her head off.

She pulled into the massive parking lot and slipped into a handicapped-only space. Before the accident, he'd often driven past those spaces, half-ashamed of the twinge of temptation to pull into one. Now that he was entitled, he loathed the idea.

She reached in the glove box, then hung a handicapped parking permit from the rearview mirror.

To Garrett, the blue and white sign with the handicapped symbol screamed Fragile. Non Person. Handle with Care! He sat on the explosion in his gut.

Maggie made no attempt to help him into his wheelchair and walked beside him as he made his way toward the sidewalk. Halfway through the traffic lane, the front wheels dropped into cracks in a fractured patch of asphalt, jerking him to a stop. Maggie reached toward him to help but retreated at his hard look.

Garrett shoved on the hand rims, but the chair didn't budge. A car pulled up, needing to drive past, but the driver waited patiently, politely trying not to watch. A swell of degradation washed over him. Open staring would have been kinder.

"Maybe you can back out," Maggie suggested softly.

"It wasn't my brain that was paralyzed in the accident, Maggie Jean. Give me some credit. I can get a couple of six-inch wheels out of a damned hole."

Resentment flared in her eyes, but she stepped back. "Go to it, then."

"Thank you," he gritted between his teeth.

By now, cars had stopped in both directions, forming lines in front of the busy shopping center, and lengthening by the moment. Garrett swore, loudly, with feeling. Every muscle in his body knotted with frustration and humiliated rage.

Through clenched teeth, he asked, "Would you help me—please?" Each syllable came out with a clipped edge.

"Certainly." Her reply was equally terse. She moved behind the chair and tipped it back. No more than an inch, by his estimation, but it was enough to free him. He looked straight ahead as he rolled forward, daring the traffic to exist. He concentrated so hard on putting distance between him and the witnesses to his failure that he hit the sidewalk's wheelchair ramp at too sharp an angle, nearly dumping over. It made for a jarring and conspicuous ordeal.

He caught sight of Maggie's reflection in the smoked-glass

doors of the mall's main entrance. Her features were pinched, her mouth pursed in a thin, pale line. It renewed his sanity as nothing else could have.

Other shoppers went around them, but he paid no attention to the fact he sat blocking pedestrian traffic as he turned to face her. "I'm always apologizing to you, babe. Today, I've given you every reason to mop the sidewalk with me, but you haven't."

Her body became even more rigid, if that were possible. Actually, he decided that helped. Instant forgiveness would have made him feel like a bigger louse than he already did.

"I really am sorry." He wanted to reach to her, but he didn't dare.

She hesitated so long, he was afraid she wouldn't accept his apology at all. He hated the sadness in her eyes, hated knowing he'd caused it.

"You're a real mess, aren't you?"

He didn't realize he'd groaned out loud until she laughed. "Babe, I'm trying not to be. It's all so…so—"

"Disabling?" she offered wickedly.

He grimaced. "You've been around Sapperstein too long."

"Tell me about it."

They then turned to face the doors. Rather than the nice convenient automatic ones, these were the swinging type with half-inch, raised metal sill plates. A normal person wouldn't notice the narrow edging, but getting a wheelchair over it while manhandling a heavy door was beyond him.

Maggie watched him assess the situation. "Do you want to tackle this yourself?"

"No, my self-esteem has taken enough of a beating for one day."

She didn't answer but held open the door while he lined up the wheels to take the maddening doorsill head-on.

"It's the little victories, right?" he muttered.

She laughed. "Onward, Sir Galahad."

In the men's department, shirts weren't a problem. He just picked out one size smaller than he usually wore. Jeans, however, were another story, and he ended up in the fitting room with two different sizes to try. Wrestling with clothing at home when he had the bed to lie back on was a whole different animal than attempting the same feat in a wheelchair in a fitting room.

Maggie waited for what seemed like hours. More than once, she was tempted to go in and check on him or send in an employee. But his explosive protests would probably raise the roof. So, she waited, checked her watch far too often, and tried to think like a therapist rather than a wife. *That's still how you see yourself, Hughes. Married to a man whose livelihood scared you to death, one who now has absolutely no idea how to pick up the pieces. What are you going to do if he leaves? Or stays, for that matter?*

When Garrett finally emerged, the air crackled with his frustration. He wore one pair of the new pants. The other pair and his own were folded haphazardly in his lap. He handed the new pair to the clerk. "Put these back on the rack, please." Then he handed the man a set of torn-off price tags. "I want four more pairs like those."

Maggie read the tension lines on his brow. So did the clerk, who apparently knew when not to argue with a customer about wearing the merchandise.

Dr. Kelly assured Garrett that the second surgery to tighten the tendons had gone well. Bandaged from fingertips to elbow and living with painkillers that barely touched the problem, Garrett reserved his own judgment. Maggie had taken the day off to get him to and from the hospital for the outpatient surgery and to get his wheelchair modified. With one arm completely out of commission, he couldn't handle his wheelchair by himself. They'd discussed everything the day before and, for once, she hadn't taken over. He found himself appreciative of her efforts, and they got through the whole day without quarreling.

Maggie pulled strings with the medical supply company and got a different type of axle and double hand rims on the left side installed in one day. No small feat apparently. The outer rim still controlled the left wheel. The new inner rim controlled the right. They were close enough together that he could grip both with one hand and propel himself forward in a straight line.

For yet another night, Maggie tossed and turned until she had the covers torn halfway off the bed. She was no closer to finding a way to keep him here permanently than she had been ten days ago when he'd moved in.

It could be years before he adjusted to his limitations. How on earth could she get him to weather the storms together? She didn't care what he did for a living as long as it wasn't dangerous. And as badly as he'd reacted to the counselor's suggestion of his "flying a desk" at the DEA, she was convinced that law enforcement was finally a part of his past.

Giving up on sleep, she hopped out of bed, but now that she was up, she didn't have the faintest idea what to do with herself. Lying back down, though, held absolutely no appeal.

She wandered through the living room and froze as she passed the downstairs hallway. Despite its being two o'clock in the morning, light shone through Garrett's open door. The wall switch was six feet from the bed. To a paraplegic six feet might just as well be in the next county. Had he forgotten to turn out the light before he lay down, and then just left it?

Maggie hesitated. Should she see if he needed anything or go on to the kitchen? Her feminine half hated to see him struggle to get from the bed to the wheelchair then back again, but her professional half clucked its tongue in disapproval.

"Get a grip," she grumbled under her breath. "He doesn't need tucking in."

Irritated, she marched to the kitchen and flung open the refrigerator door. The inside light nearly blinded her. Worse, the orange juice was gone. "Swell."

"Looking for this?" a sexy male voice asked from behind her.

Startled, she whirled around. The refrigerator light illuminated Garrett sitting beside the sink, carton in hand. He glanced upward at the cupboards. "I'd offer you a glass, but my reach is a bit short. If you don't mind drinking after me, you're welcome to some." A humorless, self-mocking smile twisted his square features as he held the carton out to her.

Maggie hated drinking out of cartons, and it was one of the few personal habits Garrett had that got under her skin. An echo of the old, petty quarrel reverberated through her mind. In Garrett's opinion, if no one but the two of them drank it— Rick detested the stuff—then where was the harm? It saved a glass to wash later. Sensible. Practical. Typical Garrett.

So many serious problems lay between them that the inconsequential old one made her smile. "Mark this date in history," she said lightly, reaching for the carton. Their fingers brushed, and fire raced up her arm. Then she tipped the carton to her lips.

He watched her attentively, but the glitter in his eyes told her the majority of his thoughts weren't on orange juice. Or was the desire wishful thinking on her part? A trick of the light combined with his painkillers?

As she finished, Garrett cleared his throat, the sound gruff in the stillness. "We haven't slept under the same roof but in separate beds since you moved in with Mom and Dad after your eighteenth birthday."

"Yeah, I was officially out of the foster care program, and your folks made me feel as if I'd been adopted. They didn't want me out in the cold, cruel world all alone." She smiled at the tender memories. "Then you promptly moved out."

"I didn't trust myself," he grunted, a melancholy smile on his lips. "Not after the first time you were in my bathroom taking a shower. You almost had company."

"I wouldn't have minded." Need hummed in her veins. "I still wouldn't."

He blanched, the passion dying from his eyes. "Good night, babe," he murmured, then left the room.

The crushing rejection nearly made her cry out. The master bedroom light winked out, and she trudged wearily back upstairs. "Something better give, Hughes, or you're going to rape that man."

Chapter 10

The next night, Rick ducked out right after dinner with a mumbled explanation of meeting John at the arcade. Finding a carburetor for that ancient beast had proved more complicated than expected, and he'd come home from the parts house twice with the wrong one.

Alone, Garrett and Maggie barely spoke two words all evening, then went to his room early. She changed into her pajamas, paced the bedroom floor, emotionally drained and wanting Garrett so badly she hurt.

Take a cold shower, Hughes, she grumbled. *He doesn't want you.*

So? came an impatient voice. *Initiate a little action. So what if he's always been the aggressor. As we've both acknowledged, things have changed.* Her hormones gave a sharp nudge.

Maggie pursed her lips, decision made. "I've got nothing to lose. It can't get any worse." She took a quick shower, changed into the dark emerald satin nightgown that she'd bought on a more hopeful day. Then she went downstairs and stared at the wedge of light that spilled onto the carpet from beneath the master bedroom door.

You're here. Now what? How does one go about seducing a man? Her courage faltered. "Oh, come on, Hughes," she muttered under her breath, disgusted. "Get a grip."

With a quick detour to the kitchen to snag a long-unopened bottle of brandy and a couple of snifters, she marched into the master bedroom.

Garrett lay stretched out on the bed, shoulders propped against the headboard, a police journal lying open in his lap. Pain lines creased his brow as he absently massaged his bandaged right arm.

The sight of the journal made her blood chill, and she tried but failed to force the old fears from her mind. He was home and safe. Would she even consider a reconciliation if he could return to police work? Firmly, she told herself that the entire issue was a moot point, but she knew better. As long as the subject had the power to make her blood run cold, she still hadn't completely laid it to rest.

The moment Garrett saw her, he stopped rubbing his arm. He took in the brandy, the snifters and her new nightgown, and a wary, remote cast settled over his features. "Did you need something?" he asked, coldly returning to his reading.

This new Garrett, the one who hid behind masks, wasn't the man Maggie had loved for twenty years, but she was determined not to let him keep shutting her out. She screwed together her resolve and took what she hoped looked like a confident step toward the bed. "Overdid it in the garage today, didn't you?"

"Some." He didn't look up.

She almost made a flip remark about providing a tasty pain-killer in the form of a brandy, then suddenly remembered the obvious. Booze and medication were a bad combination. *Damn.* "Did you take your pills tonight?"

The subtle inflection to the sigh he released clearly indicated he didn't appreciate the invasion into his privacy, but she had no intention of cutting him any slack, not tonight.

"Did you?" She stepped closer.

"No, they make me groggy." His exasperation was thick enough to cut with a chain saw.

Ooooh, better and better. She pursed her lips to keep from grinning.

"Maggie, what do you want?" It was more accusation than question.

With her heart pounding in her throat, she perched on the edge of the bed and set the bottle and glasses on the night table. "I thought I'd pour us both a drink. I'm not much for drinking alone."

The tactic had to be a step above "what's a gorgeous hunk like you doing in a place like this?" At least, she hoped so.

Garrett bristled, but she pretended not to notice. The space on the bed between his hip and the edge wasn't quite wide enough for her bottom, but she made herself at home anyway. Which gave him two choices—move over or let her fall to the floor. *Which is it going to be, my heart?*

His breathing came deep and labored. Every muscle in his body knotted up. "What are you up to?"

"Lighten up, Garrett," she said. "Rick's off with friends. The least we can do is have a quiet drink. Let's face it. Life has been a real witch lately."

As she waited for his answer, her own breathing stopped completely, and her heart beat frantically against her ribs. Almost reluctantly, he moved over. Raw feminine power swept over her in an unstoppable wave. Suddenly, the idea of seducing Garrett lost its intimidation.

"I asked you a question, Maggie Jean."

She nearly laughed out loud. *I've got you now, my love. The only time you ever call me that is when you're really furious or off balance.*

"I told you," she insisted. "I'm tired, I'm lonesome, and I could use a little companionship."

Suspicion and heat smoldered in his face, flaring into anguish before he closed his eyes. "This isn't a good idea, babe,'' he said softly. ''It really isn't.'' He flipped to the next page of his magazine.

Maggie had the sinking insight that something more was wrong here than she knew. *Well, Hughes, that won't be a first.*

Deliberately, she rested her hand on his chest, drawn as always to the smooth texture of his skin and the hard warmth of the muscles beneath. He might be forty-two and a paraplegic, but he still had looks men half his age would envy.

''What's wrong?'' she asked.

He shot her a hounded look, and once again turned a page. Faster than she could blink, Maggie snatched the magazine and flung it across the room. It hit the mirrored closet door and crumpled to the floor in a heap.

''I was reading that,'' he growled.

''No, you weren't,'' she countered. ''You were ignoring me. And not very effectively, I might add.''

The silence pulsed with the heat of passion radiating from him, the sheer intensity unnerving. She sensed primal need warring with intellect, and she waited him out, her body language deliberately projecting a signal she hoped would be interpreted as I-want-you and I'm-more-stubborn-than-you-so-give-it-up.

''You don't take hints as well as you used to.''

''Sure I do.'' She grinned. ''I've just gotten more selective about which ones I act on.''

He digested that a moment, self-loathing twisting one side of his sensuous lips. ''You're not going to let up, are you?''

She shook her head, no, and braced for the worst.

He looked off in the distance so long, she wondered if he planned to answer at all. ''I've always pitied men who had this happen to them, but, like paralysis, I never thought it would happen to me.'' He still refused at look at her. ''It's gone, babe. At RPI I thought I had it back, but...''

A sick knowing churned in the pit of her stomach. Had the signs been there and she'd missed them? Or had he been working so hard at masking them behind indifference that she couldn't have guessed on her own? ''Impotence?''

His haunted gaze flicked to the far side of the room. "Loaded word, isn't it?"

She slid her hand around his ribs into a tight embrace and rested her forehead against his shoulder. He held his body so rigid, that it was like embracing a statue. Neither spoke for long moments, but at least he didn't push her away.

"Why didn't you tell me?" she asked finally.

"Male vanity." He snorted. "I believe you call it testosterone poisoning."

Tears clogged her eyes. Defiantly, she blinked them back.

"Babe, you walked in with that bottle of brandy and scared me to death. It's a hard thing for a man to face knowing he can't finish what he wants to start."

She leaned back enough to look into his embittered, anguished eyes. "But you were fine."

His bark of laughter wasn't at all encouraging, but he explained what had happened—or more accurately what hadn't happened—in the kitchen that night. "And nothing has worked since."

"Garrett, your body suffered multiple major traumas. Almost fifteen hours of surgery. The resulting three cardiac arrests. You should be dead. From a strict medical standpoint, you're still recovering." She shook her head. "And while we're at it, human sexuality is staggeringly complex."

"Which means what?" he snapped. "That it's going to be Russian roulette for the rest of my life? Today, I'm a man? Tomorrow, I'm not?"

She mulled that over. She'd read his charts so many times, she had them memorized. It was possible that the problem was organic, but she doubted it. If she had to make a guess, it would be along the lines of his no longer viewing himself as a man. Therefore, his subconscious proved it to him in the most devastating way it could. "Have you considered that it might be stress induced?"

A vicious expletive erupted from his lips. "That's even better. I'll bet you and Blake know the perfect shrink for me, too. Well, why not? I've got every other kind of doctor working on what's left of me.''

Dear God, he's so fragile. Help me to help him. ''Counseling may not be necessary.''

He gave her a condemning look. ''How reassuring.''

''Cut yourself some slack. You've always been a take-charge man.''

''Used to be.''

''You still are.'' She took hold of his beard-shadowed chin and turned his face toward her. ''The context has changed. That's all.''

''Look, babe, I appreciate the pep talk.'' He peeled her fingers from his face. ''However, my 'context' isn't all that rosy, so take the booze and go.''

Not on a bet. A shot of brandy and a rubdown always mellowed you out when a tough case ate at you. There's no reason to believe it won't help now, too. She kept the grim determination from showing on her face. *Besides, heart of mine, there's more to making love than intercourse. I've taught countless patients the importance of cuddling, of touching, of just being together. And you're about to get a lesson infinitely more personal than a confidential chat and a suggested reading list.*

''I asked you to leave.''

''I heard.'' She poured them both a brandy, held his out to him, then swirled it gently and stared him down. He glanced at the generously filled snifter and cast her a sour look. ''I came in here because I wanted to be with you, maybe watch a movie together. If we can't make love, I'm disappointed, but I'll live.'' She held her breath, waiting for him to accuse her of lying—which she was—but he didn't. *So far, so good.*

He eyed her suspiciously.

''Look. That room upstairs gets so quiet, I can hear my hair grow.'' She swirled his brandy again and jiggled her eyebrows at him. ''Besides, there's no TV up there.''

He glowered at her for long moments, then sighed in defeat. ''You and your movies.''

Gotcha!

He took the snifter, careful not to let his fingers touch hers, and she raised her glass in wordless toast.

Her movie collection overflow was stored in a cabinet below the TV in the bedroom. Rummaging through it would be best accomplished by kneeling on the floor. Sooooo, she bent over straight-legged, knowing full well that the short, satin gown rode up in the back, nicely outlining her bottom and giving him an eyeful of bare thighs.

He cleared his throat and coughed.

That sounded a bit strangled, my heart. Knowing he couldn't see her face, she grinned evilly. *Men are such visual creatures. Poor things.*

"Found it," she purred. "One I've only seen once."

"What is it?" His voice sounded more strained.

Maggie kept her back to him as she loaded the cassette into the VCR and pushed all the right buttons. "It's a documentary on an archaeological dig in Peru."

"I don't know, babe. Don't you have anything else? Something with a plot?"

She turned and gave him an innocent smile. "Oh, but this is just what I'm in the mood for. It's quiet and relaxing." *And guaranteed to bore you to tears.*

The opening music blared, and she hopped onto the end of the king-size bed and crawled to him, her gaping neckline giving him an unobstructed view of her naked body from breasts to knees.

He whipped his gaze chastely to the door. "Maggie, wouldn't you be more comfortable wearing a robe or something?"

She snuggled in next to him and laid her head on his shoulder. "Shhh, I don't want to miss any of this." She stared back at the TV as if completely engrossed by the opening shots of the soaring emerald-and-gray cliffs.

"But you've seen it before," he snarled. "Now go put on a robe." He swallowed hard. "Or what about your pink sweat suit?"

"Thanks, but it's dirty." She'd never played dumb in her life and found the whole game exhilarating. Striving to appear unaware of her actions, she draped an arm across his abdomen and idly twirled the dark springy hair just above his waistband. His stomach muscles spasmed.

Pure need hummed in her veins, and she prayed none of it showed on her face. Giving an exaggerated perusal of his body, she drew her brows down in a heavy frown.

"What!" he demanded.

"Your skin is awfully dry. Let me get some lotion, I'll take care of it."

His eyes flew open, horrified. "Don't you dare."

Better and better, she crowed soundlessly. She forced what she hoped was a hurt look. "Come on, Garrett. You're sitting through my documentary. The least I can do is give you a proper rubdown." She tugged at the snap on his jeans fly. "Strip and roll onto your stomach."

His glare darkened.

"Oh, come on," she groused. "We've been doing this for months. Stop acting like a sacrificial virgin."

The muttering under his breath told her quite clearly that he wasn't amused. Why he complied at all, she didn't quite understand, but neither did she argue. The moment he was settled, she unprofessionally straddled the backs of his thighs and got busy. For once, it was wonderful to run her hands over his body. With a little luck, this time the sexual purgatory would end. Garrett's body was a visual and tactile feast. As she rubbed the heavy cream into his back, sides and shoulders, his olive skin took on a sheen that was a delight for feminine eyes. But when she came to the scars, she had to squelch a shudder.

Two were bullet holes. When he'd been a patrol officer, he'd been shot once while simply pulling over a motorist. The other time he'd been trying to defuse a domestic dispute. In her mind's eye, she saw the knife scar on his left collarbone, where he'd been stabbed while wrestling a man high on PCP.

Lastly, in the small of his back was the bright pink surgical scar, a memento from the plane crash. He had been coming home to her, yet she'd almost lost him, almost lost the only man she'd ever loved. What would the future hold if she couldn't get him back? Could they build something where they'd both be happy?

Sexually, Maggie wanted him more than she ever had in her life. Her instincts as a therapist screamed his impotence had to be a self-fulfilling prophecy. *What if I push this and am wrong?*

"I'm going to ask one more time, Maggie Jean. What are you up to?" His suspicion and vulnerability tore her up. Before the divorce, he would have given her one of his most demanding stares and kept after her until she confessed all. Now he was defensive, remote.

"I'm watching a movie," she muttered.

"Bull. You're not watching that thing any more than I am." He rolled over beneath her, still thigh to thigh. The wary bitterness dared her to level with him.

Blood pounded through her veins. She wasn't sure how to answer. Deceit had never been part of their relationship until now. Surely the cause was just. Her mouth went dry, and she floundered for words, her mind blank. Tentatively, her hands came to rest on his chest.

Then risking it all, she stretched out on top of him, nose to nose, hip to hip. Panicked anger flared in his eyes, but before he could speak, she placed her hand over his mouth. "I love you, Garrett, and I need to be with you tonight. Whether we have sex or not doesn't matter. Hold me."

His eyes hardened to sapphire ice, and he pulled her hand away. "It matters to me. What are you trying to do? See for yourself just how harmless I am?"

Maggie covered his lips with her own, pouring all her love into that kiss. His lips were hard and unyielding. The rejection hurt, but she kissed him again, gently brushing the tip of her tongue against his closed mouth.

Savagely, he jerked his head away. "I should have stayed at RPI. Go back upstairs."

Defiantly, she propped her elbows on either side of his head. "Garrett, I understand what you can't do, but we can still kiss, hold each other, and whatever else your inventive imagination can think up." She sharpened her gaze. "Now stop being a pain in the backside."

Glaring, he took hold of her rib cage as if to lift her off him. *Neat trick with one arm bandaged up.* Then she kissed him with everything she had. With deliberate slowness, she caressed his throat and shoulder, the heavy pulse point along his neck driving her wild.

Just as she began to lose hope, a hard tremor rippled through him. His lips softened beneath hers, and his arms imprisoned her in a passionate embrace. In a frenzy of motion, she found the bedroom door locked, two sets of clothes littering the floor and herself back in his arms.

He nuzzled her breast, the feel of his lips against her skin so sweet it was nearly pain. Gripped by a power beyond her control, she reached for him. He stilled, covering her hand with his.

"It's no good, babe," he whispered brokenly.

She gave him a challenging look. "Does it feel nice?"

His face darkened. It was as close to a blush as she'd ever seen him. "Yeah, babe, it's always good when you touch me."

She grinned seductively. "Then stop complaining and kiss me."

A self-conscious chuckle rolled from his chest, but she'd gripped him in the same fine madness that enslaved her, and they teased, tasted and caressed, driving each other into a frenzy of sensation and loving. After thirteen years of marriage, Garrett knew how and where to touch, and far too soon Maggie felt reality shatter into a kaleidoscope of color and sensation too intense for mere flesh.

"No!" she groaned as wave after wave hit. "Not yet." It had been too many years of lonely nights to hold back.

He hushed her with gentle murmurings and held her as she

writhed in his arms. The storm passed, and she lay quiescent, spent but only half-satisfied. Paradise alone wasn't right.

"Don't tense up on me, babe," he murmured. "You're the one who wanted it this way."

Refusing to think about his bitter undertone, she sought out his lips once again. His hands wandered at will, and she once again began the climb to infinity, but made an interesting discovery. From the staggering disbelief on his face, he'd just noticed the change in his body, too. The low predatory chuckle that rolled from her lips was thick with female power.

Okay, my love. You're about to get a lesson you won't soon forget. Taking advantage of his stunned immobility, she straddled his hips, taking him deep inside. Their bodies shuddered in response, and his disbelief transformed into heartrending relief.

He didn't have the motor control to move effectively, but she was far from impaired. Slowly, seductively, she established the rhythm. They'd made love in this position countless times before, but she'd never been the one in control. He'd always had a sixth sense about what she needed and when, and she'd always been content to follow wherever he led. Not now.

She felt his hold on her hips attempting to guide her, but she brushed his hands aside. The feminine predator was fully aroused, and she had no intention of relinquishing a fragment of the authority she'd established.

His initial shock finally passed. A primal groan rolled from his throat. He tried but couldn't match the pace she'd set, but it didn't matter. His body tensed with building need for release. No longer willing to take a passive role, Garrett took hold of her hips and ground her against him. Her second peak overtook her so quickly that she cried out as much from surprise as passion. Garrett's own release came with the explosive force of a man ripped apart from within. Her joy complete, she collapsed against him, reveling in his erratic breath that puffed against her hair and in the heavy throb of his heart.

She kissed the sweat-slick skin, and they floated slowly to earth.

Time swirled by unnoticed in the quiet lethargy. Eventually, she settled against his side, wrapped securely in his arms. Words would have been invasive as the echoes of their lovemaking reverberated around them, healing wounds new and old.

We're in step again, she thought muzzily. *Nothing can stop us.* She drifted toward sleep, content.

A light tension in Garrett's body kept her from anything deeper than a light doze.

She didn't want to notice it, but what started out as a niggling suspicion that he might be upset became a full Klaxon alarm as his hand ceased its gentle roaming over her bare back, his breathing shallow and far too even.

She hated herself for asking, but the words were out before she could stop them. "What's wrong?"

"Nothing." Terse, without inflection. Twenty years of loving him allowed her to translate it into "I'm furious, and we'll talk when I calm down."

Maggie knew a confrontation right now was a mistake. Their healing was too new, too fragile. She desperately needed to hang on to the closeness for just a few minutes more, and she couldn't accept that it was gone.

Keep your mouth shut, Hughes, she warned herself. *No good ever came of a discussion where either of you was mad enough to chew paint off the walls.* "Garrett, I asked what's wrong?" *Dumb! Dumb! Dumb!* Worse, she sat up to face him.

His jaws were locked, the cords in his neck stood out, and his gaze shot fire. Passion had nothing to do with it. She'd seen him angry countless times, but she'd never seen him a breath away from cold-blooded murder.

Involuntarily, she recoiled from the elemental danger. "What is it?"

"We'll talk tomorrow." He spoke through his teeth. "Right now, I think you'd better go up to your room."

Let it go, Hughes. Now obviously isn't the time. "I'm not going anywhere."

"Good night, Maggie Jean."

That fried it. "I don't think so, Garrett. This is my room— our room—and I plan on spending the night right here."

"Our room," he repeated in a low hiss. His expression twisted into a mask of betrayed rage. "So it is. And who else has been here?"

The question bewildered her. "What?"

He sat up abruptly, grabbed her upper arm and yanked her toward him. The savagery was so unlike him that it more startled than frightened her. Maggie was eye to eye with him, his gaze slicing into her as if trying to cut out the information he sought.

"Garrett, I don't understand."

"This was *our* bed, Maggie! Who else have you brought here?"

The accusation hit her like a hammer blow. Her jaw sagged open, and she shook her head helplessly.

"Are you trying to tell me I'm the only one? That you lived like a nun for the past four years?" He snorted in disbelief.

His grip had tightened with each word, and she tried to twist free.

"You're hurting me." Maggie had never thought to say those words to him and couldn't believe she'd had to say them now.

He stared down at his powerful fingers wrapped around her delicate arm and let go as if burned. He didn't apologize, but the horror on his face said it more eloquently than words. Maggie got up from the bed, putting a safe distance between the two of them. Garrett's big body trembled with the force of reining in his temper. He wouldn't look at her.

"Garrett?"

He shook his head as if trying to make her voice, as well as her presence, disappear.

"What makes you think—?"

"Go!"

Unbidden, tears sprang to her eyes. "You're the one who always wants to talk—"

"Get out! Now!"

Confused, hurt and embarrassed, Maggie pulled on the emerald satin nightgown and backed toward the door, unable to take her eyes from him. How could her first attempt at seducing Garrett—the only man she'd ever been to bed with—backfire so badly? Realizing she needed distance as badly as he did, she fumbled with the door and fled down the darkened hallway.

The door slammed behind her with enough force to rattle the windows. Listening to her retreating footsteps, Garrett trembled with jealousy, his fist knotted at his side. He should have been prepared that she'd led her own life since the divorce. He'd thought he was.

To make it worse, he'd physically hurt her. No matter how angry he'd been before, he'd never even come close to harming her. The fact that it had been an accident did nothing to remove the vile taste in his mouth.

Unanswerable questions reverberated through his mind. All during their marriage, he'd always taken the lead in their sex life. Never once had she hinted that she wanted a more dominant role. If she had, he certainly wouldn't have turned her down. But that was then.

Who had taught her what she'd done tonight? That seduction—complete with all the little body signals that said she wasn't too sure about what she was doing—was too perfectly executed for this to have been the first time she'd tried it out. It wasn't just that. Nothing she'd done was like her.

A small voice in the back of his head told him he was being irrational. The life she'd lived without him was none of his business. He should be ecstatic that he'd made love to her again after their being apart for so long, that he'd been *able* to make love to her. But the heart scream that Maggie, *his* Maggie, had been with another man drowned it out.

He turned off the TV, but he didn't sleep much that night.

* * *

Saturday morning, he rose at dawn. Maggie had already left. A note on the refrigerator said that she had a bunch of paperwork to finish and would probably work all day.

Grinding his teeth, Garrett translated that as "I don't want to deal with it right now, so I'm running. Don't bother to call because I won't pick up the phone."

The jealousy that had ridden him all night settled in for the duration, and he couldn't concentrate on even a simple task like fixing coffee. Who was it? Someone at work? His mind raced. Carl Sapperstein? He'd seen them together often enough, even having lunch in the courtyard the day he apologized for the furlough disaster. He did a mental replay of all the times he'd seen them talking. No, there'd been camaraderie beyond the employer-employee relationship, but no sexual undercurrents that he'd picked up on.

Garrett conquered the coffeepot as Rick sauntered into the kitchen. He snagged a whole-grain-and-fruit breakfast bar and a jumbo glass of milk, his body language radiating tension.

"What did you and Mom fight about last night?" Rick asked around a crunchy bite, his expression guarded. His green eyes, so much like Maggie's, were bright with apprehension.

"What makes you think we had another argument?" Garrett flipped the switch on the coffeepot.

Rick's lip curled in disgust. "A fight's the only time Mom *ever* slams a door that hard." Then the teen added softly, "Is everything okay?" The childlike insecurity caught at Garrett's heart. More than anything, Rick wanted his family back together, even though he'd been told that wasn't going to happen.

"Your mother was very generous in giving me a place to stay, but divorced people living under the same roof can get sticky."

"So you're really going to move out in another week?"

Garrett's heart filled with compassion. "There were never any other plans."

Rick barely acknowledged the truth, shrugging his shoulders. As a ploy to cover disappointment, it failed abysmally.

Once Rick left for work, Garrett went into the garage and took to his exercises with insane fervor. It kept his mind off Maggie and their son.

The garage phone rang. He glowered at it. Putting an extension out here had been another of the conveniences Maggie had installed for him. A nice thought, but in practice, all it did was remind him that if the phone rang while he was in the garage, he couldn't get in the house fast enough to answer it.

"Hey, big brother," came Blake's cheery voice. "Desi's not contagious anymore and Ash still hasn't come down with it, so we're going on a picnic. Would you and yours like to come? As long as you're not in close contact with Ash if she does break out—like if you were living with us—you should be safe."

"Thanks for the invitation, but Maggie and Rick are already gone."

Temptation needled him. His brother had assured him he'd kept watch over Maggie and Rick after the divorce. He'd already said Maggie hadn't dated much, and Garrett had been content with that—until now. Even as he opened his mouth, he knew he was out of line, but he couldn't seem to get hold of himself.

"Blake, I need to ask you a tough question, and I need a completely honest answer."

The low whistle on the other end of the line was subdued. "Why do I feel like I'm about to get dropped into a snake pit?"

Garrett snorted. "You always did have good instincts."

"Thanks." Blake sounded cornered but willing to get it over with. "Fire away."

"Before I came home was Maggie serious about anyone?"

"Is that all?" He sounded irked. "I told you. She dated a few times, but no involvement that I know of."

"Few," Garrett hissed. "How many is few, and who were they?"

"Garrett, what's gotten into you? You sound like a hard-nosed cop interrogating a suspect. Don't I get to hear your rendition of the Miranda rights first?''

"Stop clowning around. Who did she see?"

"Okay," Blake grumbled in disgust. "Number one, I'm not clowning around. Two clowns in one family would be excessive, and you're handling the job quite nicely. Number two, to my knowledge the most she dated anyone was twice. Mag just isn't the singles-scene type."

Garrett wanted to believe, wanted to plead temporary insanity—which he strongly suspected was the case—but he couldn't. In his mind's eye, all he could see was a shadowy, faceless man putting his hands all over Maggie's body, and her letting him. "Who was he?"

"Officer Hughes, may I ask what my client is being charged with?"

"Pretty obvious, isn't it?"

"What's obvious is that you've got a hornet up your hind end over Maggie's nonexistent love life. Want to explain why?"

"No."

"Suit yourself."

Before Garrett had the chance to reply, Blake said he'd call later, then hung up. More than anything, Garrett wished his brother was right. He'd gladly grovel for Maggie's forgiveness if he was wrong. But one thing stuck in his mind that he couldn't dismiss. Maggie had denied nothing.

Late in the afternoon, she came home, her face drawn. Heavy shadows beneath her eyes added to the overall picture of a woman who hadn't slept any better than he had. Yet those same eyes threw daggers at him as she dropped her purse on the side table at the bottom of the stairs. Tension sizzled, a full-blown quarrel a heartbeat away.

"Did you get all the work finished you needed to?" he asked, trying not to talk through his teeth.

"Yeah," she muttered. "Humiliation and hurt always helps my productivity."

"Meaning?"

"Garrett, I'm trying to be understanding. I really am.

You're cut off from the world, and you've had more on your plate than any human being should—''

''But what?''

''When Blake arrived for his rounds, he was surprised to see me there on a Saturday, but he didn't waste the opportunity.'' She looked mad enough to spit nails. ''What gives you the right to grill him about my sex life?''

Garrett turned cold eyes on her. ''The right? How about thirteen years of marriage.''

''Well, four-and-a-half years of divorce makes it none of your concern. I didn't ask if you'd lived like a saint that whole time, did I?'' She paled, as if the idea of him being with another woman just occurred to her.

That goaded his jealousy to new depths. ''Didn't you care? Didn't you ever lie awake at night and wonder if I'd found someone else? God knows, I had enough nights where—''

''What's gotten into you!''

He snorted bitterly. ''Unlike you, I never accepted the divorce as anything more than an abstract legal concept. If I hadn't gotten wrapped up in a case that took years instead of weeks, I would have come back for you and Rick long before this. But you're right, Maggie. We're not married anymore. I'm nothing more than an ex-husband, a charity case you gave a place to stay until he gets his life together.''

''This is a side of you I've never seen.''

He sighed heavily and leaned back in his chair, defeated. ''It never existed before.''

Her expressive face ran the gamut from stunned disbelief to hurt to righteous indignation. ''I'm going to take a lesson from your book. If you're too furious to talk civilly, you find something to do until you calm down.'' She snatched up her purse and headed for the door.

''Where are you going?'' It came out authoritarian and demanding as hell, not at all how he meant.

Her face suffused with color. ''It's Saturday night. Party time, buster!''

Chapter 11

Maggie shook so hard as she drove, she had serious reservations about how safe it was for her to be behind the wheel. Besides, she didn't have the faintest idea where to go. Her first thought had been Blake's house. Ever since she was Rick's age, he'd always been the brother she could turn to. But that poor man had been dragged enough into her and Garrett's problems, and she couldn't bring herself to inflict any more on him.

"How could Garrett think that?" The idea of making love with anyone but him made her sick inside. She'd tried to date. She really had. But she'd felt foolish, like a small child pretending to be something she wasn't.

Her brain felt sluggish, and thinking seemed too much effort. Her parting shot to Garrett echoed in her ears. *Party time?* Had it really sounded that stupid?

Sapperstein grinned at Maggie, standing on his front porch. "I'm sorry I didn't call first. Can I come in?"

His initial surprise passed, and he happily motioned her inside. "We've been trying to get you over here for months." He lowered his brows. "You look horrible. What's wrong?"

She stepped into the entry just as his wife peeked around the corner. Cindy Sapperstein's face brightened into a welcoming smile. Maggie had always liked her. She was charming and gracious and looked like an elf on the inside track of a good joke, the perfect match for her incorrigible husband. Unfortunately, she was just as perceptive. Her smile turned sympathetic, and she wrapped Maggie into a warm hug.

"Carl said you've been looking a little worse for wear lately." Leading her to the family room, Cindy parked her on a well-worn couch. Before Maggie quite knew what had happened, Sapperstein handed her a glass of wine.

"Here. Drink. It'll clean out your arteries and whatever else ails you." He waggled his brows.

Despite herself, Maggie chuckled. "I knew there was a reason I came here." She looked tentatively at both of them. "Are you sure I'm not interrupting anything?"

He crossed his arms and looked smug. "We *were* going out to dinner."

Maggie groaned. "I'm sorry."

"*Now,* you're going to tell us all your woes, and *then* we're going to stuff you full of linguine." He handed Cindy a glass and sprawled on a chair. "Talk."

"I feel like an idiot." Maggie stood to go.

"Oh, no, you don't," both Sappersteins said at once.

Maggie froze, then sank back onto the couch.

Cindy took her hand. "Carl told me about your husband. Does this have to do with him?"

Aggravating tears burned her eyes, and she blinked them back. Before she knew it, the whole story rolled out and she had a pathetic pile of soggy tissues in her lap.

Sapperstein squared his shoulders and tried to look pompous. "Madam Boss Lady, fearful as I am of incurring your wrath, might I suggest that you get your rosy rump into RPI's family and caregivers support group? It's called Whole Family—in case you didn't know."

Maggie scowled at the sarcasm. "Come on. What am I going to learn there that I don't already—"

"Come on, yourself," he groused. "Just because your brain knows the answers doesn't mean you can apply them when your own emotions are being ripped into little pieces. Your husband—"

"Ex," she corrected.

He glared. "*Husband* has been the central focus of everyone's concern for more than half a year. But you're the healthy spouse, which means you've gone through your own hell. Do you want me to drag out the Family Care Objectives that you ram down our throats?" He shot a look to Cindy. "She and the staff psychologist update them every year."

Cindy smiled, enlightened, and shook her head again. Maggie felt like a kindergartner being told why her thumb hurt after she'd hit it with a hammer.

"They state—and I quote—'The patient and all members of his/her support network are to be considered a whole unit in need of care. Family members and all caregivers are to be strongly encouraged to—'"

"Sapperstein, if you can quote the FCOs, why can't you do your charting properly?"

He looked affronted. "Too mundane."

Maggie whimpered in overwhelmed frustration.

Sapperstein's good humor faded, and he leaned forward compassionately in his chair. "Boss, if it were Cindy in Garrett's place, you'd have dragged me to those meetings months ago. You need TLC just like anyone else in your position."

For a long time, Maggie stared at her wine. Admitting he was right was hard. "How long are you going to rub this in?"

"I don't know." He shrugged. "When is my next performance evaluation? I want a *big* raise this year."

Maggie's breath eased out in a half laugh.

"Drink up, noble leader. Once we finish getting your head screwed on straight, we've got some linguine to hunt down."

Stuffed to the point of swearing off Italian food for a year, Maggie turned the key in the lock and pushed open the front door. Predictably, it squeaked its welcoming chorus. Tonight she wished it hadn't. Walking in unannounced would have been nice. *Wimp.*

As she stepped into the living room, she discovered it wouldn't have made any difference. Garrett sat on the couch, legs stretched out on the coffee table and crossed at the ankles. A passing thought acknowledged the effort it had taken to effect the natural-looking pose. The rest of her attention latched onto the brandy bottle clutched in his hand. There wasn't a glass.

"Where have you been?" he asked low.

She wished she could tell how drunk he was, but with Garrett the only outward sign was a slight change in body language, and since he sat perfectly still on the couch, she had no clue how far gone he was.

"Are you going to answer?"

"I went to Sappersteins."

His eyes flared with self-contempt. "I knew it had to be him, but I talked myself out of it."

Maggie's temper flared. "Sappersteins plural, Garrett. Not Sapperstein's single person possessive. I spent the evening with Carl and Cindy and their five cats."

"Oh."

She wanted to scream at him that he'd worked himself into a stew then added alcohol to the mix, but she held her breath, trying to apply the professional knowledge she demanded of everyone else.

Rule one for tonight: Don't take responsibility for the patient's problems and decisions. It's his life. "Garrett, it's too bad you're sitting there swilling perfectly good brandy from the bottle, but I'm not your mother and you can do what you want. We'll talk when you're sober. Good night." *Sapperstein would be proud.*

"There weren't any clean glasses I could reach."

"Sorry." She didn't turn around.

"I'm not drunk either."

"Yippee for your team." Her foot had barely touched the first step when his voice stopped her.

"It's a little late to ask, but are you taking any birth control?"

After a stunned moment, Maggie sucked in her breath. How could she have been so stupid? So careless?

"Well," he drawled, "I guess that answers that." There was a slight pause. "What time of the month is it?"

Maggie made some quick mental calculations. "Bad. Really bad."

"Well, we only made love once. That'll help. It's not as if we've been together every night for a week."

"Once is all it takes," she squeaked. "Your legs may have a few problems, but you're still dangerous."

His startled look turned to a restrained flush of masculine pleasure. Only then did she realize what a stroke to his male ego she'd just delivered.

She sagged down onto the steps and did more mental calculations. "Nine months of pregnancy, plus eighteen years, means I'll be fifty-five when this kid graduates high school."

"And that will make me sixty-one." Garrett shuddered.

They stared at each other, bonded by shock, neither able to speak, but then, they knew they didn't need to. The crisis—real or imagined—abruptly put them on the same side of the fence.

He looked at her with such tenderness, her heart constricted, and when he reached to her, Maggie felt like a starving deer being offered food. She came to him as if in a trance, started to reach to him. But his accusation rang in her ears, and she shook her head and shied away.

Disappointment saddened his eyes, and he sipped the brandy. "When I was in a coma, you told me you couldn't take me shredding your life anymore."

She flinched.

"I'm trying not to, babe."

"I know." She perched on the edge of an overstuffed chair. Drunk or not, Garrett picked up on it and laid his hand on her thigh. The warmth burned through her slacks and created an unwanted ache in her soul. Nothing had been resolved. They'd merely piled a new crisis onto the stack.

"I can't be the type of man you've always needed. My life has been anything but tranquil."

A harsh laugh burst from her throat.

"If you're pregnant, we'll find a way to work through it."

Maggie covered her face with her hands. "I'm tired. I don't want to be here. I want to just disappear."

He smiled faintly. "Babe, I've said it before. You might fantasize about running away from problems, and you *definitely* hate talking about them. But when it comes down to it, you always manage to meet everything head-on—even when that meant divorcing me."

"Thanks. I think." She looked at him, more weary than ever. "Can we talk about something else now?"

His deep, sad laughter only made her more tired.

For the rest of the weekend, each time they looked at each other, desire and unspoken worry hung with equal weight between them. Garrett could move in a week if Ashleigh remained "pox free," as Blake worded it. The thought made Maggie shrivel up inside. How could she let him go again? Making him walk out of her life before had nearly killed her and it had been her idea. Now, their time together had passed so quickly, and they'd accomplished so little.

After work Monday, she tucked the clandestine purchase from the drugstore in the bedside table drawer in her room. That night Rick actually ate at home. His intense regard for the way she and Garrett interacted felt like being on trial.

"Why don't I do dishes and give you two the night off?" he asked. "I'm sure you can think of something more fun than kitchen duty."

The effect was no less drastic than if he'd doused them with cold water. The walls came down.

"That would be great, son."

The poor kid didn't say a word, but the remorse on his face said it all.

"How about I flip you for scrubbing counters," Garrett added in an obvious attempt to ease Rick's guilt. "Heads I win. Tails you lose."

That grabbed his attention. "Fat chance, Dad."

Garrett motioned Maggie into the other room. Then he and Rick headed into the kitchen.

"I didn't mean to make a mess for you guys," Rick said quietly.

Garrett thought a moment before he answered. "One thing about the Hughes family, son, we're never short of messes or apologies." He softened it further with a wink, and Rick smiled.

They worked in silence for a few minutes, but inside Garrett roiled. How much worse could life get? A baby. If true, had Maggie gotten pregnant on purpose?

The accusation hit him like a punch to the gut. How far had he slid into self-pity that he could even think such a thing? Maggie of all people. *Never.* Something snapped, and Garrett felt as if he suddenly saw himself clearly for the first time in eight long months. The sight disgusted him worse than anything had so far.

The bombing of Flight 1251 hadn't turned him into a victim. He'd done that to himself in the prison of his own mind. His life had never been particularly easy. So why did he look back on it as a lost paradise? Yes, it was harder now, but he didn't need to act as if he had one foot in the grave.

You're still breathing. You've got all your mental faculties. Garrett writhed with fury at the mistakes he'd made since the accident. *So get your head out of your ass. This is your life— at least for now. Make it work. You don't have any choice, especially if you're going to be a father again.*

God, he felt better. No. He felt like himself.

Despite legitimate reservations about starting parenting over, a soft spot warmed within him. He and Maggie might have created another new life together. A smile crept from his soul to his face. Rick shot him a questioning look as he scraped a plate, but Garrett waved him off and looked long and hard at his firstborn. Rick was a good kid—a bit scrambled right now—but the remains of that was about to change.

"I saw your soccer schedule on the fridge. I'm going to rearrange my therapy so I don't miss any practices."

Rick nearly dropped the plate into the garbage. "What if you can't?"

"Then I'll do without. The problem will come in when I move to Blake's."

"You're still moving?" Rick asked in a small voice.

Garrett reached for the plate, and the teen gave him a troubled look. "No farther away than Blake's. Promise. I'm not leaving the Bay area ever again. And once I settle into my own place, count on spending half your time there. I plan on exercising my joint custody rights."

Rick's barely masked agitation turned his motions into a jerky parody of his normally smooth stride as he retrieved the glasses from the table. "Every practice?"

"I may have trouble getting from Blake's house to your school. If Faith can't give me a ride, would you come get me?"

Agitation deepened as Rick picked up a dirty glass then set it into the cupboard. Garrett doubted the kid even noticed what he'd done.

"It would be easier if you just stayed here." Rick turned away and leaned on the counter, fists knotted.

"I can't." The tone Garrett used was pitched low to invite trust. "But I won't be far, and we'll be together—a lot."

Rick leveled accusing eyes on his father. "Why can't you and Mom just get back together?"

"I already explained that, son."

"Hurting her isn't the real reason," Rick snapped. "We're just not that important to you."

That hurt. "I could tell you otherwise, but words are cheap." Garrett turned his chair around. "From the looks of your car, it's going to take us months to get it in shape, and we might as well get at it. Plan on putting in a couple of hours each day.''

''Months?''

Garrett left the kitchen as truth sank in and belief glowed on Rick's face. Definite plans meant permanence.

One down. One to go.

Maggie paced in the living room, struggling not to eavesdrop. What were they talking about in there? Their voices weren't raised, so they weren't arguing. Or were they?

Cool it, Hughes. Wasn't it only yesterday that you decided to turn over a healthier leaf? Love them. Care for them. But don't take over. Sticking to it was harder than she ever imagined. *Hughes, you need Whole Family more than they do. You're a mess.*

The phone rang, and she heard Rick answer it. Garrett emerged from the kitchen smiling. The look in his eyes had changed. It was like looking into the past. The desperation she'd seen for months had been replaced by the absolute calm of a man who'd mapped out a war he couldn't possibly lose. This was the old Garrett, the same yet different. It unnerved her.

He motioned Maggie down the hall to the master bedroom. Maggie followed but hesitated at the doorway. For years, this had been her room, their room. Yet within the space of the two days since their disastrous lovemaking, it had taken on the air of Garrett's private domain. She wasn't all that anxious to invade it, particularly when she sensed something major had just transpired.

You're being paranoid, Hughes. Irritated with herself, she suppressed the irrational reaction and sat on the edge of the bed.

Rick yelled from the other room. ''Dad, can I meet John at the arcade?''

Maggie arched a brow. ''He's asking *you?*''

Garrett took a deep, satisfied breath. ''Not tonight. We've got a long day tomorrow, remember?''

"Okay," he called back cheerfully.

Such self-confidence radiated from the man she loved. It gave rise to a newborn hope that maybe they had a chance after all. Garrett rested his elbows on the arms of his wheelchair, obviously savoring the moment as he recounted the latest chunks he'd chipped away at Rick's wall. This was more like the old Garrett, one who faced the world head-on. She would have rejoiced, except this particular mood of his made her feel like a cornered rabbit, one that was about to get eaten.

"I think it's time to talk about us."

"Good subject," she said, sounding more confident than she felt. "There's a support group at RPI. It's called Whole Family. I think we all need to go."

He looked mildly repelled. "Is this the same one Sapperstein kept ramming down my throat?"

"Good. You heard about it."

"Frequently."

Maggie felt more uncomfortable by the minute. Being together in their old bedroom was hard enough. So was trying to figure out why he was so different. He didn't have to make it worse by treating the conversation like an interrogation.

Garrett transferred from the chair to the bed. "You're squirming."

Logic told her he wasn't close enough for his body heat to burn into her skin, but she felt it nonetheless. "I don't squirm," she retorted irritably.

"Why do you bother lying, babe?" He sounded tired. The weekend with all its ups and downs was demanding its due. "We have things to discuss."

Like the fact that you're going to tell me goodbye. Desperate, she turned and faced him. A mistake. A big one. His eyes bored into her, extracting secrets and churning her emotions. Standing up was the quickest way to put space between them. He frowned in disapproval.

"Look, Garrett. You've just made major progress with Rick. Now you think you can tackle *us*. I'm just not up to being steamrollered tonight. Can it wait? Besides, what's wrong with the RPI group?''

He stared at her for so long she decided he didn't plan to answer at all.

''Garrett, we've made so many mistakes on our own that I think it's time to get some help.'' She paced from the TV to the door and back.

Slowly, his expression shuttered, he said, ''I can't see myself baring my soul to a room full of strangers.''

''It's not that type of group.'' Maggie sat beside him. ''It's learning life skills and how to redefine relationships. Patients and their families exchange ideas and experiences.''

He looked appalled.

''How can you say you want to 'talk about us,' yet be unwilling to try something that might work?''

His carefully neutral expression gave nothing away. Her heart pounded against her chest.

''Make what work?'' he asked softly. ''A reconciliation?''

That time she believed she really did squirm under his probing gaze. She thought about lying, but what was the point? ''In part.'' His lips tightened, but she plunged on. ''Whether anything ever happens between us isn't the only issue. We are all in this mess together—you, me, Blake, our parents, our son. We need to learn to adjust, and that's going to take outside help. Whole Family has an excellent success record.''

She watched each word penetrate. Then he spared an acid glance at the wheelchair. ''I can't see that I'll ever adjust to that thing, but I'm through wallowing in it.''

Then he gently took her hand, but she found no pleasure in the deliberateness of his touch. Apprehension flooded her.

''Coming home was a mistake, babe. I've done nothing but hurt you.''

''That's not true!'' Her stomach knotted, and her heart screamed against what was to come.

''I know you want to get back together. Friday night made that pretty clear.''

Each word hit like a hammer. She was losing him. They

weren't married anymore. Their relationship had no safety net, not even the illusion of one. Tears burned, but she fought them back. "I won't give up on us. I love you too much."

That wasn't quite what he expected, and it showed in his suddenly tense shoulders. He rubbed his thumb across her knuckles. "I've explained this in bits and pieces, but you need to understand—"

"I understand just fine!" The tears clouded her vision, but she wouldn't let them fall. "You're going to ride off into the sunset without me."

He blinked, startled. "Babe, I'm not the cowboy hero in some movie."

"White knight," she muttered, aggravated that the words slipped out.

"What?" he frowned.

"Nothing." She waved a hand dismissively. "You were about to give me a I'm-walking-out-on-you-for-your-own-good speech. Get it over with."

"You make it sound as if I feel nothing."

"Won't feel. There's a difference."

He cupped her chin. "I will always love you. I've never denied that, or even tried to. It's because I love you that I won't be a burden to you for the rest of our lives."

Maggie shrieked in outraged pain, launched off the bed and whirled on him. "Do you know how many paraplegics are out there changing the world? You'll be one of them, too, and I want to be with you when you do!"

Dismay twisted his beloved features. "Babe, you've got an unrealistic view of me."

Her arms fell limply to her side. "What *really* happened in the kitchen? You came out different."

"You're right." He sighed.

"It's scaring me." The tears finally spilled, blinding her. Before she turned her back on him to wipe them away, she saw his dismay turn into an open need to comfort her, to make it all go away. She didn't yield. A temporary fix wouldn't cut it.

"There's no reason to be afraid."

"Give me one good reason why I shouldn't be," she said with a sob.

She heard the mattress squeak a split second before an iron grip closed around her waist, dragging them both to the floor. Maggie yelped in surprise, and Garrett shifted his weight to cover hers, effectively pinning her to the floor.

"Sorry," he muttered gruffly. "You were too far away to grab and pull back to the bed."

She almost asked if he'd hurt himself, but swallowed it back. One look at the steely purpose in those eyes screamed that he was just fine. So she settled for, "Are you nuts?"

"Probably."

In a flash of movement too quick to follow, his lips descended on hers and muffled any further protest. He plundered her mouth, and it took her a moment to react. She squeaked in protest and pushed against him, but he ignored her. His lips slanted across hers, tasting, coaxing, insisting.

Heat coiled in the pit of her belly. She tried to fight her way out from under him but got nowhere except making her more aware of his body against hers.

"Open to me, babe," he murmured, his breath sweet against her cheek.

"No," she snapped. *Hughes, you're an idiot. He's kissing you, not saying goodbye. Wake up!*

"Let go, babe. Let it happen."

Without conscious will, she drew in his scent. Her arms stole around his neck, and a low groan of approval rumbled from his chest.

She had no idea why he'd so completely contradicted himself, but she wanted him so badly the last of her resistance vaporized in the inferno of passion. She eased her tightly pursed lips. His tongue stole inside, reestablishing his mastery. With a little maneuvering, he got her blouse unbuttoned, and his hands roamed her skin at will, igniting a trail of fire wherever he touched. Maggie grabbed his shirt and tugged it free of his waistband, then commanded the same freedom with his body as he had with hers. Her fingers swept up his sides and circled his back, the satin skin heating beneath her hands.

"Yes, babe." His voice came caressing soft. "Touch me."

The brief break in contact with his mouth became intolerable, and she pulled him back to her. Garrett shifted yet again, fitting himself intimately into the cradle of her hips. Maggie shuddered, arching toward his blatant arousal, the layers of clothing between them a torturous barrier.

He tasted her neck and throat, slipping his hand behind her back to unhook her bra. When her breasts were free, he lavished his attention freely just as he always had so long ago. She held him close, running her fingers through his dark hair as he stoked her fire into sweet agony.

Rolling aside, he then slipped the zipper down on her slacks and drew the fabric away. She reached for him, and he froze. His lack of movement barely registered in her fevered mind. Not until he covered her hand with his own and pulled her away did she sense disaster.

Her body throbbed with want, and she couldn't bear to face another rejection. Whimpering silently, she tried to bury her face in his passion-damp neck.

He held her from him. "We can't, babe," he rasped, his breathing heavy and labored. "Risking pregnancy once was insane, but an accident. Twice won't be so forgivable."

"It's okay," she murmured, her body straining to regain the lost contact.

Garrett's eyes widened incredulously. "That's your body talking. You'll hate yourself in the morning—not to mention the next nine months and eighteen years."

She slithered against him and gently bit at his ear.

He shuddered and swore. "Tempt me a little more, though...." He extricated himself and sat up.

The fog cleared a little. "You don't understand. Today, just in case something like this happened again, I bought some...uhmmm...." She blushed. *Come on, Hughes. You're a health-care professional. You've talked to patients about them before. So why the embarrassment? Because this time it's me and Garrett, not other people.* Identifying the problem didn't make the word any easier to say. "Uhmmm... supplies." *Wimp.*

Garrett looked a bit startled at first, but his eyes became molten sapphires as it sank in. "You bought condoms?"

The intense blush burned clear to her toes. During their marriage, she'd always been on the pill. Condoms seemed so mechanical, cumbersome and obvious. She half expected him to chuckle at her ridiculous discomfort, but his gaze heated with single-minded intent.

"Where are they?" The whispered question carried the impact of a lightning strike. Her blood fired anew.

"Upstairs," she mouthed, swallowing past a mouth gone cotton dry.

"Get them."

Maggie trembled with anticipation, and her legs didn't want to hold her as she tried to stand. He watched in silence as she repaired her clothes, his regard more erotic than words.

Quietly, she slipped up the stairs to the spare bedroom. The discordant sounds of a universe-altering, video game war came from down the hall.

"Hi, Mom," Rick called absently.

As Maggie raided the night table, the repetitive sound effects abruptly stopped, and Rick appeared in the doorway. He looked curiously at the small, brown paper bag in her hand.

"What's that?"

Maggie panicked. "It's..uhmmm...something for your father." She felt the blood drain from her face. *I didn't really say that, did I?* She wanted to crawl under a rock.

Rick tilted his head. "An early birthday present?"

"Sort of," she hedged. *Hughes, if you don't get out of here, the* Titanic *will look like a minor mishap.*

"Can I see?"

"No," she choked out, then coughed to cover up her discomfort. Brushing past him, she mumbled, "See you in the morning," hideously aware of his puzzled expression as he stared after her.

Chapter 12

By the time Maggie got back downstairs, Garrett was sitting on the edge of the bed, waiting. He'd changed his mind. She saw it in the regret and self-condemnation in his eyes. Maggie's heart sank as she realized what had happened earlier. Her tears had punched all his buttons, bypassing his brain and hitting him straight in his male, sex-solves-everything reaction. The little brown bag in her hands became even more conspicuous, but she clutched it tightly. It was either that or throw it at him.

"Babe, I—"

"Don't you dare," she snarled. "Do you have any idea what I just went through up there? We're going to finish what we started, even if I have to club you over the head first."

He gaped at her. "Come again?"

She gave a brief recap. She wasn't quite certain what she'd expected, but his leaning back, roaring with laughter, wasn't it.

"You told him what?" Garrett could hardly breathe.

"It's not funny," she snapped, stung.

Her tart denial sent him into new paroxysms of hilarity.

More humiliated than she thought a human being could be, Maggie stiffened her spine. Tonight was too much. She'd been nearly dumped, *again*. Nearly made love to, *again*. Now laughed at. "Good night, Garrett. I'm going to bed—upstairs."

"No, you're not," he wheezed, fighting for his wind. Even though he could barely talk, the order carried enough weight to give her pause. "Babe, lock the door and come here. You're not going anywhere."

"Oh, you've changed your mind again? Lucky me."

He looked at her, slowly bringing his mirth under control. "Nothing's changed, but we *are* going to talk." He reached to her.

Her heart felt like lead as it sank farther into her stomach. No matter what the situation, Garrett always had the power to entice her. *Hughes, if you ever had to face a firing squad, you'd probably give them tips on how to improve their aim.* Taking his hand, she let him draw her beside him on the bed.

"Dump away," she muttered irritably.

An annoyed sound rolled from his throat. "One day, in the future, if I find that—"

"I want you now. For better or worse. This is the worse, and we'll get through it." Her conscience nailed her with the divorce, but she didn't bring it up.

"Babe," he whispered softly, agonized. "You've sacrificed more for me than I had any right to ask. I can't expect you—"

"I can live with it."

"I can't!" The intensity of the outburst caught her off guard. "Once I get—"

Maggie leaped to her feet. "I'm not sixteen anymore! You don't have to protect me or wait for me to grow up. You don't have to make things perfect for us before you pop the question. We've been through all that. Don't bring back the wars of twenty years ago." Breathless, she gulped in air. "Life didn't line up the way we wanted it. The divorce happened. The plane crash happened. But we've loved each other through it all. Aren't we worth fighting for?''

Her soul lay bare between them, engulfed in a silence so profound, any reply would have dropped into the depths unheard.

Garrett opened and closed his mouth several times before he could speak. Even then, it was little more than a choked whisper. ''I can't live with you taking care of me like Mom does Dad. She's killing herself.''

Her knees nearly buckled. ''Is that how you see us? Dad needs constant supervision, and Mom flatly refuses any help. *That's* what's killing her. You've got decades of vital living ahead. As you get stronger and more independent, I won't be any more of a caregiver than I was for thirteen years.''

Thoughts roiled behind his eyes, and she watched him weigh her words. Her lungs started to scream, and she realized she held her breath waiting for his decision.

He shook his head, bewildered. ''How can you willingly walk into this mess?''

Her breath rushed out in a bark of laughter. ''Garrett, I've been in it since the beginning. I even watched live coverage of the crash on TV. Yes, it's rough now, but look how far we've come.''

The inner war showed clearly in the torment on his face. ''I don't know,'' he said slowly, looking at legs unnaturally still.

''Let's define rough, Garrett. Rough is sitting in a waiting room while a team of doctors fights to save your life. Rough is doing a death watch on you in intensive care. Rough is seeing your face after Blake told you about your spinal cord.'' She waved a dismissive hand. ''By comparison, the garbage since your discharge has been a snap.''

Maggie clamped her jaws shut to keep from saying any more. She'd either made her case, or nothing ever would. Unconsciously, she turned away, unable to face another rejection.

''Babe, I don't know whether you just made a whole lot of sense or if you're telling me everything I want to hear.''

Her heart slammed into her throat, and she stole a peek. His tortured expression sent a fresh batch of tears flowing down her cheeks.

"Don't cry, babe." In his eyes she saw the ravages of a man completely out of his depth. "I can't change gears this fast, but I can't let you go either."

She wasn't sure which one of them moved first, but she found herself locked in his arms. A whirlwind of kisses and murmured endearments followed, and her carefully buttoned blouse wound up on the floor.

"Did you lock the door?" he asked.

Her blood heated a few more degrees. "I don't remember." As she got up to check, she looked back at the love shining on his beloved face. There'd be time enough to hash out their problems another day.

She flipped out the overhead light, leaving only the romantic glow of a reading lamp, then went back to his arms.

"No promises, babe," he whispered against her hair.

"I know." She pulled back and kissed him full on the lips. "Just think about it."

Words became meaningless as they lost themselves to their love. Experimentation was abandoned in the need to reestablish the basic rights of belonging to each other. When they finally lay replete in each other's arms, their breathing still slightly labored, a deep peace settled over her. The thought of ever leaving that bed was totally repellent. They dozed for a while, but she eventually forced herself to stir.

"Where are you going?" he murmured, making a sleepy attempt to pull her back to him.

"As much as I hate to, I have to go upstairs."

His eyes snapped open. "Why?"

"If I spend the night with you, Rick's going to know more than I'm comfortable with. He's sixteen, not six."

Incoherent muttering was his first response. Then he sat up, looking patiently amused. "There's going to be a first morning after," he said tenderly. "Facing our son over breakfast won't be a picnic, especially if he grins like a village idiot."

Maggie groaned.

"Babe, you know this is what he wants."

She wanted to disappear. "Any chance you'd let me sneak upstairs before dawn?"

"Nope." He patted the mattress. "Lie back down."

She sat there, wishing he was as miserable as she. "You don't understand at all."

"Yes, I do, but dwelling on it won't change anything."

She crossed her arms over her naked breasts and stood up. "It's not that simple."

He clenched and unclenched his jaw. "Yes, it is. Now, as much as I'm enjoying the view, are you coming back here, or do I have to tackle you again?"

Still deeply rattled, she couldn't take any more. "I see. It's okay for you to badger me into talking when I don't want to, but there are different rules when you're on the hot seat."

"Maggie," he ground out in exasperation. "You're trying to pick a fight because you don't want to face our son."

That struck home, and she flinched. Her gaze skittered to his legs, then to his wheelchair.

Garrett scowled, patience strained. "What I lack in speed, I make up for in persistence."

She stood there, suspended in time, sorting through the scrambled mess in her brain. He draped the sheet haphazardly across his lap, his aggravation melting away.

"Aren't we worth fighting for?" he asked, softly repeating her own words.

"You fight dirty," she groaned.

"No, I don't. I fight to win."

She crawled back between the sheets. The kiss was a mutual endeavor, as were the flames that followed.

Garrett decided Maggie had been right about the morning after. He'd never felt so uncomfortable in his life. Despite the rather explicit talks with Rick about sex, it was still hard to think of his child as a sexual being, particularly one entirely too happy about what he guessed had gone on between his parents the night before. Garrett would have preferred the village idiot over what he and Maggie got. Every time he looked over the rim of his coffee cup, he saw sparkling green eyes and a too knowing smile. He supposed the lack of verbal comment was a teenager's idea of subtlety. Maggie inhaled her food and vanished for the day. Garrett wished he had a job and could have done the same.

The door had scarcely closed behind her when Rick turned hopeful eyes on his father. "Well?"

Garrett wiped his mouth on a napkin.

"Well?"

"We're working on it."

"Yes!" He practically leaped off the floor.

Garrett gave him a cautionary glance. "No guarantees. I'm still not convinced this was the right decision." Rick looked crestfallen, and Garrett held up a soothing hand. "Don't borrow trouble."

"One day at a time, right, Dad?"

Garrett nodded, unsettled, and watched his son head off for school. Waking with Maggie curled up at his side had been paradise. For a moment, half-asleep, he'd even forgotten the mountain of problems they had to dig through, and he lost himself in gathering her back into his arms and kissing the sleep from her eyes.

The jealousy had nailed him again, but he'd managed to keep his mouth shut this time. He had no right to grill her about anything. She'd had every legal right to start over with someone new. Somehow he needed to learn to live with that truth. There'd been no marriage, so there'd been no betrayal. He knew that, but he prayed that in time he'd believe it, too.

Her arguments for a reconciliation made sense, but would they hold up to the daily brutalities? Granted, he didn't need the care many spinal patients did. Once he could afford a van, he'd be more self-reliant and could find work. With his coming settlement, he didn't need to, but if he didn't find *something,* they'd haul him off in a rubber truck before too long. He just wished the career options held more appeal.

I'm a cop. It's not a job. It's who I am. How can I ever be anything else? He propped his elbows on the table and buried his face in his hands. *And Maggie can't live with it.*

That afternoon, after he'd recovered from Mike the Wonder Boy's therapy session, Garrett took the exercise ball outside in the fresh air and worked on his grip. It would be another several days before the doctor took out the stitches in his wrist, and the joint had stiffened up after the surgery. Maggie had told him that was to be expected, but it was frustrating. Before, he'd at least had a clawlike range of motion. Now he could hardly keep the ball centered in his palm.

He overcorrected, the ball bounced on the concrete, then rolled out onto the lawn. Maneuvering a wheelchair across grass wasn't his favorite pastime.

Hairy, asleep at his feet, had lifted his head, watched the ball roll away, then laid his head back onto his paws.

"If I promise never to ask again, will you get it?" Garrett asked. Hairy ignored him. He was a Frisbee dog. Period.

"Need some help, Dad?"

Garrett looked up, surprised to see Rick in the doorway. The teen's euphoria was only slightly more restrained than it had been at breakfast. Not for the first time, Garrett wished Rick was still six.

"Thanks, but I've got it." The ball had rolled a surprising distance out in the yard.

Pride was particularly noticeable today. If Maggie had been watching, she'd have made one of her absurd comments about his testosterone level. Despite his new resolve not to let his limitations victimize him, Garrett still found himself embarrassed over his son seeing how difficult picking up a rubber ball from the grass really was.

Rick was suddenly by his side. "Anything I can do?"

Yes, son, stop hovering. I finally broke your mother of it, now please don't pick up where she left off. "I've got it."

"But I want to help." Challenge bordering on insolence lashed out, and Garrett whipped his head around. Rick stood there looking helpless and hostile.

Now what? "I know, and I appreciate it, but I don't need—"

"I understand, Dad." The challenge darkened. "You still don't need me for anything."

Garrett froze. Surely, they couldn't possibly be back to square one.

Rick turned to go, and a new truth hit Garrett, one he'd completely overlooked. He'd been wrapped up in his own desperate need to be needed, and in his fears that the people he loved would turn into drudges. He hadn't stopped to consider perhaps they might need to be needed, too. So obvious, yet he'd missed it.

"Rick, wait."

The boy stopped but didn't turn back around.

"There's a group at RPI called Whole Family."

Rick turned, hurt accusation still in his eyes.

"I think all of us should go."

"Whatever." There was no inflection to his voice at all.

"Right now, though, if you wouldn't mind, I'd get more done if I didn't have to chase down the ball every time I drop it."

A half smile tugged at the corner of the teenager's lips.

Garrett smiled self-consciously. "While we're at it, we'll talk about my hang-ups on that subject, too."

In two long strides, Rick reached him, pushed the chair back to the patio. Garrett would have preferred to get there himself, but Rick's needs were more important.

Friday after work, Maggie walked into the house, feeling as if her bulging purse was extremely conspicuous. The black leather bag wasn't designed to hold all her regular junk, plus a home pregnancy test and a new box of condoms.

The joy of falling asleep in Garrett's arms every night all week had made breakfasts tolerable. Rick had settled down some since that first horrible morning, but not by much. Garrett's approach to therapy had changed as dramatically as he had. Gone was the desperation to succeed. He was quiet, methodical, a man with a purpose. She'd heard about this side of him from other cops on the force. This was the Garrett Hughes who got the job done. No frills. No excuses. It scared the hell out of her.

Hairy's muffled barking and human laughter drew her outside. Rick tossed the Frisbee, both dog and boy providing entertainment for Garrett, Patrick and Laverne.

The three adults sat together around the patio table. Patrick was animated, using the familiar hand gestures that had always accompanied his speech. Maggie's heart skipped lightly. Dad was having one of his rare good days.

Garrett listening attentively, a sad introspective look in his eyes. Laverne looked exhausted to the point of collapse, her spine ramrod straight with commitment to care for her husband. Deliberately, Maggie didn't look at Garrett until she'd given the elder Hugheses a hug. Long suppressed hormones had been unleashed, and she didn't know how successful she'd be at hiding the hunger she felt every time she came near him.

She bent to Garrett and gave him what she intended to be a fleeting kiss. Desire flared in his eyes. The moment their lips touched, sparks ignited, sending a fiery chain reaction throughout her body. He reached up to tunnel his fingers deep into the hair at her nape to hold her close for a more lingering, second kiss. Maggie's knees went weak.

"That's enough," Patrick teased, feigning a grumpy air. "You can kiss each other anytime you want." He turned to Laverne. "Seventeen years and they still act like newlyweds."

Heart-weary, Maggie sagged into the chair. "Tell me, Dad. What's new with you?"

"My boy's been setting my thinking straight on a few things," he said matter-of-factly.

"Oh?"

"Yep." He cast a fond look at his wife of forty-seven years. "I put in forty years with the railroad and got to retire. But my Vernie is still working, what with cooking, taking care of the house and all. It's time she retired, too. Come Monday, we'll be looking into a part-time cook and housekeeper.

Maybe a college girl who needs a job that'll fit around classes.''

Maggie shared a look with Garrett. *Or a nurse who knows to keep her mouth shut.* For all her and Blake's arguing with Mom, neither had ever thought to go to Patrick, the one person she'd never refuse. *You've been busy today, my heart.*

Garrett interlaced his fingers with hers. Surely nothing could go wrong now. The moment the thought formed, she wished she could have killed it. A mindless foreboding came over her strong enough to take her breath away. She squeezed Garrett's hand a little tighter. He frowned a question at her, but she wouldn't look back, afraid he'd see foolishness in her eyes.

"Phone for you, Dad," Rick called, poking his head out the garage door. She hadn't heard it ring.

Garrett pulled his hand away, and Maggie sucked in her breath. The broken contact left her drowning in irrational terror.

"Are you okay, babe?" he asked, frowning.

She nodded, unable to speak. He shot her a skeptical look.

"Are you coming, Dad, or should I take a message?"

"Be right there." Garrett gave her another worried glance, then turned toward the garage.

Once inside, he took the receiver. What was wrong with Maggie? She looked about ready to faint. "Hello?"

"Garrett? It's me, Tom White."

His partner on that case at the DEA. Worry about Maggie was pushed to the side. "Tom! Where are you?"

"D.C. I just called to see how you're doing."

"More complaints than I'd like," he quipped. They exchanged pleasantries for a few minutes. Then Tom dropped the bomb.

"I started back to work last week."

Garrett's stomach knotted. "Oh?"

"Yeah, my doctors had a fit. They wanted to do another round of skin grafts on these damn burn scars first, but I couldn't stand sitting around anymore. It's not like they're on my face or anything. So I'm back in harness."

Each word hit Garrett with sledgehammer force.

"I miss you, partner. They've got me paired up with a real pain in the backside. No finesse. I'm sure he's got redeeming qualities somewhere, but I haven't found any yet."

Envy screamed through Garrett, making speech impossible. Tom had his life back. *His life back!* Garrett looked down at his legs, legs that had betrayed him, locking him in a prison called paraplegia. He reeled under the weight of it.

"You there, partner?"

He cleared his throat and tried to sound normal. "Yeah, you working a case I'd know about, or something new?"

"Oh, you'd know this one," he drawled, smug. "The name DeWitt ring any bells?"

"You're kidding."

"Nope." He laughed. "You were right. That slime bag kept records. File boxes full. He got himself blown away yesterday. Sorting through this stuff is better than Christmas."

"That's great." Garrett thought the envy might strangle him. He bluffed and fumbled his way through the conversation for another few minutes before he found a way to end it. When he hung up he was as drained and breathless as if he'd run a marathon. He didn't want to resent Tom's good fortune, but he resented it so deeply, he nearly hated the man.

DeWitt only rubbed salt into it. Three years ago, Garrett had used every argument he could think of to convince the higher ups that DeWitt had been worth going after. He hadn't established himself yet, and nobody listened. Pointlessly, he ran through the old arguments again. How many of the records Tom found justified them? Garrett's mind whirled with details, one case spilling over into another.

"Garrett, are you okay?" came Maggie's worried voice behind him. "You've been in here a long time."

Had he? How long had he sat staring at the phone, his guts churning? Tom had picked up the pieces, all of them. Garrett's breathing sounded unnaturally harsh in his ears. All he could see was his wheelchair.

* * *

Maggie had debated long and hard before following Garrett into the garage. Now that she had, her apprehension went into overdrive. He looked wired enough to chew steel.

"I almost hate to ask," she said, "but what's wrong?"

The explosion came trip-wire fast. "Maggie, would you marry me again if I could return to the DEA? Or are you only interested because I'll be the nice stay-at-home husband you always wanted?"

"Who was that on the phone?" she demanded.

"Tom." He glowered at the exercise equipment that surrounded him. "He's working the DeWitt case."

"The what?"

"I wanted it, Maggie. Wanted it bad. Instead, I got stuck with that import cartel. I shouldn't have been on that plane."

Maggie didn't have an immediate answer. He'd hit on one of her deepest worries. Would she take him back if he were still a cop? She wanted to say, yes. She wanted to believe that she'd overcome the fear that one day he wouldn't come home, but it still lurked just below the surface, waiting to shred her.

Focusing on Garrett's turmoil instead of her own, she knelt beside him. Whatever buttons Tom White had pushed, she'd be the one to clean up the mess. "Garrett, I take it Tom returned to work and you're not handling it well."

He glared at her. "Would you?"

She shrugged. "I don't know. Women don't wrap so much of their self-identity into their careers. From what I understand, cops are more prone to what you're feeling than most professions."

"You sound like a shrink," he bit out under his breath.

She ached for him and slid her arms around his rigid shoulders. "Please, Garrett, let the past go. What matters is how we live the rest of our lives."

He didn't answer. Had he even heard?

"Don't lock me out," she pleaded.

Dispassionately, he peeled her arms off him. "Go back to Mom and Dad. I'll be out in a minute."

Every fiber of her being said to stay, to ride out the storm with him, but he didn't want her. Deep down where it mattered, she knew that this crisis would have a shattering effect on their chances to reunite forever. *And he locked me out.*

For the next two days, Maggie walked a fragile tightrope between control and insane worry. Never, in all the years of their relationship, had she seen Garrett brood like this. At night, his need for her didn't diminish, but she sensed that part of him was closed to her.

"Are we going to figure out a wedding date?" she asked when the languor of lovemaking had worn off. He hadn't specifically stated that he again wanted to marry her, but she thought it was a safe assumption and she needed the security of solid plans.

He stroked her hair and held her close. "Not for a while, babe. Not until I get a few things settled."

Disappointment set a choking knot in her throat.

The next night at quarter to eleven, Garrett still hadn't come in from the garage. Worried, she went looking for him.

The sight that greeted her was both glorious and horrifying. Garrett had parked his wheelchair at the end of the newly installed parallel bars, his back to her, and levered himself upright. His feet were planted squarely on the floor, but she couldn't tell how much weight, if any, rested on them.

"I told you to stay away from those things without me!" she shrieked. Her gaze latched onto his right hand. The steel pipes were wide enough in diameter for him to close his fingers around, but what kind of a grip did he have? Dr. Kelly believed the surgery would eventually give Garrett seventy percent or better function in that hand, but that didn't mean he had anywhere near that much now.

"It's rather pathetic to feel like I conquered the world when all I did was stand up." His voice came out in a ragged whisper almost too low to hear as he looked over his shoulder at her. Tears gleamed on his lower lashes. "But, Maggie, I'm *standing.*"

She rushed to him, buried her face against his back, locking her arms around his waist. Her own tears dripped down her cheeks and dampened his shirt. "How long have you been doing this?"

He cleared his throat. "First time."

They stood in silence, words inadequate. Living day by day through his recovery had seemed like a lifetime, but given his injuries, he'd come impossibly far in an impossibly short time.

He still might never walk again, she conceded, but with the feat he had just accomplished, leg braces and crutches were real possibilities. She nuzzled his back and kissed him between the shoulder blades.

"Babe, I have a problem," he said uncomfortably.

Maggie was instantly alert. "What?"

"My hand is about to give out, and I don't have a clue how to get down." It ended on a tremulous laugh.

Between the two of them, they got him seated in his wheelchair. Garrett covered his face with his hands, rubbing a bit too hard. She almost asked what he was doing, but when she saw his shoulders tremble with silent tears, Maggie knelt beside him and wrapped her arms around his neck. Not quite aware of how it happened, she found herself locked in a tight embrace. They held each other and cried. Later, they laughed under the realization that there wasn't a box of tissue in sight.

"We make quite a pair, babe," he whispered, brushing at both their wet faces.

Such love shone in his eyes, and she kissed a salty tear from his cheek. "We always did."

Maggie hadn't thought about how much garbage that remark would dredge up until the words tumbled from her mouth. "There really hasn't been anyone but you, Garrett."

He tipped her face up to stare deeply into her eyes. Was he seeing the truth there? He didn't answer for so long that she regretted saying anything at all.

His expression twisted into dismay. "I'm sorry I doubted you, babe. You'd changed. I didn't know what else to think.

Even if you had found someone else, we were divorced. I had no right to hurl accusations.''

She groaned with relief. "If I thought you'd been with another woman, I'd get a little crazy, too."

Shadows clouded his eyes, and she panicked. *No!* Suddenly she understood his irrational jealousy. It ripped into her so fast, she couldn't think past the rage and hurt. "Who was it!" She wanted to rip the unknown woman's lungs out.

"Babe, I've never made love to anyone but you."

He'd worded that too carefully for her to trust, like a used car salesman hiding a loophole in a warranty. A distant thread of sanity condemned this whole discussion. He'd just stood up for the first time. Dissecting past fidelity, or lack of it, showed extremely poor judgment.

She plowed ahead anyway. "You're lying."

Anger flashed. "Maggie, I've never lied to you about anything. Never."

His offended vehemence startled her, but she conceded that he had the right to be annoyed. He'd diluted the truth a few times, but never lied.

"You're not telling me everything, though."

He gave her an appraising look, as if weighing how much to say. She thought her heart would break.

"I want to know."

He sighed. "Let it go, babe. Nothing happened."

"Then why is it bothering you?"

"Because I love you, and the situation wasn't something I'm particularly proud of," he said exasperated.

"Tell me."

"Why won't you drop it?"

She swallowed against the lump in her throat. "Would you?"

"I'd like to think I would, but I know better." He sighed. "Just remember. You insisted."

She held on to him and braced herself.

"Do you remember the last time I called home on the safe line and you answered instead of Rick?"

"Yeah." How could she not remember? He'd sounded so alone her heart started making up all kinds of excuses to ask him to come home. She'd held firm, telling him that unless it pertained to their son, she had nothing to say. After she'd hung up on him, she'd cried half the night.

"When you wouldn't talk to me, not even small talk, it hit me pretty hard. Getting you back seemed hopeless, and I felt like a fool for carrying a torch that long. The case had been dragging on interminably, and I was at a real low.

"There was a woman I'd met during the investigation, not a suspect, just a hanger-on, a wannabe. She'd been rather blatant about wanting to get involved, but I'd pretended not to notice. I ran into her later that night, and we ended up at a motel. I left before anything happened."

She couldn't imagine anyone calling it off after it'd gone that far. "Why did you leave?"

"When we were getting undressed, she called me Gary. That's who she thought I was—Gary Reeves, drug trafficker." Sad mockery dulled his eyes. "She didn't want *me* any more than you did."

A sob escaped before Maggie could stop it. What she'd put him through, put them both through. How could she live with it?

He tilted her face up. "I know you, babe. Don't start blaming yourself. It was my choice to walk into that motel room and my choice to walk out." Garrett drew her to him for another kiss. When they came up for air, he whispered, "No more dwelling on the past, all right?"

"Promise." She poured all her love into her smile.

He kissed her fingers, his eyes devouring her. "There are a few other things I'd rather dwell on," he murmured, "but I'm so tired, sleep is about all I can manage."

"I'd settle for you holding me all night."

"That could be arranged." When she went to draw her hand away, he grasped it and frowned. "That reminds me. Wasn't your monthly due today?"

Maggie felt her smile freeze, and she looked away.

He drew her face back to meet his gaze. "What is it, babe?"

She sighed. "It was, and it didn't happen." She'd only been late once in her life—with Rick.

Instead of getting upset as she'd feared, his square-cut features softened. "We'll work it out."

"I bought a home pregnancy test a few days ago, just in case. I'll use it tomorrow morning. Then we'll know for sure."

Supportively, he squeezed her hand. "I've heard that parenthood after thirty can be more fun."

Amazed, she stared at him. He had so much to cope with. Yet he was willing to accept more? "You wouldn't mind?"

He shook his head in slow, but emphatic, denial. "The timing's not the best, but in another eight months, our lives should be more settled."

They cuddled close that night, enjoying just sharing a bed. Idly, she traced the swirls of soft black hair on his chest, and he caressed her side, his hand coming to rest low on her stomach.

As impractical as a baby was, she found herself wishing it were true. Irrational, she knew, but how much of life made sense? Would another child be such a disaster? Her salary could handle it, and whatever occupation Garrett decided to pursue would only help. Actually, when she thought about the financial end of things, having babies after thirty made sense. In most instances the parents were financially stable, and they definitely had a lot more life experience to draw from. Garrett seemed to be thinking along the same lines as he kissed her forehead and sleepily pulled her closer.

"This is where we belong," he murmured, gathering her to him. He closed his eyes. "Remember that."

The words echoed through her mind until apprehension raked her heart with vicious claws. What wasn't he telling her? She sat up. He'd fallen asleep instantly, and his face wrinkled in protest at the loss of her body heat.

"What are you talking about?"

His breathing slowed to the even rhythm of deep sleep.

* * *

The next morning, Maggie stood in the bathroom, staring at the test kit set up on the counter. "Come on," she muttered. "Turn blue."

"Anything yet?" came Garrett's soft inquiry from behind her.

She turned and shook her head. "We're being really stupid about this."

"Having another child with you doesn't feel that way."

Maggie flushed with the primitive desire to give the man she loved a baby. Afraid of the intensity of her feelings, she strove for a nonchalant air. "Watching this thing isn't going to speed it up. Do you want breakfast?" She tried to squeeze past him, but he captured her by the waist.

"Yeah, I do, but coffee doesn't sound particularly appealing." The naked desire that radiated from him formed a heated knot low in her stomach.

The prospect of having made a baby added an extra poignancy to their lovemaking, and they accepted the challenges of his body's restrictions, basking in the freedom of no preset roles or rules.

The pregnancy test came up negative, and she felt ridiculously disappointed. So did the one the following day. Ten minutes later, she discovered that her period was starting and she hopped into the shower to hide grief she still thought was stupid. By the time she'd shampooed her scalp raw, she was ready to get out. Unfortunately, Garrett waited for her.

From the disappointment on his face, he'd seen the supplies for the normal monthly maintenance of the feminine body and drawn his own conclusions.

"I suppose it's for the best," he said, obviously talking past a knot in his throat.

"Probably." Whether he noticed the puffiness she felt in her face or not, she didn't know.

"Mag's going to carve you up into little pieces," Blake warned as he negotiated the parking lot. It wasn't a joke, and he didn't smile.

"I've never asked her to be anything less than she is," Garrett said irritably. "If it's going to work between us, she's got to accept me for who I am, too."

"If you say so." Blake pulled into a parking space and cut the engine. "I've given you my best doctor lecture, and I don't think you heard a word I said."

"Yes, I did," he countered, wrestling his wheelchair from the back seat. "I just don't believe you. Not yet, at least."

As Garrett transferred neatly from car to chair, Blake snorted, and grabbed a patient file and a tape recorder from his briefcase. "Let a guy stand up once," he muttered, "and he thinks he's back to being Dirty Harry."

Garrett glowered at him. "Give me a little credit, Blake. There's no guarantee I can pull this off."

"Win or lose, you're dog chow," he replied absently, already absorbed in mentally composing a letter to a patient's insurance company.

As Garrett headed across the parking lot alone, a grim determination gripped him, just as it had that long-ago day when he'd seen the bomb wired into the instrument panel of the plane. In Garrett's mind, he could no more walk away from this war than he had that one.

Chapter 13

Maggie felt the blood drain from her face. A nameless, seething mass of emotions crushed her chest. Yet Garrett sat in their bedroom as calm and at ease as if he'd just announced he planned to read the newspaper.

"I know you're upset, babe," he said soothingly, "but this is an entirely different situation than before. I won't be out on the streets at all."

"But you'll still be a cop." Even to her own ears her voice sounded thready, on the verge of hysteria.

"A training officer for the city. Nice and safe. No bullet tag with drug dealers as you call it. No cases at all, in fact. You always wanted me to work a nine-to-five job. This solves both our problems."

She tried to speak, but only a strangled croak came out. She cleared her throat and tried again, but it didn't help much. "I'm not hearing this." Out of the morass of emotion, rage clearly identified itself, and she ran with it. "How can you do this to us? How can you go back?"

"There's a big difference between a street cop and what I'll be doing," he stated flatly. "You're not thinking this through."

"*I'm* not thinking this through?" She stared pointedly at his legs then into his face. "You're just now getting some motor function back in your legs. You aren't anywhere near ready to return to the workforce—any workforce."

"Larsen doesn't retire for another three months. I have—"

"Three months? Garrett, your recovery could take two or three more *years*."

He shook his head. As far as she could see, it was a refusal to even consider that she might be right.

"When you first joined the force, you had to pass a monster physical. Perfectly healthy people fail it all the time. Want to explain how you plan to scale a six-foot wall?"

"I won't have to," he said quietly.

That stopped her. "Why not? Are the powers that be going to waive it?"

"They're working on it."

How could he be so calm? Didn't he realize he was tearing her apart all over again?

"If they can't, they'll try to hire me as a civilian adviser. Either way, because of budget problems they can only put me on for twenty hours a week tops. That will fit well with what I estimate my limitations—"

"This is insane!"

"I knew you'd be upset, but you're reacting, not thinking."

"Upset!" she squeaked. "Upset doesn't begin to cover it." Hemmed in between the bed, closet, TV and him, she started pacing erratically. "Three times I rushed down to the emergency room because you'd gotten shot or stabbed."

His eyes darkened in compassion. She knew he loved her, but he loved being a cop more. And she'd lost to the competition.

"Maggie, calm down," he whispered, reaching toward her.

She recoiled. If she didn't touch him, maybe this ancient nightmare would go back to the past where it belonged.

"I'll be safe. No streets. I promise."

He'd never lied to her, not about anything, but she couldn't believe him, not in this. "No, you won't. Your safety record speaks for itself. Most cops never get seriously injured their entire careers. Not you. If there's a way, it'll happen." She sat miserably on the bed and buried her face in her hands. "Garrett, I can't be a cop's wife again. I just can't."

She heard Garrett sigh heavily and heard the soft squeak of his wheelchair, realizing too late that he was approaching her, not leaving the room. She jumped to her feet. He still managed to grab one of her hands before she could get out of reach. The warmth of his skin deepened the ache in her heart. Hadn't it been just this morning he'd held her, promising they'd always be together?

She didn't want to lose him. Yet how could she stay with him? The pain on his face nearly made her cry.

"What do you want me to do, babe? Sell shoes? Be an insurance adjuster?"

The idea made her slightly ill. "I don't know."

He pulled her down to the bed where they could be relatively eye to eye. "You have to trust me."

"You want too much."

He covered her hand with his bad one. "Do you love me? Or do you love what you want me to be?"

If he'd stabbed her, it couldn't have hurt worse or made her feel more guilty. In his mind, she'd rejected him on the most basic level. The pain triggered her temper. She jerked out of his hold so quickly, he couldn't react fast enough, and she stepped out of his reach. "Why won't anything else make you happy? People change careers all the time."

As she watched him debate how to answer, she felt their love slip further and further from her grasp.

His chest rose infinitely slowly as he took a deep, silent, controlled breath. "I have to go back, babe. It's what I am."

If her heart bled before, surely he'd cut it from her body this time. "That's what I thought." Her words came out breathless and weak. She was drained. Yanking open the closet door, she pulled out an armful of clothes.

"What are you doing?" His own heartbreak tore her up, but she hardened herself to it. Survival depended on it.

"I'm moving upstairs until you come to your senses."

"You don't mean that."

"I worked too hard to free myself of a life where I jump every time the phone rings when I know you're out there somewhere." She gestured wildly with a pair of slacks clutched in her hands. "I can't go back to that."

"I love you, Maggie. Don't do this to us."

"Me?" she wheezed. "We're just starting to be okay again, and now you're changing things."

She sensed the change come over him before she actually saw it. The pain on his face congealed into a resolve that scared her clear to the bone. There was an elemental danger here, and it was focused exclusively on her.

"I let you go without a fight last time." He was breathing fire. "I won't make that mistake again. There's a Whole Family meeting tonight, and we're going."

"No, I'm not." She took an involuntary step backward at the determination in his eyes.

"Then Rick and I will go alone." He pivoted his chair around and rolled out the door.

Garrett made his way to the living room, so wrapped up in turmoil that he didn't immediately see Rick standing by the couch, eyes as wide as dinner plates.

Not again! Garrett took a steadying breath. He needed time to get himself under control before he dealt with any more, but that wasn't an option. Maggie's soft crying from the bedroom didn't help matters. "What are you doing home this early? It's barely noon."

"Somebody stuffed a bunch of firecrackers in the electrical box at school. It could have burned the whole place down, but it just knocked out the power. They sent us home."

Garrett wanted to swear. He needed all day alone with Maggie to straighten things out. That was why he'd asked her to take the day off. He hadn't allowed for idiot teenagers playing with matches. "How much did you hear?"

Rick was reeling from shock. "Everything from 'Blake took me to the department yesterday.'"

So he'd heard it all. Garrett's heart sank. "Rick, look at me." The eyes swiveled around, but Garrett had doubts about how much they saw. "I'm not leaving home, not yet."

The teenager pointed down the hall. "She's moving back upstairs. I know what that means." A new thought seemed to strike him, and he darted down the hall before Garrett could stop him.

"Mom, you can't do this," Rick wailed. "We're supposed to be a family again!"

Garrett's first impulse was to follow him, but getting in the middle of the hysteria in that room would serve no purpose at all. If he hoped to salvage this mess, he needed to approach it logically and with great care. Perhaps the best course would be to wait them out. Once a little exhaustion set in maybe he could get something accomplished.

Maggie was the first to storm out, her eyes swollen and red. "How can you put us through this?"

"You're the one moving your clothes."

"I don't want to." She wiped at her face. All he wanted to do was hold her and get her to trust him. "I just don't want you to be a cop anymore."

"No one's going to be shooting at me."

Rick stood at the edge of the hall, and Garrett motioned him on into the room. Another problem with teenagers was that realistically you couldn't send them out of the room. They'd eavesdrop anyway, focus on the worst and make controlling the situation that much harder.

"Garrett, I don't believe for one minute that you can be around other cops, ones who go out on the streets, while you sit back on your heels. It's in your blood. The first chance you get, you'll be right out there with them. I can't live with that."

"I know you can't. That's why I won't put you through it again." He turned to Rick, who looked on the verge of tears.

"Son, you and I are going to Whole Family tonight, okay? Obviously, we had problems before the plane crash put me in this thing. We're going to get them straightened out." There was such hunger and fear on the boy's face that Garrett wanted to scream out in frustration. "Will you come?"

He nodded slowly, and as one, they looked to Maggie.

"Oh, thanks a lot, Garrett. That makes me the bad guy." Maggie gave Rick a desperate hug. "I'm sorry. This is all my fault. I should never have asked him to come home. It only got everyone's hopes up. I didn't mean to set you up for this kind of hurt." Tears got the better of her again, and she left the room.

Garrett met Rick's eyes. For once, he saw himself there, the determination, the will to make tough decisions. All the boy needed was a little guidance.

"Son, I can't guarantee that I can pull any of this off, but do you trust me to try?"

He watched, holding his breath as Rick weighed the request.

"Yeah, Dad," he said slowly. "I trust you."

He let out his breath. *One down, one to go.* "It's going to be a rough trip."

Rick shrugged self-consciously, still pretty strung out. "How can I help?"

Maggie walked into Blake's office as he was rummaging through a file cabinet. "How could you have taken him down there?"

He looked up, then walked around his desk to pull her close, letting her cry into his lab coat. "The timetable on this little fiasco is running late," he murmured. "I expected the compost to hit the fan last night."

The next thing she knew he handed her a tissue with terse instructions to blow her nose.

"He's my brother, Mag. What would you have me do?"

"Care enough about him to want him to stay alive."

"And you have to love him enough to want him to live."

That stopped her. As angry as she was at Blake, she'd hoped

she could convince him how foolish Garrett's actions were, but hope for an ally dwindled to nothingness. "What about the medical end of this? He simply can't work yet, not at anything."

"I know that. So does he."

"How can you be so calm?"

He hitched a hip on the corner of his desk. "Mag, I've been a surgeon for eight years. He has made a joke out of every prognosis I've come up with. After the crash, when we wheeled him into surgery, I truly believed we'd never get him off that table alive. Now he's standing up—granted, he supported all his weight on his arms, but the bottom line is he got his feet underneath him *by himself.* I can't tell you what he'll be capable of in three months. I simply don't know."

She started pacing. "It may take him years, but he's going back to the streets. Just as soon as he can get there."

Blake looked thunderstruck. "That's not what he told me."

"He doesn't think he is," she said dismissively, "but I know him. He won't be able to stay out of it. A juicy case will come along, and he'll go right back to undercover work."

"Number one, he never got hurt working plainclothes. It was that uniform that acted like a target. Number two, he doesn't lie. Even if he pulls off another miracle and recovers *completely,* he said he wouldn't go back, and he won't. He made a major concession to keep from losing you." Blake scrubbed his fingers through his dark hair. "Mag, you're not thinking this through."

"That's what he said."

He stepped away from the desk, put his arms around her again and kissed the top of her head. "Then stop listening to the battle scars and listen to your head."

She mulled it all over, trying to sort out the truth. Surely it was in there somewhere, but all her mind's eye could see was another torn and bloodied uniform.

When Maggie got back home, her house looked like a cop convention, and she had to park two doors down. Cruisers and private cars came and went. Police officers—in uniform and out—swarmed on the lawn. At first she thought something horrible might have happened, but several men in civilian gear stood around nursing beers. Garrett Hughes had come back to the fold, and his old cronies had come to call.

A sick, hollow feeling settled into the pit of her stomach as she walked up the sidewalk. A group of four men she recognized descended on her as she crossed the yard. They all wore identical expressions of bewilderment and horrified shock. Few things were worse than cops with unanswered questions.

"Maggie, why didn't you let us know what happened?" asked the tallest one. She'd met him once but couldn't remember his name. "We would have been here."

She knew she needed to be polite so she forced a smile but kept walking nonetheless. "The press kept quiet because of his undercover work and Garrett didn't seem to want any contact with the outside world. I left it up to him." She shrugged apologetically. Actually, calling his friends on the force had never entered her mind.

In the house were more cops. Pizza boxes littered the dining room table, and Garrett's rolling laughter rumbled from the kitchen. The entourage still followed her. She kept moving.

"Hey, Hughes," called someone, pawing through the food. "Do you want pepperoni or that mushroom mess Steuben brought?"

"Get a life, Roberts," fired back a voice from the crowd.

The man closest to her touched her shoulder. Reluctantly, she stopped and turned. He didn't really have a face, just a uniform.

"Maggie, we're his friends. Did he think we wouldn't want to know because he's a Fed now?"

A jeans-clad buddy added in a lowered voice, "It's rough seeing him like that. What can we do?"

It was all too much. "Guys, I've had a really rotten morning. If you want to know anything, ask him. I'm just his ex-wife. Nothing more." She turned back around as Garrett came from the kitchen. The fading smile said he'd heard what she'd said, and it had hurt him deeply.

Guilt seared her heart. What more could she have said to let him know she didn't want him? But with their attentive audience, she could hardly explain. They all knew about the divorce, and probably burned with curiosity over what Garrett was doing here in the first place.

A sudden pounding went off in her head, and she rubbed her temples. "I've got a headache, and I'm going upstairs where it's quiet and lie down."

She and Garrett stared at each other across the room, silent in the midst of the noisy crowd. *Garrett, I love you. Why can't it be enough? Why did you have to do this?* Unable to think of anything to say, she retreated upstairs and scooped the clothes off the bed.

"Hi, Mom," Rick called from behind her. "Did you get any pizza?"

She didn't turn around for fear he'd see the agony that ripped her into pieces. "I'm not very hungry right now." Passionately, she prayed he wouldn't come into the room. For the moment, he didn't seem upset at all. She supposed she ought to say something encouraging and supportive. After all, she was the parent. But how could she tell him that her worst nightmare had come true and that she couldn't remarry Garrett if it meant marriage to a cop?

"You really ought to trust him, Mom," he said softly. He sounded so much like his father that Maggie cringed.

She took a slow breath to keep from coming completely unglued. "It's not him I don't trust, honey. It's a bullet."

She felt him watch her as she hung up her clothes, then heard his footsteps as he went downstairs. Maggie took something for her head, then lay down, trying to figure out what had happened to her world.

Upstairs was anything but quiet. Masculine laughter and voices echoed from below. Occasionally, she picked out something Garrett said. Newcomers asked the usual plethora of hushed questions. Their more subdued tones made it hard to

pick out words, but she had no trouble reading the emotions—
horror over one of their own being in a wheelchair and fear
of facing their own mortality. The impromptu open house
ended as people needed to get home to their families or back
on patrol.

"Maggie?" Garrett called from the bottom of the stairs.
"It's time to leave for the meeting. Are you ready?"

She wanted to put the pillow over her head. How could he
expect her to go to Whole Family with all this hanging over
them? How could she face patients and their families on an
equal footing when she was supposedly the one with all the
answers?

"I love you, babe. Come downstairs."

"Dad, do you want me to go up and get her?" Rick asked.
She couldn't hear Garrett's answer. "Are you sure?" After
another pause, Maggie heard the front door squeak open and
close.

"Maggie, Rick's getting the car started, so it's just the two
of us. Since you're not answering, I'll assume you fell asleep
and we'll talk in the morning."

Maggie rolled over. He knew full well she was awake but
gave her a face-saving out anyway. She almost hated him for
it.

The next morning, Maggie buried herself in paperwork in
her office. At midmorning, a familiar knock sounded on her
door. Her heart leaped into her throat, and Garrett let himself
in. He wore a gray and black sweat suit and looked as dignified
as if it were a tuxedo, the casual outfit setting off his dark hair
and olive skin.

"Morning, babe." Love, sadness and loneliness shone in
his eyes and slightly crooked smile, but no censure.

She'd successfully avoided him since the day before. "What
are you doing here? *How'd* you get here?"

He studied the wall a moment. "Steuben lives about a mile
from the house. I called him and he brought me. As to the
why... You forgot me."

Maggie sucked in her breath. "Today is water therapy." She almost threw up. Despite their problems, she'd agreed to handle his case. In essence, she'd forgotten a patient, morally unpardonable.

Then she heard what he'd really said. You forgot *me*. The first tears of the day started. "I hate crying."

Without a word, Garrett moved around behind her desk and tried to gather her into his arms.

"Don't touch me," she demanded brokenly, pulling back. "Sapperstein can handle—"

"No, he can't, babe. You assigned him to other cases. He's busy. Besides, I'm *your* patient."

Her head snapped up. Love radiated from him, enveloping her in a warm blanket where nothing bad ever happened. But she knew better. "I can't."

"Yes, you can. You're a professional, and a patient comes first."

"You're fighting dirty again."

"Whatever works. I told you I'm not giving up without a fight this time."

The instinct for survival kicked in. "You have to choose, Garrett—me or being a cop. You can't have both."

He met her gaze without a twitch of emotion. "Why not?"

That stunned her. "How can you even ask?"

"What exactly about law enforcement can't you live with?"

"You know full well what it is."

"Humor me. Please?"

She let her breath out, and she put some distance between them. "It's the danger. The not knowing."

He looked unnervingly thoughtful. "So it's not a fundamental hatred of cops?"

She glowered at him. "Don't be absurd."

"If it was safe and predictable would you object?"

He was setting her up, but she didn't see how. If only she didn't hurt so much, maybe she could think. "Stop playing mind games!"

"Our marriage isn't a game, Maggie. Now answer me. If it was a nine-to-five job, could you live with it?"

"Yes, but no matter what you tell me, I'll never believe you won't go back to wrestling suspects with guns and knives and—" Her throat closed up.

He looked at her hard. She could see thoughts churning behind his eyes, and it frightened her. What if he found an argument to drag her back in? She loved him enough that she knew part of her would grasp at straws.

"Babe, I never intended to tell you this, but while I was in a coma, I could read your emotions."

She felt her jaw go slack. He might as well have announced he was the tooth fairy.

"Don't look at me like that. I'm not nuts."

"What you just said didn't sound particularly...normal." If Blake or Sapperstein had said such a thing she'd instantly brace herself to be the butt of one of their jokes, but no hint of amusement lurked in Garrett's eyes.

"Maggie, when I came out of surgery, I was dying. I wasn't quite connected to my body anymore. New senses opened up. Old ones shut down. I felt what you felt, babe. Until then, I didn't understand that you really couldn't handle the stress. During our marriage, I didn't completely believe it. I do now. That's why I'm compromising."

She still couldn't quite comprehend she was hearing this. "You could read my mind?"

"No. Just your emotions. For a week I couldn't see. I had no physical sensations at all. But I could hear, and I knew what people around me felt. Anger. Fear. Love."

She shuddered.

"I learned what you went through when I got shot." His voice caressed her with its gentleness and warmth. "Your worries about Rick scared me to death. You never said what was wrong, and I worked myself into a real stew thinking he'd been busted or worse. Being absolutely helpless was hell." He gave her a crooked smile. "I never did thank you and Mom for reading to me every day. It gave my mind something constructive to chew on.''

Maggie remembered back to those first terrifying days. He'd been aware of everything. She didn't know what to say, and she found herself staring into his eyes. The intensity of the love and truth that burned there was too much, and she turned away.

"Garrett, that's too bizarre."

"I know, babe, and I lived through it."

Neither spoke for long moments.

"Whether you believe what happened or not, at least think about everything I've said," he murmured. "For now, we need to hit the pool, remember?"

Maggie changed into her suit in the staff locker room. When she came out, Garrett had peeled off his sweats and was waiting for her. The sight of his magnificent body reawakened things better left alone. She swallowed hard and tried not to think about it.

Their gazes met, and her heart grabbed on to the treasure of his smile, knowing it was emotional suicide but unable to stop herself. These remaining moments were all she'd have for a lifetime.

She wasn't sure she believed the entire story about his coma experience, but she sensed a credibility that made her at least consider the possibility. Maybe he really did understand now. Not that it changed anything. He'd decided to go back anyway. Somehow that made it worse.

"Ready?" he asked, moving toward the pool's edge.

"Can I be petulant and say no?"

He laughed, locked the wheels and slid down to the decking. She hopped into the water and waited for him as he maneuvered his legs over the edge. The overall scope of his accomplishments still amazed her.

"Have you tried standing again?"

"No," he snorted. "My arm ached so bad afterward it kept me awake most of the night."

Maggie was instantly alert. "Why didn't you tell me? Did you tell Kelly what you did? I should have thought… Garrett, you could have undone the surgery." She pressed her fingertips to her temples. "Why didn't I—"

"That's enough, babe," he scolded gently. "Blake already chewed my tail." With a quick shift, he dropped into the pool, treading water with his arms to keep his head above water. "It was something I had to do."

Like being a cop. No matter what the cost. "Okay, let's get at this."

As she approached him, open desire flared in his eyes. An answering cry echoed deep within her, but she refused to let him know. He had a strong enough hold on her.

They went through the exercise routine, ending with the part she dreaded most, his lying flat in her arms as he worked his legs. The simple contact of skin against skin was nearly her undoing. Worse, the evidence of his desire was blatant.

"You're not going to apologize for that either, are you?" she said pointedly.

He chuckled. "Not on your life." He sobered slightly. "Last night at Whole Family, after they broke up into small groups, the adults talked about sex and disabilities." He stopped working and looked deeply into her eyes. "I'm sorry I accused you of being with anyone else. I was so eaten up by jealousy that I couldn't see what should have been obvious. What you showed me was merely what you knew as a therapist, not as another man's lover."

Choked up, Maggie could hardly speak. "We've been through all this. It's over. Can we talk about something else?"

"Sure," he said low in his throat. "How about how long it's been since we made love in a pool? Do you remember the spa in Bodega Bay?"

Heat jolted through her.

"Babe, I've always believed that's where we conceived Rick."

He'd voiced her most secret fantasy. Maggie recoiled so fast that she lost her grip, and he went under. Why did he torture

her like this? He surfaced, water streaming from his smiling
face.

"Garrett, I ought to let you drown."

His chuckle was positively lethal.

"Why are you pushing all my buttons?"

"You know why, babe," he said, treading water. "Swim
with me." The seductive tone sent her blood raging with need.
He couldn't have made the invitation sound more erotic if he'd
openly propositioned her.

He flipped over and swam off, desire blazing in his face.
She'd seen the state of his body. Survival dictated that the last
thing she do was go after him. "But he's your patient,
Hughes," she gritted out.

Then, with long strokes, she caught up with him, pacing his
slow, steady progress. They reached the end of the pool, turned
and swam back, together, matching stroke for stroke. Fatigue
settled in, demanding he spend more and more of his attention
on swimming. The familiar gray cast settled over his features,
but he kept going.

"Marry me, babe. We'll get it right this time."

She nearly gasped aloud from the pain. "Time to get out.
You've had enough. So have I." She stood up, and he stopped.
Still, his gaze never wavered.

Exhaustion had taken its toll, and he could barely stay
afloat. With an inward cry, Maggie took hold of him, heartbreakingly aware of the moment he stopped forcing his body
to do what it no longer could and he rested trustingly in her
strength, his breathing labored.

"When I was on the plane and I saw that bomb, I only
resented dying because I'd never see you and Rick again,
never tell you one more time that I love you."

The lump in her throat made it hard to swallow. She was a
heartbeat away from collapsing and promising him everything.

"I bet you can still wear your wedding dress. When we get
married again would you wear it for me?" He studied her
figure. "You were gorgeous at nineteen, but I love your body
better now. You're a woman, not a girl."

Her mouth went dry. His lips were so close, so inviting in their promise of taking her once again to paradise. With an inarticulate cry, she turned away, dragging him through the water as she headed back to the side. His ribs vibrated with silent chuckling.

Chapter 14

Garrett's calculated assaults on Maggie's heart got sneakier from there. One night she came home to a catered candlelight dinner for two. The next night she found painstakingly handwritten coupons tucked in odd places throughout the house. One entitled her to a free bubble bath, complete with back rub. Another promised an entire week free from housework. The latter made her smile. There was no question in her mind that Rick was in cahoots with him on that one.

In spite of herself, she found herself anticipating what she'd find next when she got off work every night. Tonight, Garrett was nowhere to be found, but a trail of rose petals led from the front door to the kitchen—where she found a glass of zinfandel on the counter. The trail then led to the master bedroom where she found a single red rose on the pillow on what had always been her side of the bed. The note reminded her of their honeymoon in a cabin at Lake Tahoe, most particularly the night they'd made love by the fire. With trembling fingers, she folded up the note, tucked it in her uniform pocket and went upstairs to change.

Her willpower cracked. Defeated but caring only that they'd be together for however long they had, she descended the stairs. Halfway down she heard two low-toned masculine voices. One was Garrett's. The other she didn't recognize. As she got closer, the stranger's words became clear.

"If the prison guards hadn't reported his threats to kill you, I wouldn't think much about it."

Maggie's knees buckled, and she grabbed the railing to keep from falling down the stairs.

"I still don't," Garrett muttered. "That slime bag's a hot-head, but he's not a triggerman and he doesn't have the follow-through to hire it done."

Somehow, Maggie made it to the living room. Garrett's gaze riveted onto her, anguished dismay twisting his features. The other man, clad in a three-piece suit, barely spared her more than a polite nod of greeting.

"I agree with you, Hughes. He's the type who'll say whatever makes him look like a bigger bad guy than the next idiot. Not much on initiative. Since he's being paroled, I thought you'd want to know." As he spoke, he apparently caught the troubled air between Garrett and Maggie and discreetly moved toward the door.

"Thanks, I appreciate the courtesy," Garrett said, showing him out.

"Who was he?" she demanded the moment the door closed. "A detective or someone from the D.A.'s office?"

"Not important." He sliced the air with one hand and wheeled himself to her. "What you heard sounded worse than—"

"Sure, Garrett." Her voice trembled. "Just like you said you'll be safe if you go back to the department."

"You're not thinking this through."

"So people keep telling me!" Her fists balled into knots at her sides. "I want you out of here. Now! Get out of my life!"

Rick sauntered in, his contented smile fracturing.

"I swear somebody ought to patent that kid's radar," Garrett muttered under his breath, then added louder, "Son, come here."

The teenager stood trembling, his mouth opening and closing soundlessly. Maggie wanted to crawl under the floor and die.

Thoughts ricocheted behind Garrett's eyes with lightning speed. "Listen to me," he said, his voice sharp with command. Rick's eyes slowly focused. "I want you to go into the kitchen and make a pot of coffee. My gold and red Fortyniners mug is dirty. Wash it by hand, fill it and bring it to me."

Rick, still dazed, gave him an uncomprehending look.

"Now, son. It's important."

Like an automaton, the boy wandered into the kitchen.

Maggie recognized Garrett's ploy and was grateful for it, but too consumed by her own pain to visibly react. She had to end this now, or she'd be trapped for the rest of her life. *A death threat. How can he act like it's no big deal?* "Garrett, I want you out of my life. I don't ever want to see you again."

He didn't answer, but his face looked like a road map of heartache. She couldn't look anymore and ran to the garage and took two large suitcases down from the rafters.

Dropping them at his feet in the living room, she put her hands on her hips. It was either that or throw herself into his arms. "I want you packed and out of here in an hour. I'll call Blake to come get you."

As she turned away, he said, "Rick can take me. Blake had a heavy surgery scheduled for today and probably isn't home yet."

Garrett's sudden resignation should have been a relief, but it wasn't. She'd made the right choice. Maybe he'd finally realized that he couldn't have her and his career. Whatever the case, he hadn't chosen her, so they'd all lost.

"I've got one request," he said as calmly as if they were discussing the weather. Rick came back with the coffee, and Garrett thanked him. "Did you remember the sugar?"

Rick blinked and frowned. "You drink it black."

"Not today. One spoon, please."

"Okay." The boy turned bleak eyes on his parents and went back to the kitchen. Maggie bled inside for her child's suffering, but it couldn't be helped. She had to survive, and *this* time, she'd make sure Rick got the counseling he needed so he could live with parents who led separate lives.

"What's the request?" she asked, her voice as broken as her heart.

"That you get in your car and leave now. Go find something to do while Rick helps me pack. It'll make it easier on us all."

"But Rick needs me."

"Later, Maggie," he said, his voice taking on an edge. "For now, I'll handle him alone."

"And if I refuse?" She couldn't leave her son in a near catatonic state.

His expression hardened, as unyielding as steel. "In case you've forgotten, we have joint custody. I don't recommend that you put him in a position where he has to choose. If you do, you'll have to call 911 and have me thrown out. Since there's a strong possibility we'll know the responding officers, that'll embarrass all of us. Now which is it going to be?"

Maggie's stomach lurched, and she made a run for the bathroom. When she was finished being sick and had washed her face, she dragged herself back into the living room. Surely death itself would be less painful than this.

Garrett sent Rick back to the kitchen to add cream. Rick was more coherent now and balked.

"You don't really want this coffee, Dad, so stop running me all over the place."

Garrett looked a bit frustrated that Rick wouldn't be controlled just a little longer, but he nodded. "Go upstairs and get your mother's purse and car keys."

Rick glowered through moist eyes and crossed his arms.

"For real," Garrett said almost too quietly for her to hear.

Rick nodded, and trotted upstairs.

"Maggie, go to a movie, or maybe over to the Sappersteins. All right?"

Rick came back with the requested items and handed them to her. She didn't want to go anywhere, but the idea of watching Garrett pack nearly sent her back to the bathroom.

She gave him one last look, one she hoped didn't show the longing in her heart. She kissed their son and walked out the door as Garrett turned his back on her and told Rick to sit down before he fell over.

He didn't even watch me leave.

Maggie felt cold and dead as she sat down on the worn, brown couch in the Sappersteins' family room.

"You're shivering," Cindy said. "Here." She took a tiger-print throw from the back of a chair and draped it over Maggie's trembling shoulders. "Carl is picking up Mitzy from the vet and should be back any minute."

"I'm sorry to be such a bother lately."

Cindy turned on her hundred-watt smile. "You're supposed to impose on friends. It's what they're for."

Maggie almost laughed, but it hurt too much. Cindy plopped unceremoniously on the coffee table and faced her, not saying a word. Maggie didn't want to take the invitation to talk, but found the whole story tripping from her mouth anyway.

"A death threat," Cindy whispered, horrified. "And he expects you to pretend it's nothing?"

Maggie shrugged. "To Garrett it *is* nothing. It makes me wonder how many other threats there were over the years that I didn't know about."

"Since somebody came to warn him, does that mean the convict will be getting out soon?"

"Apparently." Maggie leaned back and wrapped the throw more tightly around her, the blanket provided no warmth. The warmth she needed was Garrett's arms, but she'd closed them to her. "He turned his back as I left. It was like twisting the knife."

The other woman patted Maggie's knee, trying to offer what little comfort she could. Later, she disappeared into the kitchen, returning in a moment with a hot mug. "Try this. It's a little weird but pretty soothing."

Maggie took a sip. The warm tang surprised her. "Hot orange juice?

Cindy nodded. "Unbeatable."

Maggie smiled. "It's good." She took another sip and remembered back to the juice she and Garrett had shared in the middle of the night, the brush of their fingers as she'd taken the carton from his hands. "I need him, Cindy. I built a life without him once, but I don't know how to do it again."

"You can't live with that kind of fear either."

A disgruntled Siamese's yowling heralded Sapperstein's arrival. "Mitzy, if you'd stay out of fights, your life would be a lot easier." He set the cat carrier down, opened the door, and the unhappy animal shot under an antique hutch. He shook his head in exasperation and looked up. "Hey, boss, what are you..." His grin froze as he took a good look at her. "You look awful."

"Thanks." Maggie laughed miserably. "I feel like that cat. I know how to avoid getting beat-up, but I can't help myself." She loosed another shuddery laugh and took a too large swallow of hot juice. It burned a little as it went down but left a mellow warmth in her stomach. "I think I'll be drinking a lot of this for a while."

Sapperstein sat beside her, his dark eyes riveted on her. For the second time, the story was coaxed from her. Telling it again wasn't any easier.

He leaned back on the couch, stared thoughtfully at the ceiling and stretched his long legs out in front of him. The cat, deprived of being the center of attention, meowed pitifully from her hiding place.

"I know, Mitzy," he said dryly. "Men are scum."

Garrett's not, Maggie defended involuntarily, then swallowed hard.

"I wish I had a magic rabbit I could pull out of the hat for you, boss," he said softly. "I really do."

"Thanks," she said quietly. Maybe if she tried hard enough,

she could keep the love suppressed and out of sight until she learned to live with it.

The two Sappersteins cajoled her into sharing their leftovers for dinner, then indulging in a rousing game of Monopoly. Her mind wasn't on that either. Most of the time she kept forgetting what property she owned. By ten o'clock she felt as if she'd been run over by a tractor.

"Your ex is a very dynamic man," Sapperstein observed absently, counting out the Monopoly money he owed her for landing on Baltic with the two hotels he insisted she buy. "He's not someone I'd ever want to annoy. Wheelchair or not, I think it could get dangerous. It doesn't really surprise me that he'd drop such an uncompromising ultimatum on you."

"He said he'd never go back."

Sapperstein shook his head. "Too bad you can't trust him to keep his word."

Maggie bristled. If Garrett was anything, it was truthful. *He promised he wouldn't go back to the streets. All he asked was that I trust him.* "Oh, God, what have I done?"

"What are you talking about?" Cindy asked.

"I did it again." Maggie came to her feet. "In the early days after the crash I believed he *couldn't* go back to being a cop, and I wanted him back. Then everything blew up in our faces, and he pushed *me* away. This time, all I had to do was trust him to be who he is—an honest man. I had everything I ever wanted right in my hands, and I threw it away."

"I still don't follow you," he said, "but are you forming a plan?"

"Oh, yes," she moaned. "Plead temporary insanity. If that doesn't work, I'm not beneath groveling." Maggie laid the tiger-print throw on the back of the overstuffed chair. "Garrett has never lied to me in his life, and he said he'll be safe."

She drove like a madwoman to get home. Maybe he hadn't left yet. *It's been hours, Hughes. He didn't have that much to pack.* She clung to the feeble hope anyway.

When she pulled into the driveway, Rick's car was gone,

and the two-story stucco was dark. Not even the porch light was on. The only illumination came from the street lamp in the neighbor's yard. "If I lose, I'm going to sell this place. Too many memories."

Reluctantly, she got out of the car and trudged up the front walk. Garrett had told her before that he'd left hoping she'd get lonely enough to ask him back. In essence, he'd called her bluff. Maybe he was doing it again. It was a desperate hope, but the only one she had.

She reached the porch, and her heart plummeted at the sight. The wheelchair ramp had been dismantled virtually nail by nail. Only the concrete footings and the old porch beneath it remained. The lumber had been stacked neatly to the side in a clear message. He was gone, and he'd returned her house to as close to its previous condition as possible.

Then she found the note taped to the front door. Tearing it off, she stepped inside and flipped on a light.

In Garrett's blocky, determined, left-handed script, she read:

Maggie,
Rick promised to get the mess out of the yard this weekend. If he decides to spend the night with me, I'll have him call. I'll also see that he gets to school on time. We used the last of the bread for sandwiches. I put money to cover on the table.

Garrett

Tears cascaded down her face, and she crumpled into a chair. The note had been functional, to the point and cold as ice. This time, he'd taken her at her word. She desperately wished she'd taken him at his.

Maggie wanted to crawl into a hole and disappear, but something Garrett had told her whispered in her ear.

Babe, when are you going to stop seeing yourself as a coward? You're the most courageous woman I know. You're al-

*ways strong when you need to be. The rest is just baggage
you don't need to carry around.*

"I am not that strong!" she yelled at the note, the only
thing of his she had. *Yes, you are, Hughes. He loves you. If
you want him, go get him. It may not work. You hurt him bad
this time. But maybe over time, you can show him you can
handle the uniform.* She shuddered. The fear hadn't abated one
iota. "But I'll be damned if I let it rule one more day of my
life." Maggie got to her feet.

She washed her face, scrubbing so hard she wondered if
she'd taken some skin off as well. Patting it dry, she stared
hard into the mirror. Emerald eyes flashed fire.

"I know it's late, Faith, but may I come in?" Maggie
looked past her startled sister-in-law, hoping to see suitcases
in the foyer, anything to indicate Garrett might be having second thoughts, but she saw nothing. Knowing Garrett, his be-
longings were already neatly put away in his new home.

Faith squealed and pulled her into a quick hug. "You're
here! From the shape he and Rick were in, I didn't expect to
see you." She pushed Maggie through the living room.
"They're all out back."

Maggie nodded, stuffing her hands self-consciously into her
pockets. The idea of begging Garrett's forgiveness in front of
an audience didn't sit well, but pride made a lonely bedmate.

Patio lights blazed as she stepped outside. A basketball hoop
was bolted to the pool house, and Garrett bounced a basketball
with deadly intent. Blake was in another wheelchair, one undoubtedly purloined from his office. Rick and the girls were
sprawled in a patio lounger, cheering them on.

"Get it together, Dad, or you'll be scrubbing his tires with
a toothbrush tomorrow."

"Thanks," Garrett groused. "Just what I need. More pressure."

Maggie had been wrong about this, too. No matter Garrett's
future, the two brothers would still have their hard-fought basketball games, a ridiculous bet riding on the outcome.

With a quick flick of his wrist, Garrett flipped the ball over and shot. It bounced off the backboard, then he and Blake scrambled after it, wheelchairs colliding. Garrett got to the ball first.

"Unfair advantage!" Blake whined. "You've had more practice with these things than I have."

Garrett snorted. "Right. That's why you're eight points ahead." The words were jovial enough, but she didn't miss the somber tone.

None of them had seen her. Maggie stepped into the light as Garrett prepared to shoot again. His head snapped around. Unguarded heartache and love racked his features. He lost control of the ball, and it bounced away. Blake started for it, but stopped when he saw her. Rick turned and stood, and Maggie felt as if she faced the ultimate firing squad. She wished they'd just execute her and be done with it.

Her attention locked onto Garrett. Closer, he looked even worse. What she'd mistaken for concentration on the game was in actuality a deliberate attempt to survive one moment at a time. She swallowed hard, acknowledging with a grateful nod Blake's suggestion to the kids that he and they go in the house.

Rick said nothing to her as he walked past, but the condemnation in his set jaw spoke volumes.

Once she and Garrett were alone, her mouth went dry. The carefully rehearsed speech that she'd memorized on the drive over vanished.

"Didn't you find my note?" he asked. "I told you I'd let you know what Rick's plans were for the night."

"That's not why I'm here."

He didn't say a word, merely waited, the seasoned cop giving a suspect enough rope to hang himself.

"I love you, Garrett," she said past the strangling knot her throat had become.

"So?" He turned away to retrieve the basketball.

She flinched, but she doubted he saw it. He tried to dribble the ball but couldn't maintain control, and it bounced away again. A tiny spark of hope flared. He'd demonstrated much more skill before he'd noticed her. Maybe he wasn't as hardened to her as he appeared.

She lifted her chin. "You've never lied to me, Garrett. I'm sorry I let fear blind me to that. You have no reason to trust me, but I want to try to—"

"Stop it!" His voice cracked. "You tried. I tried. I'm tired of trying. You either love me—wheelchair, uniform and all—or you don't."

"I do." It came out whisper soft but cased in iron.

He stared. "You what?"

She stepped toward him, burying her hands deeper into her pockets. It was the only way she had to keep from throwing herself at him. How could she have brought this magnificent man to his knees? Could she ever forgive herself for that? "I love who you are, Garrett, not who I want you to be."

His eyes narrowed, and she held her breath as he wheeled himself to her. Up close, she could see the ravages grief had made of his face.

"Your fear is real, Maggie. I told you how I know that. You can't turn it on and off at will. So what's the point of all this?"

"I need your help."

He lifted his brows at the audacious pronouncement.

She plunged on. "I'm ready to deal with it, even if it means parking myself in the staff psychologist's office seven days a week until it's conquered."

A shudder racked his big body, but he forced it down. "What does this have to do with me?"

"I want you home where you can remind me that I'm strong, that you never lie, that I can always trust you." She took a shallow breath. "That if you say a—" she swallowed hard and nearly gagged "—a death threat isn't worth worrying about, then it really isn't."

He looked thunderstruck.

"Garrett, I'll fight this battle alone if I have to. If that's what it takes to prove to you—"

"Oh, babe," He opened his arms and she flung herself into his embrace so hard it nearly dumped them both onto the ground. He crushed her to him, and she felt the moistness of his tears on her hair. She closed her eyes, unable to bear it. *Have we won? Or is this just another emotional hit-and-run?*

Determined to face even this head-on, she pulled back. If she could just see his eyes, then she'd know. But she didn't get the chance. His lips descended on hers, his usual finesse completely gone as he drank deeply, frantically of her. They drew strength from each other, their kisses healing wounds and promising endless tomorrows.

"Do you really want me to come home? If you do, it's got to be forever. I can't move out again. It'd kill me." The shadows of mistrust were still there.

If it takes a lifetime, I'll erase them, she vowed silently. "Do you want to get married in your uniform or civilian gear?"

He laughed, the tension leaching from his body. They wiped the moisture from each other's faces.

Then she remembered something. "You tore out the ramps. How are we going to get you into the house?"

He looked thoughtful, then amused. "Watch me. I'll crawl up those steps if I have to."

They held each other in silence, soaking up their love, both indulging in an occasional nibble. Much still needed to be worked through, but not now.

Rick came out, Blake holding a supportive grip on the boy's shoulder. Faith trailed behind, wringing her hands. The kid looked as if he'd been battling his own war, which Maggie acknowledged that he had. "Mom? Dad?"

That was all he got out before Garrett opened an arm to him. He flew across the yard. The latest impact again threatened the stability of the chair. Hugs were fierce and long.

"Is it for real this time?" Rick asked.

Garrett ruffled his hair. "How would you like to give the bride away?"

The war whoop blasted painfully in Maggie's ear, but she laughed and kissed his cheek.

"Son, would you go get my suitcases?"

He was off like a rocket. Blake and Faith retreated into the house as well, but at a slower pace and chuckling.

Garrett looked at Maggie. "I couldn't bring myself to unpack."

She gave him a confused look. "I thought you'd have completely settled in by now. You sure got out of there fast enough."

He shook his head. "At that point, Rick's needs were more important than ours. I had to do something to defuse the situation so I could help him."

"In other words, you conceded the battle but not the war."

He didn't answer, didn't need to. The truth shone in his eyes.

"What about the ramps, and that note?"

"I dismantled the ramps because I was afraid if they were still there, I'd end up on your porch about dawn tomorrow. Sabotaging my only reasonable means of getting into the house was the best way to keep me away until I could come up with a workable plan."

She laughed tremulously. It hadn't been as bleak as she'd feared. That word again—fear. Garrett would never abandon her, no matter what she did. A bomb that had taken nearly two hundred lives hadn't kept them apart. Neither would anything else.

He kissed her again. "Are the blue satin sheets clean?"

Her blood fired. "If they're not, give me an hour."

"Too long. We'll do without."

Epilogue

In the small anteroom at the front of the church, the sense of well-being that had started in Blake's backyard remained as Maggie prepared to walk down the aisle. Rick smiled at her, the picture of contentment. He looked good in a tux.

"How badly did you and the girls decorate the van?"

He grinned, smug. "Uncle Blake gave us pointers."

"Oh, swell. Whatever it is had better come off easily. You know how your dad is about his baby." Maggie had surprised Garrett with the fully equipped van for his birthday the month before.

Rick chortled, but didn't deny a thing.

Sapperstein knocked, then poked his head in. "Ready, boss?"

A new flock of butterflies took flight in her stomach.

He sauntered in and checked his tux in the mirror. "I love the new wedding etiquette. This matron of honor stuff is fun."

Shaking her head affectionately, she smiled. "I think the proper term for you is attendant."

"Matron of honor still sounds better." His teasing expression sobered a little. "Thanks for asking me."

"You're the closest friend I have." *Outside Garrett.*

"Remember that at raise time, will you?" The music started, and he slipped out the door.

Maggie smoothed the satin gown. Garrett had been serious when he'd asked her to wear the dress she'd worn when they'd married eighteen years ago today. The alterations hadn't taken the heroic measures she'd been afraid they might. She felt a little silly wearing white, but this was for Garrett, and somehow that made it okay.

Taking a deep breath, she draped her wrist over the crook of Rick's arm and stepped into the sanctuary. Family and friends filled the small church. A corner of her mind noted Laverne, Patrick and his nurse in the front pew beside Faith and the girls. With skilled help, Mom looked rested, and Dad was doing much better. Blake and the minister stood at the altar, but her attention and her heart locked onto Garrett.

His presence was commanding, the wheelchair an irrelevant detail. His attempt to get back on the police force had failed, at least temporarily, but she took no joy in it. Patients with concrete goals were the ones who made their own miracles. He was still a long way from walking, if ever, but his courage and determination got him closer to it every day. If anyone could come back all the way, he would. When he did, he'd once again wear a police uniform with pride, making a difference in his corner of the world—but behind the scenes. He'd promised.

Undisguised devotion shone from his face, warming her from across the room.

"I love you," he mouthed as she walked toward him, the aisle strewn with rose petals.

"I love you, too," she mouthed back.

The formalities exchanged between Rick and the minister were lost to her as Rick placed her hand in Garrett's. Of one mind, she and Garrett tightened their hold, the unspoken promise as binding as the vows to come.

"I want to grow old with you, babe," he whispered to her as they turned to face the minister.

"I think that can be arranged." Her promise lodged itself forever in his heart.

Garrett suddenly couldn't help himself and pulled her to him for a kiss totally inappropriate to the traditions of the ceremony. His heart swelled to overflowing. At that moment, he couldn't have cared less about propriety.

Last week had seen the first anniversary of the bombing of Flight 1251, and his settlement was due in soon. With careful investing, he'd never have to work again, but he couldn't see himself as ever living a sedentary life-style.

He hadn't come close to giving up on one day returning to law enforcement. In fact, he'd figured out another proposal to pitch to the powers that be. Even if his dream never became a reality, he was beginning to see life as having new possibilities. He'd even checked into going back to school to get his master's degree. The future was wide open, and he had every intention of making it count.

"Would you two stop necking long enough to make it legal?" Blake groused. "Some of us are tired of waiting."

Garrett felt Maggie's laughter against his lips, and he gave her one more hard kiss before releasing her enough to look into her radiant face. They'd decided to start a second family, complete with a private ceremony tonight that consisted of throwing away the box of "supplies."

He had his family back, and this time, they'd get it right.

* * * * *

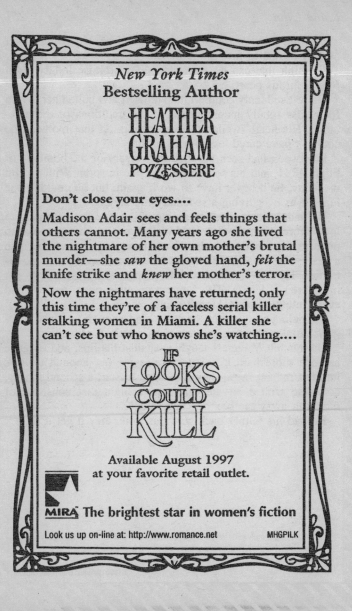

Take 4 bestselling love stories FREE

Plus get a FREE surprise gift!

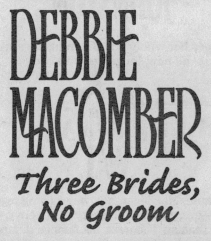

Bestselling author

JOAN JOHNSTON

continues her wildly popular miniseries with an
all-new, longer-length novel

The Virgin Groom

HAWK'S WAY

One minute, Mac Macready was a living legend in
Texas—every kid's idol, every man's envy, every
woman's fantasy. The next, his fiancée dumped him,
his career was hanging in the balance and his future
was looking mighty uncertain. Then there was the
matter of his scandalous secret, which didn't stand a
chance of staying a secret. So would he succumb to
Jewel Whitelaw's shocking proposal—or take cold
showers for the rest of the long, hot summer...?

Available August 1997
wherever Silhouette books are sold.

Silhouette®